KING OF
CLUBS

KING OF CLUBS

Aces & Eights — Book Two

SANDRA OWENS

Published by Montlake Romance, Seattle

www.apub.com

Amazon, the Amazon logo, and Montlake Romance are trademarks of Amazon.com, Inc., or its affiliates.

ISBN-13: 9781542045803
ISBN-10: 1542045800

Cover design by Letitia Hasser

Printed in the United States of America

This book is dedicated to Melody Guy because after editing six of my books, believe me, she deserves at least one of them dedicated to her. So thank you, Melody, for being an awesome editor and for never saying, "Have you ever considered a different career?"

PROLOGUE

Lauren Montgomery slid the key into the lock of her small off-campus apartment, happier than she'd ever been in her twenty-one years. As soon as she got inside, she'd call Court, let him know she'd arrived home safely. *Court.* Just thinking his name sent a spine-tingling sigh through her. It didn't matter that she'd only known him for six days. He was her soul mate, and even though she'd seen him nine hours ago, she missed him terribly already.

She'd left for spring break on the spur of the moment to celebrate her divorce, never expecting to fall in love. After Stephan, she hadn't wanted anything to do with men. But she *had* fallen in love. The insta-love kind that she'd always rolled her eyes at. It had been like right out of a romance novel, the way her gaze had connected with Court's. From that moment until they'd parted, each to return to school, they had been inseparable.

Even as she closed the door behind her, she was pulling her cell phone from her purse, anxious to talk to him. Court Gentry. A cool name for an awesome guy. She grinned, thinking about how many textbook margins she was going to doodle his name in.

"That's a smile I haven't seen in a long time. Who put it on your face, Lauren?"

Ice flowed through Lauren's veins. *Run,* her brain screamed, but her feet were frozen to the floor. She tried to look away, but Stephan's eyes held hers. During the two years she'd been married to him, he'd specialized in training her to fear him.

"I asked you a question."

There had been a time when she'd loved his Russian accent, but no longer. Now she equated the sound of his voice to fingernails scraping down a chalkboard. She hated it. Hated him. But her hate wasn't greater than her fear, the reason she stood like a statue, too terrified to move.

"Answer me, Lauren. Where have you been?"

"I was . . ." She swallowed past the lump of dread in her throat, willing herself not to automatically obey his commands. *Stop being a coward,* her brain said. *If you don't stand up to him now, you never will.* She straightened her spine and lifted her chin in defiance. "None of your damn business, Stephan."

She flung the door open. "Get the hell out of my house." It felt good to finally be free, not shivering like a cornered little mouse whenever he decided she'd done something wrong. They were divorced. She owed him nothing.

Like a striking cobra, his face was inches from hers in the blink of an eye. He wrapped his fingers around her throat, rubbing his nose in her hair. "I can smell him on you. Tell me his name."

He was guessing. He had to be. "There is no name to tell you. If you don't get out, I'll call the police." She lifted the phone in her hand, pushing her thumb down on the 9. She never got to the 1-1.

Stephan's fists rained down on her face, her stomach, every place on her body, beating her so badly that she wished he'd just kill her and be done with it so the pain would go away. She never breathed Court's name during the assault. She learned later that a neighbor heard her cries and had called the police; otherwise she was sure Stephan would have ended her life that night.

"You're all brown, which tells me you've been at the beach. Who was he?" He hit her again. "A name, wife."

"I'm not your wife anymore," she tried to yell, but her jaw refused to work. She put her hand on her cheek, already swelling from his fist. "Not wife," she finally managed, her mouth protesting the movement by shooting excruciating pain though her eyeballs, up to her skull. "H-hurts," she whimpered.

"You will always be my wife. Get that through your fucking head. You're mine, Lauren." He pressed his big hand against her sex, squeezing so hard stinging pain shot down her legs. "This is mine." Next, he gripped a breast, digging his fingers into her skin, bringing another whimper from her. "This is mine. No one touches what is mine." He grabbed her hair again. "I will find out who he is. You can trust me on that. It will go easier on you if you give me his name right now."

"No . . ." It hurt so badly to talk. Even breathing was almost impossible, but she had to convince him. She pushed the words out of her aching mouth. "N-no one." Her vision blurred from the tears flooding her eyes, and the metallic taste of blood was sharp on her tongue. "S-swear."

Stephan wrapped his hands around her neck, cutting off her air, and leaned down, putting his mouth next to her ear. "I will find out his name, Lauren, and when I do . . ." The police broke through the door before he could finish.

The threat was left unsaid, but she knew. To protect Court, she coldly cut him out of her life.

CHAPTER ONE

Six years later . . .

Eight members of the Miami Cubanos Motorcycle Club surrounded Spider, Aces & Eights' . . . What was Spider exactly? Their mascot?

Court Gentry paused to consider the question. Whatever the dude was, he was about to lose a few teeth. Most of the clubs tolerated Spider, even thought he was some kind of good-luck charm and would rub his bald head on the way out the door as they headed for their bikes. The Cubanos, however, hated him.

That might be because he'd stumbled out of the bar drunk as a skunk one night and had fallen on the motorcycle belonging to the club's president, knocking it over. The rest of the gang's bikes had gone down like dominos.

Court sighed. Spider had been told to make himself scarce whenever the Cubanos showed up, but there he was, grinning like an idiot at the eight dudes giving him death glares as they tightened the circle, moving in for the kill. Where the hell were Nate and Alex when he needed them?

"You dudes make him bleed, you're banned from here for life," he said, pushing his way into the circle and grabbing Spider's ear. He pulled Spider away before the Cubanos sent them both to la-la land. The only reason the Cubanos let him make off with Spider was because Court and his brothers were mean sons of bitches, an image the Gentry brothers worked hard to project. No one had bested them in a fight, although many had tried.

"Dammit, Spider, what part of *become invisible when those dudes are around* don't you get?" Court asked, dragging Spider to the kitchen. "John Boy, put Spider to work washing dishes, and then feed him." Their all-around do-whatever-job-needed-to-be-done employee nodded.

"You got it, boss."

Court caught a glimpse of his older brother in the poolroom and headed that way. Nate was on the phone, a frown on his face. As Court waited for him to finish, he glanced around the bar. The Cubanos had settled down now that they didn't have Spider to play with, all four pool tables were occupied, and several couples were on the dance floor.

Court and his two brothers, all FBI agents, operated Aces & Eights as a cover for their covert operations. It was the perfect setup. None of the biker gangs guarded their speech around the brothers, allowing them to pick up all kinds of intel. Like the talk over a beer Court had had with a few of them that had given him a lead on the car and motorcycle theft ring he was investigating.

"Alex wants you to go to Madison's apartment and wait for her roommate to come home," Nate said, sticking his phone into the back pocket of his jeans.

"I thought he was home sick. What's he gotten into now?" Where their baby brother was concerned, nothing would surprise him.

"Ramon attacked Madison."

"The hell?" Alex was head over heels for Madison Parker, Ramon Alonzo's cousin, which was a complication considering Alex was ass deep in an investigation of the Alonzo drug cartel.

"Alex is there now, but he's taking Madison back to his condo."

"And I need to wait for her roommate to come home because . . . ?"

Nate shrugged. "I guess he's worried Ramon will come back. He doesn't want the roommate there by herself."

"Why me? Why don't you do it?"

"I'm not a babysitter."

Court knew he'd already lost this battle, but he wasn't going down quietly. "And I am?"

"Tonight you are."

"I hate it when you pull rank, bro." That was the problem with being the middle brother. As the oldest and the one who'd raised him and Alex, Nate got to make the rules. As the youngest, Alex got away with breaking the rules—like falling for the cousin of the target of his investigation. Court thrived on rules and planning ahead. He had not planned on being reduced to *babysitter*.

Nate patted him on the shoulder. "You'll live."

"So you say. Madison okay?" He supposed he should have thought to ask about her right away.

"Alex said she's shook up, but otherwise unhurt."

"That's good. Well, I guess I'm off to babysit. What's the going rate these days?"

Court parked his Harley in front of High Tea and Black Cat Books. After getting no answer when he rang the doorbell, he called Alex. He'd never been to the bookstore that Madison and her friend owned, and he eyed the Art Deco building washed in the pastel colors typical of South Miami Beach's architecture. He loved South Beach, sometimes referred to as the American Riviera—a playground for the rich and famous, as well as sweaty, wide-eyed tourists and local South Florida residents coming over the MacArthur Causeway for a day at the beach.

"No one's here," he said when Alex answered.

"Madison just talked to her. She'll be there in about twenty minutes. Mad didn't tell her what happened or that you'd be there. She didn't want to upset her roommate while she was driving."

"So I get to deliver the bad news? News flash, Alex. I don't like you."

His idiot brother laughed. "Yeah you do. We left you a key taped behind the mailbox."

There was a two-inch gap between the wall and the back of the box. Court slipped his finger in and felt the key. "Got it."

"Go on in and make yourself at home. Madison said you can sleep in her bed tonight."

"Dude, I'm not spending the night. I thought I was just supposed to make sure she was locked up safe."

"I need you to stay over. I don't trust Ramon not to come back. She shouldn't be there alone if he does."

Court pulled the phone away from his ear, scowling at the screen. Had Nate left that bit of information out knowing Court would flatly refuse? His brothers were going to owe him big for this one. He put the phone back to his ear. "Fine, but I'm not a happy camper. I didn't know I was supposed to bring my jammies."

"Stop your whining, bro. You don't own a pair of jammies."

He hung up on Alex. Key in hand, he went into the apartment above the bookshop that Madison shared with her roommate. His first order of business was to get the lay of the land, so he toured the place, checking to make sure the windows were closed and locked in each room. Since the apartment was on the second floor, the only way Ramon could get in would be through the front door or up the fire escape. He located the fire escape, checking to make sure the window leading to it was locked.

Satisfied everything was locked tight and he knew the entry points, he returned to the living room. The TV remote was on the coffee table. He picked it up, tuning in to a Marlins baseball game. A black cat jumped onto the couch, sat, and stared at him.

"Hey, buddy. You come to watch the game with me?"

The cat blinked. Court blinked in return before turning his attention back to the game. As he watched the pitcher shake off the catcher's call, he wondered if he could have made it to the big leagues given half a chance. His high school coach had thought Court had the talent to go all the way, but his sonofabitch father had nixed any hope of that. After-school baseball practice and games took time away from Court's chores at the piece of shit dirt farm the old man called a ranch.

Court snorted, thinking of the *ranch*—a five-acre plot consisting of three pigs, one mean cow, and a dozen or so scrawny chickens running around, pecking at the dirt for insects. The one time he'd tried to stand up to the bastard, demanding he be allowed to play ball, he'd ended up with his pitching arm broken. He'd never pitched the same since.

Although he'd lost his dream that day, he was happy as an FBI agent. The few times he thought about what might have been, it was more with nostalgia than disappointment. Why cry over something he couldn't change? And if there were times when he felt like there was something missing in his life, he shrugged it off. He had a great job, two brothers he would die for, and a pretty woman in his bed whenever he wanted. Best of all, his sonofabitch father was dead and no longer able to make their lives miserable.

As for his mother, it was only recently that he'd begun thinking of her, and only because Alex had been wondering lately what had happened to her. Court had tried hard to forget her. She'd left them in the hands of the meanest man on the planet, walking away without a backward glance. He'd been nine the last day he'd seen her, and good riddance.

"Now whatcha gonna do?" he asked the pitcher when he walked the batter, loading the bases.

At the sound of a key in the lock of the apartment's front door, he muted the game. The door opened, bringing Court to his feet. The last person on earth he'd ever expected to see again walked in, and why in hell hadn't he asked Alex the roommate's name?

"Lauren?"

Lauren froze, unable to believe her eyes. Why was Court Gentry standing in her living room?

He swiped a hand through his hair. "I don't fucking believe this."

That made two of them. It had been six years since she'd last seen him, and she hated how her heart raced at the sight of him. He'd always had that effect on her, still did, apparently, and that made her angry. She didn't want to have that reaction to him because he no doubt hated her, and rightly so.

"Why are you here?" she asked, finally finding her tongue. Except for filling out his body, which appeared to be pure muscle, he hadn't changed much since she'd last seen him. The man she'd turned her back on after the most amazing week of her life for reasons she would never, ever tell him was still mouthwateringly gorgeous. Tall, dark, and dangerous was how she'd always thought of him.

Black eyes glittered with irritation. "Because I drew the shortest straw?"

"Is that a question?" Yes, he hated her, but he still wanted her. The truth was in his eyes. No matter how hard he tried to hide his desire, she saw through his smoke screen. This was how it had been between them—tense, burning-up-the-sheets chemistry. The kind that made her want to happily go down in flames.

But that was then, before she'd let him go to keep him safe. Nothing had changed, and he could never know what that week with him had meant to her. Now he stood in her living room vibrating with anger.

"I asked my questions six years ago, and you refused to answer." After getting that dig in, he sat, picked up the remote, and unmuted the TV, dismissing her.

"You have three seconds before I call the police. Why are you in my home, Court?" It was a cruel joke the universe was playing on her.

"Call your roommate."

"Why?" He continued to ignore her, so she fished her phone out of her purse. "Fine. I'll call Madison. Then I'll call the police." When he snorted, she came close to throwing her phone at him. Madison had called earlier to find out if she was on the way home, but hadn't warned her that a blast from her past was about to happen. Not that her roommate would have known to warn her. Lauren hadn't told a soul about Court.

As she waited for her friend to answer, it dawned on her that Court had the same last name as Madison's boyfriend, Alex. Although she'd only seen Alex a few times since Madison had started dating him, she wondered why she hadn't seen the resemblance. Alex wore his hair longer than Court's military cut, but they both had black eyes, nearly black hair, and high cheekbones. It wouldn't surprise her if they had some American Indian blood in them. Whatever flowed through their veins, it had created two very fine-looking men.

Maybe she'd never made the connection because it hurt too much to think of Court and what might have been, so she'd blocked any thought of him from her mind.

"Wow, are you okay?" she asked after Madison told her about Ramon's assault. Lauren had never cared for her friend's cousin. She'd thought him too controlling, too demanding, too much like Stephan. His actions tonight only proved her right.

"I'm fine. I think Alex is more upset than I am. I didn't say anything when I called you earlier because I didn't want you to refuse to let Court come over."

Lauren eyed Court. He appeared to be engrossed in the baseball game, but she was sure he was listening. "Tell Alex I want him to call off his dog."

Madison laughed. "I thought you'd take one look at him and fall in love."

Oh, she'd done that six years ago. "Nope. I want him gone."

"Alex wants him to stay tonight in case Ramon comes back. You shouldn't be there alone if he does."

"Don't I have any say in this?" She didn't want Court to think she wanted him here, but what if Ramon did come back? If Court left, she'd be here alone. What if he went into a rage because Madison wasn't here and attacked her instead?

"Nope," Court said, proving he was paying attention even though he hadn't taken his gaze off the TV.

She stuck out her tongue, not caring if she was being childish, and got a chuckle from the man on her couch. What? Did he have eyes on the side of his head? After hanging up with Madison, she went to the kitchen. Hemingway followed her, sat, and stared at his empty food dish.

"Your friend didn't feed you?" She took Hemingway's drawn-out meow to mean no. When she'd gotten over the shock of seeing Court in her living room, she'd been surprised to see the cat hanging out with him. After Court had sat down, Hemingway had curled up on his lap. Hemingway was the bookstore's cat and tolerated customers petting him when he was downstairs, but he only snuggled with people he liked.

After filling his bowl, she made a cup of mint tea, then took it with her to her bedroom. Before she closed herself in, she got a lightweight blanket and the extra pillow from her bed, walked back to the living room, tossed them at Court, and then returned to her bedroom. She probably should have said good night or something, but the less she and Court talked, the better. What was there left to say?

She went to her closet, and took down a shoebox filled with photos of her and Court. She hesitated. For six years she'd tried her best to forget the week she'd spent with him, but she'd never been able to throw away the pictures she'd taken during that spring break. Did she really want to take a trip down memory lane?

CHAPTER TWO

Seven months later . . .

"Going in," Court said, the microphone in the overhead light sending his words out to his brothers and the FBI SWAT team standing by. He sat behind the wheel of a metallic-blue "stolen" Lamborghini, which was actually borrowed from a local dealer who'd had two high-dollar cars stolen off his lot.

Months of slowly working his way into the auto theft ring had paid off. Tonight, he was finally meeting the ringleader. The promise of a container ship to move automobiles overseas, along with the Lamborghini, had sealed the deal.

The container ship was real. It just wasn't going to be carrying any stolen cars on its decks. But Dan Woods, aka Dragon, president of the Satan's Minions Motorcycle Club, had taken a tour of the ship borrowed for that purpose, even meeting the supposed captain. In truth, he'd met Rand Stevens, a fellow agent. That had finally convinced Dragon to introduce Court to the leader of the operation.

Court turned the car into a lot with weeds growing up through the cracks in the pavement. The warehouse appeared to be abandoned, but he pulled up to the garage door on the left as instructed, beeping the horn once before pausing, then giving three beeps in a row. He rolled down both windows so his team would hopefully be able to hear what was happening after he was out of the car.

A few seconds later, the door lifted and he drove into the warehouse. Without moving his lips, he said, "Six that I can see. All armed. Two with AKs." He pulled to a stop a foot from the dudes with the AK-47s.

Court recognized all four of the guards as Dragon's club members. After turning off the engine, he stepped out of the car, his gaze zeroing in on the man next to Dragon. The guy was average height but built like a heavyweight boxer. He had a shaved head, a swastika neck tat, and a teardrop inked under his eye. An ex-con, a thief, and a racist. Court was going to enjoy taking him down.

"You armed?" the bald man said.

Court snorted. "Of course I'm armed." He pointedly looked at the AK-47s. "It's not like we're here to play chess now, is it?"

"You have a smart mouth," Baldy said.

"So I've been told."

"Dragon vouches for you, but I'm not the trusting sort." He jerked his chin at one of the men standing near him. "Frisk him for wires."

Court held out his arms. "I'm cool with you checking. I'd do the same, but your man tries to take my guns, we're gonna have a problem." The glimmer of respect in the dude's eyes confirmed he was playing this right.

"Just keep them where they are, and we're good."

There were no introductions, and he hadn't expected any. They'd find out the dude's name soon enough. After a pat down confirmed he wasn't wired, Court motioned to the car. "She's a sweet ride. Tempted to keep her myself."

"How hot is it?" Dragon asked.

"Close-by hot, so you don't want to be taking it for a joyride around town. Now, if you'd be so kind as to hand over my money, I'll be on my way."

"Not so fast," Baldy said. "I want to see that ship for myself."

"No problem. Be at Aces and Eights in the morning at nine, and I'll take you to it." Not that the dude would be free to go anywhere in the morning. "My money, please. I got a hot date waiting for me."

The bald man nodded, and Dragon picked up the briefcase at his feet, bringing it to Court. "The beginning of a profitable association."

Not. "You bet." He eyed the ringleader. "Don't be offended that I'm going to count it."

"And don't be offended that it's ten grand short."

Court narrowed his eyes. "Well now, that does offend me. We had an agreement. Forty thou on the delivery of one late-model Lamborghini."

Baldy crossed his arms over his massive chest. "You'll get the rest tomorrow after I see proof that there really *is* a container ship, along with assurances from the captain that he's on board with moving my merchandise."

"That wasn't the deal." Court mimicked the man's stance. "I'm almost pissed off enough to shoot you." He ignored the AK-47s now pointed at him. One thing you could never do with men like this was show any weakness. "But I won't. Not today. Tomorrow, different story if I don't get my money."

He took a few steps back, putting him near the rear of the car, squatted, set the briefcase on the floor, and opened it. "Still gonna count it, though." By now, his team would be in place, waiting for the magic words. After thumbing through the packs of bills, he said, "We're good to go."

"The first one of you fuckers that moves a finger, dies," said a voice from the catwalk above them. Men in black, their faces covered by ski masks, *FBI* emblazoned on their Kevlar vests, stepped out of the shadows, weapons raised, their fingers on the triggers.

Court glared at Baldy. "You shithead. You set me up?"

One of the idiots guarding Baldy and Dragon lifted his gun. Before he could fire, a shot sounded and the gun flew out of his hand. The man yelped as he fell to his knees, holding his bloody hand to his chest.

"Next time I aim to kill," one of the SWAT team members said, picking up the gun.

Court flattened himself on the cement floor, hands stretched out above his head. Apparently not as stupid as they looked, Baldy and Dragon did the same thing. The other three men darted looks at each other as if trying to decide if doing their appointed job of protecting the two leaders was worth dying for.

Nate and Alex were present—not trusting anyone else to make sure Court came out of this alive—but they stood back in the shadows. After Alex had almost died during an investigation last year, Nate's protective streak had gone into overdrive where his two younger brothers were concerned. If he didn't back off soon, Court was going to start calling him *Mommy*.

The SWAT team leader raised his weapon, pointing it at one of the dudes holding an AK-47. "See that red dot right there between his eyes?" he asked calmly. The other thugs stared at the dot, one even nodding. "He has three seconds to live if you boys don't set down your weapons nice and easy like."

The man in question's eyes widened, then fear flashed in them. Before Court could shout a warning, the dude pulled the trigger, firing wildly, and in his panic, he took down one of his own men. The other one decided it was a good idea to join the fray, and took wild shots, one of the bullets hitting the floor near Court's head. A shard of concrete hit his cheek, just missing his eye.

"Dammit," he grunted.

Within seconds, it was over, with three of the guards dead. The one with the bleeding hand was curled up in a whimpering ball. Like Court, Baldy and Dragon had hugged the garage floor for dear life. They were all jerked up, two SWAT members assigned to each of them. They were frisked, relieved of their weapons, handcuffed, and then read their rights.

Court glared at Dragon and Baldy. "I find out it was one of you that ratted, I'm coming after you."

"You were just told you have the right to remain silent," Reggie Duncan, the SWAT team leader said, pushing Court in the chest. "Use it."

For good measure, Court gave his fellow FBI agent a death glare, getting the hint of a lip twitch from Reggie.

Reggie pushed him again. "Get these scumbags out of my sight."

The man was having way too much fun at his expense. Court *accidently* stepped on Reggie's foot as he was yanked away. He, Baldy, and Dragon were each put in the backs of different unmarked cars. EMTs carted the wounded guard away, two agents tagging along.

Court's driver twisted in his seat. "You need to go to the hospital?" Nate asked.

"Dude messed up my pretty face," he complained.

"What a shame. Now the girls are gonna run from you, screaming," Alex said beside him.

"Nah, a scar will just make me look dangerous. Women like that."

Alex snorted. "If you say so, bro."

Truthfully, he'd lost interest in other women ever since Lauren had unexpectedly popped up again in his life, which pissed him off. She was old history. Her mere presence shouldn't have affected him in the slightest. But for seven months now, he'd been celibate. That just wasn't right.

He couldn't begin to conceive how it was possible that Lauren just happened to be his brother's wife's best friend. Whenever he tried to process that, it tied him up in knots, so each time she crept into his mind, he pushed her away.

The car with Baldy left first, followed a few minutes later by the one with Dragon in it. The plan was for both men to be taken to separate jails to be booked so they'd not pick up on the fact that Court wasn't thrown in a cell with them.

He turned his back to Alex. "Get these things off." Once free of the handcuffs, he slapped Nate on the back of the head. "Let me out."

The FBI car didn't have interior door handles in the back, and he waited impatiently for Nate to open the rear door. With his brothers flanking him, he returned to the warehouse.

"Glenmore's not going to be happy," he said, eyeing the Lamborghini. He'd promised the dealer that the car would be returned intact, but there were two bullet holes in the driver's door.

Nate ran his hand over the damage. "Just needs a new door. Tell him we'll pay the cost."

"There's money to cover a Lamborghini door? Who knew?"

"Didn't say Rothmire was going to be happy." Nate suddenly had him in a bear hug. "What counts is you're okay."

He patted his big brother on the back. "I'm fine, Mommy."

Rothmire was their boss, and no, he wasn't going to be happy. A Lamborghini door probably cost as much as Court's annual salary. Hopefully, their bureau chief wouldn't deduct the cost of a replacement door from his paycheck.

"You're bleeding all over Nate's shirt." Alex's lips twitched as he eyed Court's face. "I think you need stitches, dude. Maybe like dozens and dozens of them."

Court leaned away, meeting Nate's eyes.

Nate smirked. "Go for it."

At Nate's encouragement, Court spun, scissored his legs around Alex's, taking them both down. In the end, Alex—a Krav Maga black belt—had him pinned. No surprise there. Court had only earned a brown belt, but it had been worth a try.

"You lose," Alex said. Then, being the tenderhearted brother that he was, he pulled his shirt over his head, cleaning the blood from Court's face.

Court gave Nate an eye roll. "Why do you always encourage me to fight him when you know I'm gonna lose?"

"Cause it's fun?" Nate leaned down, examining Court's face. "Might actually need a stitch or two."

They left the SWAT team to clean up the scene. An hour after making a stop at the emergency room—which resulted in four stitches to Court's cut—they returned home. A few years earlier, during Miami's real estate bust, they'd each bought condos in the same oceanfront building in Surfside, a little north of South Beach. Their homes were directly above and below one another's with Nate's unit on the tenth floor, Court's on the ninth, and Alex's on the eighth.

After making some renovations, they'd settled in, living in the kind of luxury they'd never even dreamed about as young boys. Along with not wanting to remember his week with Lauren, Court didn't want to think of his childhood either.

He'd just stepped out of the shower, a towel wrapped around his waist, his aim his bed, when Alex walked into his bedroom. Sometimes he regretted they each had keys to each other's condos. Tonight, he wanted to just crawl onto his king-sized mattress and try to go to sleep, forgetting the day he'd had. Unfortunately, there was a mountain of paperwork to deal with before his debriefing in the morning.

"I'm on the way to pick up Madison," Alex said. "Come with me. We'll grab a late dinner."

"No."

"No, why?"

That was Alex for you. Never settling for an easy answer. "No because no." He scowled when his baby brother, ignoring him, disappeared into his walk-in closet.

"Just something casual." Alex came out, tossing a pair of jeans and a T-shirt on the bed. "Mad loves the food trucks, so probably we'll get fish tacos." He looked up, fucking love stars shining in his eyes. "She's crazy about those."

Court refused to feel jealous that Alex had found the love of his life. He'd once thought he had, but that only proved what a fool he'd been. "What part of *no* don't you get?"

"Bro, you're hurting my feelings."

Those pitiful eyes weren't going to work on him. Which was why, thirty minutes later, he wanted to put his hands around his own throat and choke himself when he walked alongside Alex as they approached High Tea and Black Cat Books. Damn Alex. His baby brother had a way of getting everyone to do what he wanted.

There was one reason, and a really big one at that, for his not wanting to be anywhere near the bookstore. Her name was Lauren Montgomery. Since he'd kept that secret to himself, he couldn't exactly blame Alex for dragging him along.

He hadn't seen Lauren since Madison and Alex's wedding two months ago, and even then, he'd avoided her as much as possible. She'd almost destroyed him once. Damn if he'd give her a chance to do it again.

Whenever Alex mentioned that Lauren was coming over to see Madison, Court made a point of not being home on the off chance they might decide to pop up one floor to see him. The only reason he was tagging along now was because when he'd tried to use the cut on his face as an excuse to stay home, Alex had called him a crybaby.

That had resulted in a round of wrestling before Court had thrown in the towel, agreeing to come as far as the door to the bookstore before heading on over to Aces & Eights, where he'd have to hide out in the office since he was supposedly in a jail cell somewhere. That was fine since he had a ton of paperwork to fill out detailing what had gone down tonight, which had given him an excuse to drive his own car.

Although the outlaw biker gangs that frequented their bar rarely made their way to South Beach's touristy streets, Court wore a ball cap pulled low over his forehead and a pair of fake glasses.

"Why's Madison here this late anyway?" Usually, she came home after she and Lauren closed up for the night.

"She and Lauren wanted to get some restocking and other stuff done tonight." Alex gave him a sly look. "Maybe Lauren would like to come with us."

Court refused to take the bait. His dumbass brother was trying to play matchmaker. If he said absolutely not, that would only lead to questions he wouldn't answer. Besides, he'd never agreed to go anywhere with them.

"No comment, huh?"

"I have no comment because I'm going straight to the bar, where I'll bury myself in paperwork. You and Madison and Lauren can do whatever you want."

"You used to be fun, brother. What happened to . . . Who the hell's that?" Alex picked up his pace.

Court frowned at seeing a large man crowding Madison and Lauren. He jogged up to them beside Alex.

"Your husband isn't pleased with you, Lauren. He expects you to be home when he arrives."

Husband? Court came within seconds of walking away, but one glance at Lauren's pale face and the worry in Madison's eyes kept his feet planted in place.

"Who the hell are you?" Alex said, pushing between the man and Madison. He tucked his wife next to him. "I asked you a question."

"Not that I owe you an answer, since my business is with Lauren, but I am simply passing on a message from my brother to his wife," he said with a Russian accent.

"He's not my husband," Lauren screamed.

Court stepped next to Lauren. "You heard the lady. You need to go."

The man's vivid blue eyes shifted to Court. "And you are?"

"Her boyfriend." He clamped his mouth shut. Where the hell had that come from? And worse, was Lauren's reaction to his blurting that out.

CHAPTER THREE

Lauren gasped. What was Court doing? "No, he isn't. I swear it, Peter."

"Then why would he say such a thing?"

She was almost as afraid of Peter as she was of Stephan. Her instinct was to take off and never look back. But, unknowingly, Court had put a big, fat target on his back, and she had to make Stephan's brother believe Court meant nothing to her.

"A misplaced sense of gallantry? I hardly know the man, so how am I supposed to know how his mind works? Tell Stephan I'll come see him." She'd set foot in the prison where Stephan was serving his sentence for almost killing her when hell froze over. But she had to make Peter believe it so he would go away.

"This week, Lauren. If you don't, I'll come take you to him myself." He gave her a hard stare, letting her know he meant it. She watched him walk across the street where Grigory, his driver, waited.

Grigory gave her a nod after closing the rear door of the Mercedes. He had always been nice to her, even though she'd suspected that his true assignment was to report back to Stephan on everywhere she went and who she talked to during their marriage. Not that she was allowed to take off on her own very often.

As soon as the car was out of sight, she turned on Court. "You have no clue what you've just done."

"Seriously? You hardly know me?" he snarled.

She flinched, but she deserved that. If she told him she was trying to protect him, he'd probably go all macho on her, insulted that she didn't think he was badass enough to take care of her. But Court didn't know Stephan and what he was capable of. She intended to keep it that way. Hopefully, Peter believed Court meant nothing to her and wouldn't tell Stephan.

"What the hell just happened?" Alex said.

"Nothing happened." She forced herself to walk up the stairs to her apartment instead of running up the way she wanted to. At the sound of footsteps following her, tears burned her eyes. Madison knew most of her story, but Court and Alex would want an explanation. And once they knew, they'd want to help. That couldn't happen.

Then there was the fact that by just being her friend, Madison was in danger. If Alex knew that, he'd go ballistic, and rightfully so. When she and Madison had bought the bookstore, they'd considered it a plus that there was a two-bedroom apartment above the shop. Those had been good times, getting High Tea and Black Cat Books up and running, rooming together, hanging out at the various clubs in the area. Now, Madison lived with her husband and Stephan would be getting out of prison soon. The fun times were coming to an end.

As much as she missed Madison's company in the evenings, she was glad her friend had moved out. Madison was safer not being around at night. Lauren didn't worry about Stephan showing up during the hours they were open. There were too many customers in and out. He preferred sneak attacks, enjoyed being a night monster.

"Tell them, Lauren, or I will," Madison said. "They can help you."

She opened her mouth to remind Madison of her promise not to tell a soul, but spotted the bandage on Court's face. That she hadn't noticed it before proved how off balance Peter had made her.

"What happened to your face?"

"What do you care, G.G.?"

Gorgeous Girl. His pet name for her during a week when she'd believed in fairy tale endings. He'd used it on purpose, a reminder of what she'd done to him.

"Who's G.G.?" Alex asked. "I don't have a clue what's going on here." He raised a brow at Madison. "I gather you do?"

Lauren couldn't deal with this. Not tonight. She grabbed Madison's hand, pulling her into her bedroom. "You can't tell anyone. You promised," she said after closing the door.

"They can help. I swear it."

The tears she'd been holding back rolled down her cheeks. "You know why I won't. Oh, God, he's getting out, Maddie." She sucked in a breath. "I thought by now he'd have forgotten about me." Stupid, stupid her, so naïve. "He'll hurt anyone who gets in his way, maybe even kill them. I'd die if something happened to any of you because of me."

"Oh, sweetie." Madison hugged her. "You're not alone. Why can't you get that through your head?"

Lauren rested her chin on her friend's shoulder. "Because in this, I have to be."

"No, Lauren, you don't. I'll give you until tomorrow night. Either you tell them about Stephan or I will. And get that angry look off your face. I'm doing this for your own good."

"Okay." It wasn't okay, but there would be no reasoning with Madison. Lauren stepped back. To keep everyone safe, she needed to leave. If Madison's deadline was tomorrow night, she'd have to figure something out fast.

"I'm going to stay here tonight," Madison said. "Give me a minute to go send the guys home, and then we'll eat our weight in ice cream and drink wine while you tell me how you know Court and why he called you G.G."

"No. Go home with your husband. Between both your jobs, you guys get so little time together." The plan taking seed in her mind required everyone to be gone. "I mean it, Madison. I'm going straight to bed." She pulled the cover down to prove her words.

"Are you sure?"

"I'm sure. We'll talk about everything in the morning. I'll tell you all about me and Court."

Her friend gave her a hard hug. "I'll keep my phone nearby if you change your mind."

She wouldn't. By the time Madison arrived in the morning, she planned to be long gone. Lauren walked to the window, staring unseeingly at the traffic going by on Collins Avenue. While she waited to hear silence, letting her know they'd left, she allowed herself to remember meeting Stephan.

She'd met him the day her mother died, when she had been vulnerable to his charms. *False charms,* she amended. She'd stood next to her mother's hospital bed with her father and little sister, all of them crying.

There had been so much grief in that room that she'd had to get away for a few minutes. Without a destination in mind, she wandered through the hospital, ending up in a waiting room. If there were one thing in her life she could undo, it would be taking that walk.

Stephan had been there, waiting to get an X-ray taken of his ankle. He'd asked why she was crying, so she'd told him. Then he had taken her hand, holding it between his big, strong ones.

In that moment, she'd believed he could heal all her hurts. When he'd asked her to tell him the best story she had about her mother, she'd fallen a little in love with him. And his accent—Russian he'd told her—was charming.

By the time the technician had come to take him to get his X-ray, they'd both been laughing over what a horrible cook her mother had been. It was a family joke that her mother shouldn't be allowed in the kitchen and wasn't embarrassed to admit it.

When he'd shyly told her he was a star hockey player for the Florida Thunder, and then asked for her phone number, she'd wondered why such a good-looking celebrity would be interested in her. She'd been powerless to resist him, and even though she gave him her number, she hadn't expected to hear from him. But she had. Unfortunately.

The Stephan who'd romanced her had been everything a young girl could dream of. Because of a hairline fracture in his ankle, he'd been put on injured reserve for a few weeks with plenty of time on his hands. He'd spent those with her, even going to her mother's funeral. He'd not only made *her* fall in love with him, but her dad and sister, too.

Stephan had been there for her family during the worst days of their lives, doing everything in his power to make things easier for them. He'd claimed to understand her grief because he'd lost his mother several years earlier. She'd been so stupid to fall for his act, something she'd learned the minute he put a wedding ring on her finger. Young and naïve, she'd been no match for her new husband.

The first time he'd hit her was on their wedding night, the second time when she'd refused to quit college. By the time she'd found the courage to leave him, she'd lost count of the reasons why she deserved to be hit. She leaned her forehead against the glass pane, wondering what her life would be like now if Stephan hadn't been waiting for her when she'd returned from spring break. Would she and Court still be together? Deep in her heart, she believed they would—the magic between them had been that amazing.

At hearing a scratch at the door, she pushed away her memories. "Everyone gone?" she asked Hemingway, after letting him into her bedroom. He gave her a pitiful meow. She picked him up, put him on the bed, and scratched his chin and ears, getting deep, rumbling purrs of pleasure. Right now, she'd like to be a spoiled cat, without a worry in the world.

"I have things to do, Hemingway, my man. I can't be pampering you tonight." She was going to miss him.

Court assumed Lauren was talking to the cat, but he couldn't make out the words. After the scene he'd witnessed earlier between her and the Russian, he hadn't felt comfortable leaving her alone. Alex and Madison had offered to stay, not wanting to leave her alone either, but he'd sent them home. They were newlyweds and surely had better things to do, whereas he had absolutely nothing better to do, aside from a mountain of paperwork. Guarding a woman he'd never expected to see again was as good an excuse as any to put off that chore.

Madison had given him the pillow from her old bed, and he removed his shirt and shoes. He wished he had his computer. A little research on Lauren's life would be helpful since she was refusing to talk about her husband . . . *ex-husband*, he corrected. That was if he took her at her word that the dude really was an ex.

She probably wouldn't appreciate an invasion of her privacy, but his law enforcement instincts were screaming that she was in trouble. No matter she'd once crushed his heart so badly it would never be the same. She was a close friend of Madison's and his brother loved Madison—for that reason alone, Court would get involved.

Besides, he was going to have to lie low for a while, so this would give him something to do. He'd wanted to let her know he was here, but Madison said if he did, Lauren would just kick him out. According to Madison, Lauren intended to go straight to bed. He tilted his head, listening to the sounds coming from her bedroom. She was moving around, opening and closing drawers. She definitely hadn't gone straight to bed. What was she up to?

Suspicious, he waited. An hour later, the floorboards in the hallway creaked. A dark-clothed person walked into the kitchen, opened the refrigerator, took out two bottles of water, and stuffed them into the backpack she carried, and then headed for the door.

Lauren. Lauren. Lauren. "Going somewhere, my little midnight ghost?"

She yelped, the backpack falling to the floor with a heavy thud.

"Easy, G.G." He pushed off the sofa.

"Court?" She pressed her forehead against the door. "Why are you here?"

"Guarding you. Going to be kind of hard to do if you're not here, don't you think?" He picked up the backpack. "Where you headed?"

"None of your business." She slipped around him, backed up to the kitchen light switch, and turned it on. "You can leave now."

"Don't think so." He frowned at the sight of a gun barrel in the partially unzipped bag. He pulled it out and held up the Glock 26, also known as a Baby Glock, preferred by women because of its smaller size. "You planning on shooting someone?"

"Again, none of your business."

He shouldn't like that fire in those golden-brown eyes so much. "I'm making it my business. Do you even know how to shoot this?" When her gaze shifted away, he had his answer. Christ, she was clueless. About everything. How to use the weapon she'd been careless enough to let him find, how to disappear, and she probably didn't know how to fight off an attack.

What to do about that? As he saw it, he had two choices. Either let her go and hope she somehow managed to safely disappear or make her his project. He wasn't stupid enough to tell her that last part since he doubted there was a woman in the world who'd appreciate being any man's project.

"Are you that afraid of him?" he asked even though he was sure of the answer.

"Feeling like a broken record here because again, none of your business. I'd like you to leave now."

She crossed her arms over her chest, probably to show him she meant business. It wasn't working since she'd managed to push up her breasts so that the material of her T-shirt stretched against them, leaving her nipples outlined.

He'd had those beautiful breasts in his mouth, had explored every inch of her body, had known all her sighs of pleasure. He'd once thought she loved him. Until she'd told him in a phone call it was over, not even having the courtesy to tell him to his face.

Nor had she given him a reason. Just, "Don't call me again or try to see me." That had happened only days after she'd told him she loved him. He'd learned the hard way that women couldn't be trusted, the first lesson from his mother. The one time he'd forgotten that lesson had been with Lauren. But never again.

"What are you looking at?" She lifted one arm, snapping her fingers. "My eyes are up here."

Irritated with himself and her, he kept his gaze on her breasts to prove . . . What? That he was an ass? "So they are," he said, lifting his eyes to hers. "Here's the deal."

"There is no deal, Court. You have no say over my life. I'll ask you one more time to leave."

"Or you'll what? Call the cops?"

"Yeah, that's exactly what I'll do."

He chuckled, amused that she had no clue she was threatening to call the police on an FBI agent. "Let's sit, and I'll tell you the deal." Ignoring the little growl deep in her throat, he settled on the sofa. "Come on, G.G. Just hear me out."

"Stop calling me that."

"Why? You used to like it." She'd been his Gorgeous Girl for six days. It must have been the sun and beer and salty air that had tricked him into mistaking lust for love. He had to admit the woman had a lot to do with that, too. All six years had done to her was turn her from a cute college girl with a love of life into a beautiful woman afraid of her own shadow. He could appreciate the physical change in her, but he didn't like the fear her ex-husband had put in her eyes.

And when did she have that husband? Before he met her or after? Or even during? No, he couldn't believe that she would have given herself to him so freely, showing no sign of guilt during their time together, if she'd had a husband waiting in the wings. He wanted answers, and he planned to get them.

"Lauren, please. Sit and hear me out." Her cat jumped onto the sofa, climbed onto his lap, and peered up at him with curious blue eyes. "See, even . . . Hemingway, is it?" At her nod, he said, "Even Hemingway wants to hear what I have to say."

Like a wary crab, she inched sideways to the nearest chair. "You have five minutes."

Little did she know, he had as long as he wanted because she wasn't going anywhere. She might not like it, but it was for her own good. From all the signs she'd unknowingly given him, she fully expected bad trouble was headed her way.

"I have an offer for you." He absently stroked the cat's back, earning a loud purr. "I'll teach you how to shoot that gun, how to fight back, and if it becomes necessary, how to disappear without a trace. Right now, you don't know how to do any of those things, which, if your ex—What's his name again?"

"Stephan." She slapped her hand over her mouth.

Yeah, he'd tricked her into giving him the information, but he would've found out one way or another. She had no clue of the resources he had at his fingertips. "If Stephan comes after you right now, which you think he'll do, especially since his brother told you he would, you don't have the know-how to protect yourself."

"That's why I won't be here."

"Again, you don't know how to disappear without leaving a trail. He wants you bad enough, he'll find you. Does he want you that badly?"

She shrugged. "Maybe."

"Where is he right now, Lauren?" He sighed when she didn't answer. "Trust me, I can find out. You might as well make it easy on both of us."

He knew the second he lost her. Something he'd said triggered a reaction and not a good one. Her eyes glazed over, and she folded into herself, which he recognized as a typical response from a battered woman. When she walked away without a word, returning to her bedroom, he let her go. At her departure, the cat took off, following her.

After replaying their conversation, he came to the conclusion her trigger had been one or both of his last two sentences. What had the bastard done to her? He turned off the kitchen light, leaving the dim one under the microwave on.

He wasn't at all surprised when, a few hours later, she tiptoed to the coffee table where he'd dropped her backpack, picked it up, and then headed for the door. He rolled his eyes *and* sighed since neither gesture alone was enough to express his current exasperation. The damn woman was determined to drive him crazy.

As he saw it, he had two options. Scare the hell out of her again or prove that she didn't know how to disappear. He chose option two. She needed to learn a hard lesson, one that just might keep her alive if her ex was as dangerous as she seemed to think.

As soon as the door closed behind her, he put on his shoes and tugged on his shirt. At the bottom of the stairs, he cracked the door. She stood on the edge of the sidewalk, darting glances all around. At least she was *trying* to be aware of her surroundings, even if she was entirely too obvious about it. Another thing he needed to teach her.

A taxi pulled up, and as soon as it stopped, she jumped in. He made a mental note to explain to her how easy it was to bribe a cabbie to learn where she'd been dropped off. As the cab pulled away, he jogged across the street to his car. He made a bet with himself that he'd follow the taxi straight to the bus station.

CHAPTER FOUR

Lauren paid the driver, and after a quick look around, she hurried into the bus station. She'd forced herself to wait until she was sure Court was asleep before finally sneaking out. He wasn't going to be happy to find her gone, but she refused to put him, along with his brothers and Madison, in danger.

Everyone was safer if she disappeared, including herself. As long as Stephan couldn't find her, he couldn't hurt her. She bought a ticket for the first bus leaving, which was only going as far as Fort Lauderdale, unfortunately. At least, she'd be out of Miami where Court and Peter would be looking for her.

Her final destination was New Orleans, the city she'd settled on while waiting for Court to fall asleep. It was a place she could easily get lost in, and it should be simple enough to get a job as a waitress. If she got really lucky, the owner would agree to pay her under the table. That would probably mean working in a dive, but until she could figure out how to get a false ID, she wouldn't have much choice.

The one thing she regretted the most was not saying good-bye to her father and sister, but that was one of the first places Stephan would look for her. Their confusion as to her whereabouts would be obvious, so he would leave them alone. She had to believe that. When she thought it was safe enough, she'd call and reassure them she was okay.

As the bus headed north, she stared out the window even though it was too dark to see anything. All she saw was her reflection. The pink tips on her hair would have to go. Maybe she'd dye it red. She'd always liked dark auburn. The best color might be a mousy brown, though, something people wouldn't remember.

Court was wrong. She knew how to disappear, and when he woke up and she was nowhere to be found, he'd learn that. She'd almost told him everything, but then he'd said those words—so similar to Stephan's—that had unmercifully slung her back to that day she'd found Stephan in her home, waiting for her.

From her hospital room, she'd called Court and ended it between them to protect him. Now he was doing his best to negate everything she'd done for him, making himself a target for a vindictive and vicious man. Well, she wasn't having it.

The bus pulled into the Fort Lauderdale station, and she hoisted her backpack. As she waited to get off, she looked out the window, scanning the faces of the people milling around, relieved not to recognize anyone. She'd done it, gotten away without anyone the wiser.

After a quick stop in the restroom, she went to the ATM and withdrew as much cash as it would allow. That still left a few thousand dollars in her account as a cushion until she could find a job. When she got to New Orleans, she would write to Madison, giving her friend her share of the bookstore. If and when she could ever return to Miami, she trusted Madison to welcome her back as a partner.

She stuck the bills into the front pocket of her jeans, then went to the end of the ticket line. "New Orleans," she murmured, testing the sound of her soon-to-be new city, as she scanned the departure board.

"Not a bad choice for a city to disappear into."

Lauren froze. She knew that voice, recognized the scent of the man with his mouth next to her ear. It was impossible that he'd found her. He should just be waking up about now, puzzling over her absence. Hoping she was hallucinating, she turned her head, almost putting her mouth to mouth with Court. His breath was warm on her lips, and without any instruction to do so, her back leaned closer to his body heat, her lungs greedily soaking up his masculine scent.

She squeezed her eyes shut, willing her body not to shudder. He couldn't know the effect he had on her. "Go away, Court."

"Afraid I can't do that, G.G." He put his hand on the back of her neck. "Don't you want to know all the things you did wrong, making it easy for me to find you?"

She nodded. She did want to know what mistakes she'd made. With the gentlest of pressure from his fingers, he guided her outside. His touch was so different from Stephan's. Whenever her ex-husband had wrapped his hand around her neck, it was to dig his fingers into her skin, hurting her. After Stephan, it sometimes surprised her that she could still trust a man, yet she trusted Court. She wasn't sure why, but she knew in her heart that he would never physically hurt her.

"Do you often go around kidnapping women?" she said as he guided her toward his car.

"It's a daily occurrence. I see a woman I like, I drag her home with me."

"Lucky me to be today's woman."

"Unlike you, most are willing."

Well, that hurt. She didn't want to think of him being intimate with other women. When he opened the passenger door, she balked. "We can talk out here." As soon as she learned what she wanted to know, she was getting on that bus.

"Where we'll be noticed, and anyone questioned as to whether they've seen a woman matching your description will remember us both?" He moved his hand up to her hair, twirling a pink-tipped strand around his finger. "Your hair alone is memorable. If you're okay with that . . ." He trailed off, cocking a brow.

No, she wasn't okay with being memorable. He was making her feel totally inept, and it irritated her, but she was angrier with herself. She'd had six years to plan an escape. Should have disappeared the day Stephan went to prison. But she'd naïvely thought he would forget about her, especially when, other than one letter, he'd made no attempt to contact her after he was behind bars. She believed—or had wanted to believe—that he'd decided she wasn't worth his trouble. That bubble had burst when Peter had shown up.

Since she couldn't argue that everyone who'd seen her here wouldn't remember her hair, she got in the damn car, and pulled the door shut. She watched Court walk around the front, her eyes devouring him. From his military-style haircut to the muscles that rippled with every move he made, there wasn't a thing about him that didn't call to her. The black hair, his black, almond-shaped eyes, his chiseled features, and olive skin all added up to a very sexy man.

For six days, she'd known every inch of his body and he'd intimately known hers. By the time they'd parted, he had owned her heart. It wasn't fair. She'd been divorced, had been free to fall in love. Stephan hadn't had the right to destroy her hopes and dreams, but he had. She'd never stopped loving Court, although she'd tried.

He slid into the driver's seat, dropping his keys into the cup holder. "I made you an offer to teach you how to protect yourself, but you took off. I'm making it one more time."

"I thought it would be obvious that by leaving I didn't want you involved." She had to try to get him to stay out of her problems.

"Got that message loud and clear. But, Lauren, if I could find you, he can, too, if he knows how to look. Does he?"

That was the question, wasn't it? Toward the end, before she'd left Stephan, she'd begun to suspect there was more to her husband and his brother than they wanted her to know. There had been too many times she'd been sent to her bedroom when other Russian men would visit. And those men all radiated danger from their cold eyes.

She pressed her fingers against the bridge of her nose. "I don't know. Maybe."

"Then your first lesson is knowing your enemy down to every last detail." He pulled her hand away from her face. "Listen to me. You can't outsmart someone if you can't make an educated guess as to his next step because you don't know him inside and out."

"How did you find me?" He let out what sounded an awful lot like a snort. She wanted to punch him. Or maybe kiss him. She was too confused and bone-weary to figure out which.

"Baby, you left a trail a mile long."

"Such as?" It was hard being so close to him in the confines of the car. All she wanted to do was curl herself around him and forget everything.

"We'll get to all that." He picked up the keys, slid one into the ignition, and turned it.

She reached over to turn it off. "I'm not leaving with you. Besides dying my hair, what else?" He put his hand over hers, pulling it away from the key. He didn't let go of her hand, though; instead, he rested it on his thigh. She knew she should pull away, but it felt so good to touch him.

"Such as getting in a taxi right outside your front door to start, but this isn't the place to have this discussion." He squeezed her hand. "I told you I'd teach you what you need to know. I'm asking you to come back to Miami. You'll be safe with me, I promise."

It was so tempting to agree, but her purpose in disappearing was not only to protect herself, but him as well. He sighed, something he seemed to do a lot around her.

She'd never had a real boyfriend before Stephan. She wasn't a stupid person, but she had been sheltered. Her minister father and her mother had homeschooled her and Julie, most of their social activities involving church events. So no, she hadn't learned how to disappear without a trace. How did Court even know all these things?

He sighed again. "I can hear the wheels turning, G.G. How about trusting me for one week? If at the end of seven days you still feel like you don't need my help, I'll put you on a plane under an assumed name and send you wherever you want to go."

There was an offer she couldn't refuse. She had almost two weeks before Stephan was released, so she could be long gone by then, with whatever tricks up her sleeve that Court could teach her. Even more appealing, she would get to spend seven days with Court, something she found she couldn't resist, or even wanted to.

"Okay," she said, even though the voice in her head was calling her a fool.

Relieved, Court shifted into reverse, backing out of the space. He wasn't going to have to resort to Plan B. Kidnapping was not something an officer of the law should be considering, but he couldn't let her traipse off thinking she knew what she was doing. Truthfully, he had no idea what *he* was doing, but until he learned all the facts, including who her husband was and what he was capable of, he would have stopped her however he had to.

"You're going to stay with me for the next seven days." When she shook her head, he said, "I have a guest bedroom, which is all yours for the duration. Peter said if you didn't show up to see Stephan, he would come collect you. Do you really want to stay alone at your apartment, risking him following through on his threat?"

She paled. "No."

"Didn't think so." He pulled out of the bus station parking lot, aiming his car for home. A few minutes later, she'd unsurprisingly fallen asleep. He doubted she'd gotten much rest since Peter had delivered the message from his brother.

The sun was rising, providing enough light to see her face. In sleep, the tension lines around her eyes and mouth had eased, making her look more like the girl he'd fallen for six years ago.

He'd seen her within an hour of walking onto the beach his first day in Panama City. She'd been playing volleyball, the two teams a mix of guys and girls. Her neon green bikini was the first thing to catch his attention, followed quickly by her smoking hot body. Even then, she'd worn her hair in that short, spiky style she still favored. He'd always thought he preferred long hair on a woman, but Lauren had proven him wrong.

There was something edgy and earthy about her, and as he watched her dive for the ball, missing and falling on her face, he saw a woman not afraid to go after what she wanted. She pushed up and spit sand out of her mouth, all the while laughing. Lust hit him hard.

He moved into her line of sight, watching only her while the game lasted. Several times, she looked over at him, her gaze lingering a little longer with each glance. When she missed the ball, doing another face-plant in the sand, she came up laughing, even though her miss had lost the game for her team.

One of the male players came over to her, put his mouth close to her ear, and said something. Court gritted his teeth, wanting to step between them and claim her, but he dug his toes into the sand, anchoring himself to the spot. If the dude was her boyfriend, he had no right to interfere. She shook her head, patted the guy on the arm, and then faced Court.

She raised a brow. He mimicked her, raising one back. As if he could read the mind of a woman he'd never seen before, he understood she wanted him to come to her. He'd be damned if he would. It wasn't that he wanted to control her. He'd never been that kind of man, would never allow himself to be like his father. No, this was something different.

The stand they were each taking was a purely sexual one. Which one of them would have the other on their knees first? And at the thought of her on her knees in front of him, he went rock fucking hard. Her gaze lowered to his board shorts, and he didn't try to hide how much he wanted her. After a few seconds, her eyes roamed up his body, finally meeting his. Golden-brown eyes snared his, and he accepted that he'd lost the game. He didn't care. Without even realizing his feet were moving, he walked toward her.

The first thing he learned about her was that she didn't bask in her victories. As soon as he moved, she did, too, meeting him halfway. They were inseparable for the next six days, and he'd thought he'd known her inside and out by the time spring break was over. When they kissed good-bye, he told her that he loved her. If she hadn't said it back, and if they hadn't made plans to see each other on alternating weekends and school breaks—meeting somewhere halfway between the University of Miami, where she was going to school, and Florida State University, where he was in his final year—he might have understood her cutting him off without giving him one damn reason for doing so. Turned out, he hadn't known her at all.

But was that true? Things he'd learned about her during one of the most intense weeks of his life came flooding back. How she'd stayed glued to his side whenever they'd ventured out among the drunk, partying college guys looking to get laid.

"Most will respect a no from you, but a few won't give a damn that you don't want to be raped," he'd told her. "Don't let go of my hand." For six days, she had never let go of him.

He had learned that she was fearless but not stupid. He had learned that she could make a man feel like he'd won a once-in-a-lifetime lottery. And he'd learned that just as easily as she'd given him the world, she had as easily snatched it away, walking off without a backward glance.

♠♠♠

After Court showed her to the guest room, Lauren dropped her backpack on the floor, and then shut the door in his face. That had been two hours ago, and he hadn't heard a sound from her since. He assumed she was sleeping, but because he didn't trust her not to try to sneak out again, he'd grabbed a pillow and catnapped on his sofa.

Two hours later, he sat up, yawned, and stretched his arms above his head. He was getting too old to be up all night. After making a cup of extra-strong coffee, he got out his laptop. Time to do a little investigating, find out who Lauren had married and when. The *when* was the question that ate at him. Had she gone back home and gotten married after saying she loved him? Those three words they'd exchanged had meant something to him. If the week she'd spent with him had been nothing more than a lark before she settled down with a wedding ring on her finger, he might go ballistic.

Wasn't that what women did, though? Walk out without looking back. His mother had done it, and he should have learned his lesson then. But he'd thought Lauren was different, had believed her when she'd said she loved him. It didn't make sense that he was getting angry all over again. He'd dealt with his feelings where Lauren Montgomery was concerned and had put them behind him. He was a smarter man than he'd been six years ago, and he'd never allow another woman to hurt him again.

CHAPTER FIVE

Lauren blinked open her eyes, frowning at the light beige wall. That wasn't the wall in her bedroom. She rolled onto her back, scanning her surroundings. She'd never been in this room before. Where was she? And why was she in bed wearing her clothes?

Was that coffee she smelled? She sat up, combing her hands through her hair. Her brain finally woke up, supplying one word. *Court.*

Right. I was kidnapped.

Grabbing her backpack, she went searching for a bathroom.

Thirty minutes later, showered, clothes changed, and hair air-drying, she made her way to the kitchen, hoping there was coffee. There was, thank you God. She wandered into the living room, stopping when she saw Court sitting on the sofa, watching her.

"Morning," he said, closing his laptop.

"I haven't decided if I'm talking to you yet."

He chuckled. "Let me know when you decide. We have some things to discuss."

Things she'd hoped to never talk about, but Stephan was once again making her life miserable. To delay having that conversation until she was more alert, she went out to Court's balcony. The view was incredible. A tropical storm was supposed to make its way up the Florida coast sometime this evening, but the ocean was already stirred up.

She'd been too tired to notice what floor Court lived on when they'd arrived last night, but looking down, she guessed the eighth or ninth. Even from up here, she could hear the waves crashing onshore. A seagull caught her attention, and she watched it try to fly against the wind. She loved walking on the beach when the ocean was angry, and wished she were down there right now.

Without glancing back, she knew Court was standing behind her. How did she sense him so easily? It was as if she had some kind of invisible connection to him, the way her senses recognized his presence. She could probably close her eyes and still know if he came within ten feet of her.

"Fortunately, the storm's weakening, just a lot of rain and some wind," he said.

"I like storms. The smell and sound of the rain, the breeze blowing on me." She leaned over the rail, lifting her face to the wind.

"I remember," he said softly.

So did she. A thunderstorm had moved in one afternoon during spring break. Until the rain and lightning came, he'd walked on the beach with her, then they'd returned to his room, opened the windows so she could listen to the rain while they passed the afternoon making love.

"I'm sorry." *For so many things.* She glanced over her shoulder, but he'd gone back inside, missing her apology. Maybe it was better that he hadn't heard, because then he'd ask what she was sorry for, and she couldn't tell him the truth.

Her coffee had grown cold, but she drank it anyway, and then followed him in, ready for her inquisition. She would tell him as little as she could get away with, until she learned what she needed to know.

He was back on the sofa, working on his laptop again, so she parked herself in a chair, waiting for him to start with his questions. While his attention was on the screen, her eyes devoured him, noting the ways he was still the same versus the changes six years had brought him.

When she'd met him, he'd been happier, quick to laugh. That was one change she didn't like, and she'd hate herself if she were the reason the light was gone from his eyes. But that was silly. Weren't men famous for moving on? She was certain that he hadn't been celibate all that time. As gorgeous as he was, he could have any woman he wanted.

Did he have a girlfriend? She wasn't about to ask, but it would be surprising if he didn't. Or maybe he was a player, which would make her sad as well. The boy she'd fallen in love with had only had eyes for her. Not once from that first day had she caught him checking out another girl. She did hope he was happy, and if that meant with another woman, she had no right to resent it.

"How long you going to stare at me?" He closed the laptop lid.

Her cheeks heated, probably turning red. "I wasn't. Just waiting for you to finish."

One side of his mouth curled up. "Were, too."

That was another change she'd noticed. He didn't used to smirk. "So, what do you want to know?" she asked, changing the subject.

"My first question was going to be when did you get married, but I found that answer for myself."

"You're doing a search on me? That's an invasion of my privacy, you know."

"If you'd told me the things I need to know, I wouldn't have had to"—he made air quotes—"invade your privacy."

"If you've found out everything, then I guess our Q-and-A session is over." She stood.

"Sit, Lauren. We're not done here."

She saluted him as she plopped back down. "Yes, sir."

"Attitude, G.G. I don't feel like you're showing appreciation for what I'm trying to do for you."

They were both getting irritated, which she knew would get them nowhere. She took a calming breath. "Fine. I appreciate it, even though I didn't ask for your help. In fact, I'd prefer you stay out of it."

"No can do. Your divorce was final a few days before we met. Stephan Kozlov was a star player for the Florida Thunder. Sounds like quite a catch. Why'd you divorce him, and where is he now?"

Obviously, he hadn't discovered everything, which was a relief. If he found out she'd lied, she didn't know how he'd react. He'd be angry for sure, and he'd probably be insulted that she'd done it to protect him. An affront to his male ego, and all that.

Not that she wasn't beginning to think he was capable of going up against Stephan now, but back then, Court had been more boy than man, with a bright future ahead of him. He'd been only months from graduating, and she'd loved him too much to drag him into her mess of a life, especially when it would have put him in danger.

Truthfully, she was surprised he'd ended up owning a biker bar, but maybe his older brother had talked him into it. He'd majored in criminal justice, with a minor in computer science. Whenever she'd let herself wonder about him, she'd imagined he'd gone on to law school or maybe something to do with fraud investigations. He'd once mentioned that he thought that kind of job would be fun.

"Why did you divorce him, Lauren?"

"Because he turned out to be not such a nice man, okay?"

"That's a good reason. Where is he now?"

The answer to that would lead to all the things she didn't want him to know. "I need to use the bathroom." She paused at the hallway. "And stop invading my privacy. No more searches on your computer."

In the bathroom, she splashed cold water on her face. A week, he'd said, and then she could leave. All she had to do was keep him from discovering she'd almost died to keep his name from Stephan. If Court learned that, he'd probably decide to play knight in shining armor. He was already trying to involve himself. Somehow, she had to find a way to stop him.

"You promised to tell me how you found me," she said when she returned, hoping to steer the conversation away from personal questions.

"Why'd you leave me?"

"I told you, I had to go to the bathroom."

Court hadn't meant to ask her that, but it was the question burning a hole in his gut. Or heart. Or wherever. "I'm not asking why you left the room. Why'd you leave *me*?" He told his mouth to shut up.

She bowed her head, closing her eyes. "Please don't do this."

There was something in the way her shoulders slumped in defeat that made him want to hold her and tell her he would fix whatever the problem was. Angry with himself for even thinking about wrapping his arms around her, and angry with her for making him want to, he stood, went to the glass doors, and stared out at the ocean.

She'd asked him not to invade her privacy, which meant she was hiding something. If she hadn't come inside when she had, he would have had time to find out for himself whatever it was she didn't want him to know. It would be easy enough once he was alone to continue his investigation into her life. Although he wasn't sure why, he wanted her to trust him enough to tell him. So he would respect her privacy while working to gain her trust. He would not, however, respect Peter Kozlov's privacy. In the short time he'd had to look into the man, some worrisome things had cropped up.

"You want to know what you did wrong?" He returned to the sofa, and perched on the arm, which brought him closer to the chair she sat in. "Like I told you earlier, getting in a cab right outside your door was your first mistake. All I had to do was hand over a few dollars to find out which taxi picked you up, and then a few more bucks to learn he'd taken you to the bus station."

She didn't need to know that he'd followed her from the moment she'd tried to sneak out, making sure she stayed safe. If he told her that, she wouldn't listen to how easily he really could have found her if he'd had to pay off a cabdriver.

"Second, your hair is distinctive. You should have worn a wig or at the very least a ball cap. You never paid attention to your surroundings. At the bus station, I was able to walk right up to your back without you noticing. If I was up to no good, I could have abducted you and had you out of the building before anyone was the wiser."

"You did abduct me," she grumbled.

He hid a smile. She was adorable when she was grouchy. "Next, you used an ATM."

That got a frown. "Bank records are confidential."

"I could have your bank history in my hands by this time tomorrow, either by hacking into your bank records or by bribing an employee." He was exaggerating to an extent. It wouldn't be that easy, but a determined person could find a way. He could easily hack into her bank records, but that was another thing she didn't need to know. The goal was to make her think before she acted.

"What else?"

"That's it, but that was only for the first two hours of your attempted disappearing act. Left to your own devices, you would have continued to make mistakes. I'm not criticizing you, only trying to make you see that it's too easy to leave a trail if you don't know what you're doing."

"Then teach me."

"I said I would, but that's not all you need to know. How to defend yourself is high on that list." A plan was forming in his mind, a way to kill a whole flock of birds with one stone. He needed to talk to Nate and Alex, get them on board, get some things set up.

He stood. "I have some things to take care of today. You need to make an appearance at your bookstore. If anyone is watching, you want everything to appear normal. Tonight, we'll begin your training."

Her eyes widened. "Watching me?"

"Peter didn't seem the type to make threats he didn't mean. He said he would come collect you if he had to. If he's smart, it will occur to him that you might run, so you can't discount he has someone watching you." He didn't enjoy scaring her, but if his suspicions were correct, she needed to be scared and wary.

She wrapped her arms around her waist and rocked her body. "Why can't they just leave me alone?"

Court was beginning to think Stephan was obsessed with her, which was disturbing. A man obsessed with a woman was dangerous and unpredictable. "Get whatever you need, and I'll take you to work. Madison should be arriving about now. She's gonna be concerned that you aren't there. You should probably call her."

"Madison wants to tell Lauren that we're FBI," Alex said.

Court eyed his baby brother, wondering if he'd lost his mind. "Absolutely not." He didn't trust Lauren with their secrets.

"Why does she want to?" Nate asked.

"Because they're best friends, and some dude's hassling Lauren." Alex shrugged. "I guess Madison thinks we can help her somehow."

Nate shook his head. "Just because someone's hassling her isn't a good enough reason to blow our cover."

At least his older brother had some sense. Marriage had made Alex soft. He was all touchy-feely now. He needed to knock that shit off. They were undercover FBI agents operating a biker bar, dealing with the worst of humanity on a daily basis. Soft got you killed. Alex had almost died once, and if he went and did it for real, Court would never forgive him.

"I have something to run past you both," Court said. They could definitely help Lauren without telling her who they were. If his brothers weren't on board, he'd go it alone.

They were sitting around the dining room table in Nate's condo, Court waiting to pitch his idea. After he'd taken Lauren to the bookstore, he'd returned home to learn all he could about Peter Kozlov.

Although he'd resisted searching for information on Stephan Kozlov while investigating Peter, he'd inadvertently stumbled on the fact that Stephan was in prison. He hadn't decided yet whether that entitled him to invade Lauren's privacy. If knowing why a hockey star was sitting in a prison cell helped him keep her safe, he would invade her privacy without one iota of guilt.

"You got curious about the dude claiming to be Lauren's brother-in-law, so you went a-snooping. Am I right?" Alex asked.

"*A-snooping?* You're an idiot, bro." When Alex kicked him, Court kicked him back.

Nate sighed. "If you two don't behave, I'm going to call time-out."

"What? You have X-ray vision and can see through the table now?" Court said.

"No, I just know how your juvenile brains work." Nate leaned his chair back onto two legs. "Stop picking on your brother and tell us what you got."

"Want to learn someone's secrets, then you follow the money." He held up a hand. "And don't ask how. You don't want to know."

Nate snorted. "I wasn't about to ask. What'd you learn?"

It was a known fact among the brothers that Court could hack his way past almost any firewall. While he seldom used those skills in an investigation—since nothing he learned could be used in court—he had on occasion snooped if an investigation hit a brick wall.

"Lauren's ex was a star player for the Florida Thunder, but he's in prison now." He took some pages from the printer, stacking them on the desk. "Don't you think it's interesting that Peter Kozlov, who managed Stephan's career, hasn't had an income since his brother was sent to prison, yet he still lives in the same house, valued at twelve million, drives a Bentley valued at over two hundred thou, and throws cash around like it's cheap candy?"

"Meaning there's a steady flow of money into his bank account?" Alex replied.

"Why's Stephan in prison?" Nate asked.

"As to why he's in prison, I don't know. Lauren asked me not to invade her privacy. For the moment, I'm respecting her wishes. To answer Alex's question, a *very* steady flow of money. It's coming from accounts known to have ties to the Russian mafia."

He filled them in on all that he'd learned about Peter Kozlov. When he finished, he leveled his gaze on Nate. "I think once Rothmire hears all this, he'll open a file on the brothers. I want the case."

"Not learning what you need to know because Lauren asked you not to?" Alex said. "Who are you and what have you done with my brother?"

Nate dropped the legs of his chair to the floor. "Well, *I* didn't promise her anything. Before I'll agree to take this to Rothmire, I need to know why her ex-husband's in prison." He glanced at his watch. "I've got a meeting with the boss in an hour. I'll lay the groundwork, but I'm not asking for an investigation until I do a little snooping of my own since you're so in love with her that you're not willing to do your job."

That burned. "I'm not in love with her. I'm just respecting her wishes."

"Yeah, yeah," Nate said.

Alex waggled his eyebrows, a smirk on his face. "Welcome to the Love Club."

When Alex stood, Court stuck out his leg, tripping him, sending him stumbling across the room. "Pretty pitiful ninja, bro, when you can't even stay on your feet." Alex was already on the move. At the demonic glint in his brother's eyes, Court moved behind Nate.

"You should move aside unless you want to go down with him," Alex said to Nate.

"Gotta run. He's all yours. Try not to hurt him too badly." Nate chuckled as he walked out.

Court held up his hands. "Uncle." Two seconds later, he was on the floor, staring up at Alex. "Damn, when did you learn that move?" Laughing, he pushed up. "I guess *uncle* doesn't work anymore?"

"I've come to hate that word." No surprise, considering everything Madison's uncle had put her through.

Court left to put his plan in motion, the one he'd not shared with his brothers. Probably better that he held off on telling them he planned to make himself a target.

CHAPTER SIX

"You promised to tell me about you and Court. All you said was that you met him at spring break."

Lauren had been expecting to get the third degree from her friend and was surprised that Madison had managed to hold in her curiosity. It was the end of a busy day, and she and Madison were tidying up after locking the doors.

They'd met at the University of Miami when they'd joined the same book club. When they'd discovered that they both dreamed of owning a bookstore someday, they'd teamed up and opened High Tea and Black Cat Books.

They were perfectly matched. Lauren loved the numbers side of the business. Madison's expertise was promotion and marketing, coordinating events, and dealing with their customers.

Madison knew some details about Lauren's life with Stephan. Lauren had felt Madison needed to know because he could be a threat to them both when he got out of prison.

"So, that week I took off for spring break without telling you—"

"You had me so worried when you disappeared."

Stephan had contested the divorce, and his threats had frightened her. The divorce had been granted three days before the start of spring break, and in her need to get away from all the drama that was Stephan, she'd taken off for Panama City.

"I called you the next day, told you where I was and why. But I don't want to talk about Stephan."

"We need to talk about him soon because he gets out of prison in about two weeks, right?"

Lauren nodded. "We will, but not today."

Madison reached over and squeezed her hand. "Okay, but soon. So, back to Court."

"I met him the first day I arrived in Panama City. Have you ever looked into a man's eyes and just known there was something special between you?"

"It happened that way with Alex."

"Yeah, I could see the chemistry between the two of you the first time I saw you together. It was like that with Court. The best word I can think of to describe it is intense."

"That's a good word for all three of the Gentry brothers. Were you in love with Court?"

She sighed. "I fell hard for him. We were inseparable from the moment we met until we had to return to school. It was a week of bliss, Maddie." She blinked against the tears burning her eyes. "We made plans to see each other, you know, meet halfway on weekends, that kind of thing. Then I came home and you know the rest."

Madison leaned back against the counter. "Did you tell Court about Stephan?"

"No. What Court and I had was just so beautiful. I didn't want to spoil it with the ugliness going on in my life. I planned to tell him everything the next time I saw him, but I never had a chance." Images of the day she'd found Stephan waiting for her flashed through her mind. She involuntarily shuddered.

"Go on," Madison softly said.

"It hurts to remember, you know?" She tried to blink away the stinging tears.

Madison smiled, compassion in her eyes. "I know it does. I was afraid of my cousin, and he didn't do to me anything near what Stephan did to you. I was there at the hospital, Lauren. I saw your battered body. Of course it hurts to remember."

"Dammit, Maddie, you're going to make me cry. God, I love you." Madison's smile grew wider. "I know that, too."

Lauren took a calming breath. "Okay, so Stephan as much as said he'd go after any man who touched me. After what he did to me, I believed him. I called Court from the hospital and told him I didn't want to see him again. When he asked why, I hung up."

"Oh, sweetie." Madison stepped forward and hugged her.

The dam broke. All the hurt and fear came pouring out in fat, hot tears. For losing a man she'd known she could have loved forever, and then for finding him again, only to know she'd have to leave him a second time.

She buried her face in Madison's shoulder. Damn Stephan to hell. After his arrest for her assault, he'd been cut by his team. At his sentencing, as he was being led out of the courtroom, he'd stared hard at her with those glacier-blue eyes. She'd seen the accusation in them. He blamed her for everything—the arrest, his guilty sentence, losing his contract with the Thunder. That Stephan had only gotten six years after his brutal assault had been a blow.

"Oh God, you're crying, too. I'm sorry." Lauren pulled away.

Madison swiped at her face. "You're my best friend. Of course I'm crying with you." She reached under the counter, pulled out a box of tissues, and handed Lauren a few.

Lauren wiped her eyes. "Thanks. I thought I was done crying about all this."

"It helps to cry sometimes." Madison took her hand. "Can I tell Alex?"

"No. Please don't. You two are just married. You don't need to be worrying about me."

"Dammit, Lauren. I'm going to worry about you whether you like it or not. Alex already suspects there's something between you and Court, and—"

"Why would he think that?"

"It's obvious when the two of you are in the same room together that sparks are flying."

Lauren shook her head. "He hates me."

"I'm not so sure about that. You need to let me tell Alex everything. About both Stephan and Court."

"Let me think about it, okay?"

"You keep saying to give you time, but while you're thinking, consider this: What if Peter tells his brother about Court? Don't you think Court should know that a man who thinks nothing of beating you badly enough to put you in the hospital is gunning for him?"

Lauren buried her face in her hands. "Oh, God, that's why I ended it with him. So he wouldn't get caught up in this."

"You're underestimating Court's ability to deal with a situation like this. Not to mention, he has two brothers at his back. Stephan's no match for the three of them together. Trust me on this, Lauren. The Gentry brothers can handle a lowlife like Stephan. I know what I'm talking about."

Since there was no way to avoid Madison finding out, she said, "Court knows a little, enough that he's making me stay at his place for a few days."

"Seriously? When were you going to tell me?"

She saw Court walking up to the door. "About now. Court thought it would be safer for me at his place. I'm sleeping in the guest room."

"Yes, and that puts you close to him. You know, it gives you time to get to know him again."

Until he did as promised and put her on a plane. "Guess we should let him in." When Madison unlocked the door and he stepped inside, he gave Madison a hug. Lauren envied their closeness.

"So," Madison said, "I guess you're here to pick up Lauren?"

He glanced from Madison to her, and Lauren could see the question in his eyes. How much had she told Madison? "She knows I'm staying in your guest room for a few days because of Peter." She was still undecided as to whether she'd tell Madison she was leaving in a week, but if she did, she'd wait until it was time to go.

"You need any more clothes?" Court asked. At her nod, he said, "Go get whatever you need. I'll wait here."

Hemingway jumped out of the display window, giving them his I'm-hungry meow. Madison picked him up. "I'll go upstairs with you and get Hemingway fed and settled in while you pack."

"Spill," Madison said as soon as they were in the apartment. "You're hiding something."

"I'm not. Really." She hated lying to her friend, but the less Madison knew, the safer they'd both be. Plus, Madison would try to talk her out of leaving by arguing that the Gentry brothers could protect her. Maybe. The more she saw of them, the more she was coming to believe they could. But if what she'd long suspected about Stephan, and especially Peter, was true, then she just couldn't involve Court and his brothers.

Madison set Hemingway down. "I know you, Lauren. You're hiding something, and I will find out what."

"Your imagination's running away with you. I'll meet you downstairs." She headed for her room before Madison could start grilling her.

Court stood in the shadows, away from the display window, watching the dark-colored car parked across the street. It had pulled into the space while he was talking to Lauren and Madison, but no one had exited. Suspicious and wanting to know who was in the car, he pulled out his phone and made a call to a friend. The girls came down a few minutes later.

"Stay in the hallway," he said.

Lauren peeked around the doorway. "What's going on?"

"Not sure yet, but we're about to find out."

A police cruiser slowed as it passed the bookstore. David Markham, his cop friend, pulled up next to the car, turning on his blue lights. David exited the cruiser, going to the driver's window. A minute later, a driver's license was handed over. After a short discussion, David returned the license. The car's lights came on before it drove off.

"Don't come out until I tell you to," he said once the taillights disappeared. Court walked to the cruiser.

"You always make life interesting, Court, my man. What's the story this time?"

"Depends on who was in the car."

"Man by the name of Peter Kozlov, and somehow I don't think that surprises you."

"Wish I could say it did. What'd he say he was doing?"

David shrugged. "That he needed to text someone so he pulled over. Funny thing, when I walked up to the window, his phone was nowhere in sight. I suppose you know what he was up to?"

"Yep. Dude's harassing the woman who lives above the bookstore. She's a friend. I need one more favor."

"If it's in my power."

"I need to get her away without anyone knowing. Can you stay out here, make sure Kozlov doesn't circle back?"

"That I can do."

"Also, for the next week or so, keep an eye on the bookstore. My brother's wife is part owner. He'd be real upset if anyone messed with her in an attempt to get to her friend."

"Her friend the one upstairs?" At Court's nod, David said, "I'll pass the word around."

"Appreciate it. I owe you one." The more eyes on the bookstore the better.

David snorted. "Just one? I'm collecting them until I have enough favors from you for a fishing trip in the Bahamas on your dime."

"You drive a hard bargain, my friend." While David drove the police cruiser into a parking space, Court jumped into his car, moving it across the street in front of the shop's door.

"I'm taking you home, too, Madison," he said, poking his head in the doorway. "Let's load up before our friend comes back."

"Why's a cop here, and who was in that car?" Lauren asked.

"I'll explain everything when we get to my place."

On the way back to his condo, he made several turns, watching his rearview mirror. As he drove, he kept glancing at Lauren. She huddled in her seat, her gaze out the window, but he doubted she even noticed the passing scenery. He guessed that she'd figured out who had been in the car.

It was killing him, seeing her like that. He couldn't help comparing her to the girl he'd met on the beach. If she'd told him what was going on in her life, how different would things be today?

Had she been in danger even back then? Was that why she'd ended things between them without an explanation? Because she'd been forced to? Until he knew the full story, he could only guess, and he didn't like guessing.

In the elevator as they rode up, Lauren stood as far away from him as possible, keeping Madison between them. It irritated him how much he wanted to touch her, to somehow put the laughter back into her eyes. Being around her brought all the memories back. How soft her skin felt as his hands explored every inch of her body, how her scent intoxicated him, how she tasted, but most of all, the way she would look at him, her eyes filled with love. Or so he'd thought at the time.

He wanted to kiss her senseless, until she begged him to take her right here in the elevator. By the time they said good-bye to Madison, and he closed his condo door behind him and Lauren, he was past caring that she'd cut out his heart with a rusty hacksaw.

She stood in his entryway, silent and wary. That irritated him, too. He didn't deserve her attitude. He'd done nothing but love her. Something dark and hungry was born inside him as their eyes caught and held. Keeping his gaze on her, he stepped closer. He trailed the back of his hand down her cheek, then brushed his thumb over her bottom lip.

Satisfaction hummed through him as desire replaced the wariness in her eyes. She wasn't immune to him, and it was only fair. He sure as hell wasn't immune to her. Maybe he should lock himself in his room until he got control of his need for her, but she was here and he'd never been able to resist her.

"If you don't want me to kiss you, walk away right now." But she didn't walk away, so he cupped her chin, lifting her face. Their eyes locked as he lowered his mouth, softly pressing his lips to hers. She stood perfectly still, but her breath hitched when their lips touched.

Hungry for her, he deepened the kiss, slipping his tongue into the sweet recess of her mouth. At her quiet whimper, he wrapped his arms around her back, pulling her against him. She willingly came, snuggling into him. Their tongues tangled, and for all he knew or cared, the world could have stopped turning.

When she slid her arms around his neck, he walked her back a few steps until she was pressed against the wall. He rocked his groin against her, showing her what she did to him. She groaned, and by sheer force of will, he tore his mouth away before he took her down to the floor with him in his foyer. He shouldn't have touched her because now that he had, a fire raged inside him, wanting what he couldn't have. With his breaths coming as fast as hers, he stared down at her. His head throbbed with the knowledge that the years hadn't dimmed his desire for her.

"That was a mistake," he said, stepping back, putting space between them before the lust he felt could take over, consequences be damned. After he taught her how to disappear without a trace, she'd leave him again. Hell, he wasn't even sure if he wished she'd stay.

She turned her face away. "Just don't do it again."

He wasn't sure he could promise that where she was concerned. "I have to go out for a while. Help yourself to anything in the kitchen." There was nowhere he needed to go, but he had to get away from her so he could get his head straight.

CHAPTER SEVEN

Lauren stared at the door as it closed behind Court. It hurt hearing him say that kissing her was a mistake, and pride had made her tell him not to do it again. How was she supposed to spend seven days with him? Anytime he came near her, she wanted to touch him, wanted him to hold her the way he had when she'd still believed in happily ever afters.

She touched her lips, still tingling from his kiss as she took in her surroundings. Since Court had brought her to his home, she really hadn't taken the time to look around. Who was he today, the boy she'd fallen in love with?

Spying a bottle of wine on his kitchen counter, she poured a glass, then wandered into the living room. His furniture was all earth tones, subdued like him. He apparently liked minimalist contemporary. Other than a large, obviously expensive, brown leather couch, a matching recliner, a dark cherry coffee table, and a large-screen TV mounted on the wall, that was about it, except for a single bookcase next to the TV. She walked over to it.

She counted sixteen books, all nonfiction. There were a few biographies on famous people, a couple of criminal justice books, including one titled *Famous Cases of the FBI.* As she pulled it out to flip through it, she noticed a thin hardback in poor condition. She picked it up instead. It was one of R. L. Stine's Goosebumps books and appeared to be well read.

Inside the front cover was a message:

Happy birthday, my sweet son. You are growing into a wonderful young man, and I'm so proud of you.

Love always,

Mommy

Lauren smiled. Something about holding a book Court had obviously treasured as a boy brought tears to her eyes. What kind of childhood had he had? She hoped it had been a happy one. As she flipped through the pages, stopping to read a paragraph here and there, she couldn't help but wish she knew more about his life.

After replacing the book, she eyed the other items in the bookcase. The only photo was one of the three Gentry brothers, taken at Court's graduation from Florida State University. Why didn't he have any other family pictures, ones with his parents? It made her sad that she didn't know. She traced her finger over Court's face in the picture. It would have been taken only a few months after they'd met. Although he was smiling, it didn't reach his eyes.

Grabbing the bottle of wine and her phone, she headed out to the balcony. She'd seen her father and sister a few days before Peter had shown up, but she suddenly needed to hear her dad's voice, needed to pretend for a few minutes that everything was normal. She stared at her phone, and then set it back on the table. It would be too tempting to tell him everything—about Stephan's threat, that she needed to leave. He and Julie were safer not knowing anything.

So she sat on Court's balcony, sad and lonely and scared, and drank wine. Halfway through her second glass, she gave in, allowing herself to have a good cry. She'd lost so much already and stood to lose everything, including possibly her life. All because of a man who not only thought he owned her, but believed he had the right to dictate her every move, from her choice of clothes to who she could have as a friend. Even the books she read.

"What are you reading," Stephan had asked one afternoon after returning home from a team practice.

They'd been married two weeks when he'd asked the question, and although he'd hit her on their wedding night, he'd apologized and begged her forgiveness. She'd believed him because tears of remorse had fallen down his cheeks as he promised it would never happen again. She hadn't yet learned to be afraid of him.

Although she was well read, romances were her go-to books when she wanted an escape for a few hours. Without hesitation, she'd lifted the book, showing him the cover, which featured a sexy male model.

He snatched the book out of her hand. "What is this? You are drooling over other men?"

"Don't be silly, Stephan. It's a book, a story. It's not real."

Rage had burned in his eyes, and he'd torn the book in half with his bare hands.

After that, she'd kept her romance novels hidden, only reading them when he was playing away games. It wasn't until she left him that she could look back and see that the book-tearing episode had been the beginning of her trying to be the perfect wife, doing her best not to upset him.

Well, he could just go to hell. She refilled her glass, then lifted the goblet in a salute. "I just sent you to hell, Stephan, so take that, you bastard. And another thing. You will never touch me again." She angrily swiped at the tears streaming down her cheeks. "Ever," she whispered. She'd rather die first. She tipped her glass to her mouth, drinking the last of her wine. "And I'll read as many romance books as I want to, whenever I want to."

The balmy breeze coming off the Atlantic was soothing, and she leaned her head back, closing her eyes. What was it about the ocean that brought peace to her heart? The rhythmic crashing of the surf floated up, lulling her to sleep.

Sometime later, she jerked awake. A little drunk and half asleep, she stumbled to her room. The pillow next to her smelled like Court, as if a rain-drenched forest had been sprinkled with exotic spices. She pulled it to her, snuggling her face into it.

Court stood next to his bed, staring down at the woman sound asleep in it. Why was Lauren in his bed? Seeing her hugging his pillow as if wanting to be close to him did things to his heart, things he wasn't sure he was ready for.

He'd found a half-empty bottle of wine on the balcony. Did she even know which room she'd gone to? He debated moving her to the guest room, but it was late, he was tired, and he decided he liked her right where she was.

For tonight, he would stop thinking about their past. Other than a quick shower to get the stink of the day off, he wanted nothing more than to slide into that bed and hold close the woman he'd never been able to forget. But he couldn't.

An hour later, still wide-awake and keeping space between them, he listened to Lauren mumble in her sleep. As tired as he was, he'd been sure he'd drop right off. That wasn't happening. He wanted her. He didn't want her. Teach her what she needed to know so he could get her out of his life, or never let her go? At some point, he was going to have to make a decision. Straddling the fence wasn't his style, but this woman had him tied up in knots.

"No, Stephan." She let out a sob, her body jerking as if struck. "Please stop!"

What had the bastard done to her to make her cry out in her sleep? When she started kicking him as if trying to escape, Court gathered her into his arms. "Hush, baby. You're safe." A shudder passed through her. "I promise no one will ever hurt you again." He kept his voice soft, and as he talked to her, she calmed. Once she'd fallen back into a peaceful sleep, he continued to hold her, spooning his body around hers.

"What am I going to do about you, Lauren?" he whispered before drifting off.

The warm body snuggled up to him wiggled as if trying to get closer. Court inhaled the vanilla-lavender scent, knowing even in the haze of sleep that it was Lauren in his bed. He put his hand on her hip.

"Be still." If she kept doing that, she was going to wake up to find him buried balls deep inside her.

She tilted her head back, blinking sleepy eyes at him. "Court?"

"Mmm?" He smiled. Her short hair looked like she'd stuck a finger in an electrical socket. For some reason, he found that sexy. Although, it could be that the warm ass she kept moving against him had short-circuited his brain. Right now, he'd probably find a bald Lauren sexy.

"Why are you in my bed?"

"Look around you, G.G., and then tell me who's in whose bed."

"Did you move me here?" she asked after eyeing her surroundings.

"No, you found my bed all by yourself. What would Freud make of that, I wonder?" No answer. He leaned over to see that she had gone back to sleep. He should get up, but he couldn't resist the way she felt, snuggled up against him. Just a few more minutes, and then he'd leave, go spend the rest of the night on the guest bed.

"Court?"

"Mmm?" He opened his eyes, glancing at the alarm clock. A few more minutes had morphed into another hour. "Dreaming about you," he said. Hell. He pressed his lips together. If he hadn't been half asleep, he never would have admitted that.

"I dream about you sometimes, too," she whispered, then turned in his arms. "Is that why you brought me in here?"

Obviously, she didn't remember her nightmare or waking up. "No. The big bad bear came home and found Goldilocks already in his bed."

"Do you want to kiss me?"

"God, yes." He didn't care that he hadn't decided what he wanted from her. She was here in his bed, and if she wanted a kiss, he would oblige her. He slipped his hand behind her neck, splaying his fingers over her soft skin, intending only a small taste. The problem with kissing Lauren was that once he started, it was impossible to stop.

When he slipped his tongue into her mouth, she sighed. He remembered those breathy sighs, had loved them. This was what he'd been missing. Her. No other woman had been able to take her place. God knew, he'd tried.

From her mouth, he peppered kisses along her jaw, working his way to her neck. From there, he traveled down until his mouth reached a breast. She moaned, burying her hands in his hair when he flicked his tongue over the nipple. She'd always been responsive to his every touch, and that hadn't changed. He slid his knee between her thighs, the heat radiating from her warming his skin.

"Make love to me, Court."

"Why?" He needed to know. If their being together meant nothing to her, then he couldn't do this. They might not be back to where they were when they'd parted at the end of spring break, but it would mean *something* to him.

She captured his gaze. "I want to feel the way I did that week we were together, even if it's just for tonight."

"And if it's for more than that?"

"I don't know."

Fair enough. Neither did he. He cupped a breast. It fit perfectly in his hand. He'd thought the same thing the first time he'd touched her. "Off," he said, tugging on the hem of her top.

"You read my mind." She sat up and pulled off the T-shirt, tossing it to the floor.

"Beautiful," he said as his eyes roamed hungrily over her. She was curvier than he remembered, filled out in all the right places. "So beautiful." He put his hand on her shoulder, gently pushing her back down. "I'm going to learn you all over again."

There wasn't a place on her that he didn't want to explore, but where to start? Did she taste the same? Feel the same? He hadn't forgotten one single thing about her, but what new discoveries were awaiting him?

Impatient to find out, he put his hand under a breast as he lowered his mouth. She moaned when his teeth scraped over her nipple. He answered with one of his own. Sweet Jesus, she was as luscious as pure golden honey. After giving her other breast the same attention, he moved back to her mouth, their lips meeting in a demanding kiss.

"I need to be inside you," he said a few minutes later. "Really need it."

He pulled off her sexy boxer shorts, and after shedding the briefs he'd left on after finding her in his bed, he reached into the nightstand drawer, grabbing a condom. Later he would taste her from head to toe more thoroughly, but he'd waited six years—even though he hadn't realized it until tonight—for this moment. He moved over her, hesitating as he stared down at her. Why had she turned her face away?

"Look at me, Lauren." Intimacy with her meant something to him, although he hadn't decided exactly what yet. He needed it to mean something to her, and damn if he'd let her hide what was in her eyes. He was an expert at reading body language and expressions. If she had any doubts, he'd know and would put a stop to this right now, even if it killed him.

When she looked up at him, there were tears in her eyes. He brushed his thumb across her cheek. "Why the tears, Gorgeous Girl?"

"I don't want this night to end," she whispered.

After he'd walked out earlier, he'd ridden his bike up the coast road. Riding his Harley at night when the roads were mostly empty was something he liked to do when he needed to think. He'd decided he would keep his promise to teach her what she wanted to know, and then put her on a plane. He'd planned to maintain a hands-off policy, but then he'd come home to find her in his bed. Apparently, where Lauren Montgomery was concerned, he had the willpower of a hungry dog eyeing a big, fat, juicy steak.

"Stop thinking," he said, not sure if he meant that for her or himself. He kissed her. "Just feel." All he wanted was to lose himself in her, for them to get lost in each other. Holding her gaze, he eased into her. She was so damn hot and wet. A shiver traveled up her body, followed by a little gasp. He swallowed a satisfied smile. She definitely wasn't immune to him.

"Tell me you want this," he said, needing to hear her say it.

She put her palm on his cheek. "I do. I want you, Court. I want this."

"You have me, baby." *You always have.* Hearing those words in his head, he froze. That might have been true once, but no longer. It was just lust talking, he assured himself.

"Court?"

"I'm here." He thrust into her, then arched his hips. She wrapped her legs around his thighs as he began a push-pull rhythm while leaning into her touch. Although he'd told her to keep her eyes open, he closed his, afraid she'd see too much. He wasn't even sure what he'd see in them if he looked in a mirror, nor did he want to know. They were two people who wanted each other, nothing more and nothing less.

He slid his hands down the sides of her body to her hips, gripping them. When she wrapped her hands around his neck, pulling his face down, he covered her mouth with his. He was so hot for her that he knew this first time wasn't going to last long. They had all night, and he would love her thoroughly before the sun rose, but now, he gave in to the wildness that she brought out in him, rocking his hips harder, faster.

"Yes. Like that," she said, meeting him thrust for thrust.

"Come, Lauren," he commanded, and as if he had the power to order her to climax with him, her body tensed. He deepened the kiss, drinking in the sounds she made as they fell over the edge together. When he could think again, he gathered her into his arms as they both struggled to breathe. Rolling them over so that she lay across him, he wrapped his arms around her back, holding her close.

"You okay?" he asked.

She nodded against his neck. "I'd forgotten how amazing we are together."

He hadn't. When he'd been with her six years ago, they'd practically set the bed on fire each time they'd made love. The magic was still there, but he was older and wiser. He knew how to protect his heart.

CHAPTER EIGHT

Lauren listened to Court's even breaths, soft and contented in sleep. He should be content. They'd made love three times. She smiled, tempted to rub her palm over his morning scruff, but she didn't want to wake him. It gave him such a sexy bad-boy look, though, and unable to resist, she gently laid her hand on his cheek, loving how the stubble felt against her palm. He sighed, turning his face into her hand. Her heart responded with a painful beat. Even in sleep, he was aware of her.

What they'd done began to sink in. She'd seduced him, caught him in the haze of sleep. Would he regret it in the light of day? She hoped not because he'd given her a beautiful memory to take with her. Tears burned as her eyes roamed over him.

He was beautiful. So masculine with his hard planes and dark features. The covers were bunched around his waist, and she longed to straddle him and touch her lips to his broad shoulders, then trail her tongue slowly down his spine until he woke up. She wanted him to open his eyes, look over his shoulder at her, and give her a sleepy smile, one that said he wanted her again.

But that couldn't happen. She wouldn't add to her sins where this man was concerned. Her life was a hot mess. He didn't deserve for her to screw his up, too. She had one foot out the door, and her heart was already broken. Even with another piece of it shattered, she would survive if it meant he would be safe.

Unable to fall back asleep, she eased out of bed. Returning to the guest room, she slipped on a T-shirt and her favorite comfy jeans. After brushing her teeth, she went to the kitchen and made a pot of coffee. She took the cup out to the balcony, cleared her mind, and sought calm as she watched the sun come up over the Atlantic Ocean.

The water was as smooth as glass, and as the sun rose above the horizon, the beams of light danced across the sea like sparkling diamonds. She could live here on Court's balcony, doing nothing but listening to the soft splash of the waves hitting shore. No worries, no fear of what was to come.

Three dolphins broke through the water, their fins glistening in the sunlight. She watched them until they disappeared, wishing she could swim away with them. The worries crept back into her mind, though.

What would Peter do if he came for her and she wasn't there? Would he be able to track her to Court's? The thought of that happening made her stomach churn. If Court hadn't found her by now, she'd be in New Orleans, and he would be all the better for it.

"You're up early."

She lifted her face, looking up at Court. "Good morning."

Not replying, he leaned against the railing, gazing at the ocean as he sipped his coffee. What was he thinking? Probably searching for the words to tell her last night had been a mistake. It hadn't been for her. She'd had the opportunity both to love the boy he'd once been and the man he'd become. There were no regrets on her part. She'd treasure her memories of him until her dying day.

Her mouth watered at the sight of him wearing only a pair of sweatpants sitting low on his waist. During the night, her hands had roamed all over his body, exploring every inch. She wished she could do it again now, in the light of day, so she could watch her fingers dance over his skin. So she could see his face, watch his eyes darken with desire.

She had to stop wanting what she couldn't have, but that was impossible with him so near. It would be easier once she was away, or it should be. Who was she kidding? She hadn't been able to stop thinking of him, wanting him, since the day they'd met. Why would it be any different this time?

He turned, his eyes meeting hers. "About last night—"

"Was a mistake. I get it. I won't apologize, though." It would be a lie to say she was sorry, and she was done lying to him. She willed her eyes to stay dry, refusing to let him see her tears.

"That wasn't what I was going to say, but whatever." His gaze shifted away, then landed back on her. "Did you love him?"

"Stephan?" He nodded. She wanted to say no, she never had, but she'd promised herself there would be no more lies between them. "Yes, until the day we got married and he showed his true self." She didn't want to talk about her life with Stephan, not with Court.

"How old were you when you got married?"

Why did he want to know these things? "Nineteen. Young and stupid. Can we not talk about this?"

"Don't you think I deserve to know?"

"What we had had nothing to do with Stephan."

His eyes grew cold. "If you say so." He turned back to watch the ocean.

"I feel like my life is out of control," she said, more to herself than to him.

"It doesn't have to be that way," he said, then disappeared inside.

The tears she'd been holding back came then. Even after swearing she wouldn't, she'd just lied to him. Stephan had *everything* to do with what had happened between her and Court. And now, long after she'd thought she'd escaped Stephan, because of *him*, she was going to run away from the people she loved and the life she'd created for herself. She felt like a puppet whose strings were manipulated by an evil villain, and she hated Stephan for it.

From the day she'd walked out of her ex-husband's house, she'd worked hard to learn how to be a normal woman, one who enjoyed life and didn't feel like she needed to be punished for the slightest mistake.

Her first attempt to taste freedom had been the spur-of-the-moment decision to take off for Panama City. Then she'd come home to find the monster waiting for her. It had taken months to heal physically and much longer to stop jumping at shadows. But she had been so angry over all that he'd stolen from her. It had been that rage burning inside her that had given her the strength to find her way back to the living, determined that Stephan wouldn't win.

After a year of therapy, combined with her will to prove to herself that she could carve out a life that would give her a degree of happiness, she'd managed to do just that. She'd had the support of her family and friends, and she and Madison had made their dream of owning a bookstore come true. Hoping that word would get back to Stephan that she had moved on, she'd started dating again.

Although there had existed a lingering ache in the part of her heart that belonged to Court, she'd been content until both Stephan and Court had walked back into her life. With Stephan came fear and loathing. With Court came heartbreak all over again.

She used the hem of her T-shirt to dry her eyes. Swallowing past the lump in her throat, she moved to the railing. As she looked out over the ocean, she said a little prayer, asking God to keep both her and Court safe.

Court stood a few feet away from the glass door, watching Lauren cry. He fisted his hands, planting his feet to the floor to keep from going to her. He wanted her to trust him enough to tell him the reason she was determined to run.

Against his will, the memory of their week together filled his mind. He smiled, remembering her first words to him.

"Like what you see?" she'd said when they'd closed the distance between them.

He'd grinned. "That should be obvious." The heat from the sun beating down on his back, the rowdy shouts of the college students around him, and the calls from his friends to come join them had all faded to nothing.

"You're beautiful," he'd said.

"I bet you say that to all the girls you want to take home."

He hesitated as he tried to remember if he'd ever said anything like that to a woman he didn't know, but he couldn't recall one single time.

"Yeah, thought so." The glimmer faded from her eyes as she turned away.

"I've never said that before." When she faced him again, he brushed the sand off her nose. He wanted to trail his finger over her lips, also sandy, but that might be pushing his luck. "It's the truth, Gorgeous Girl. I'd like to take you to lunch."

She tilted her head, peering up at him. "Are you a serial killer?"

"No."

"A rapist?"

"Absolutely not."

"Crazy?"

He smiled. "I think I'm going to be crazy about you, but other than that, no."

"Okay." She held out her hand. "I'm Lauren Montgomery."

"Court Gentry." Her hand was also coated with sand, but he didn't care. Instead of shaking, he laced their fingers together. Something he'd never felt before settled in his heart.

He still didn't understand how he'd fallen in love with her so fast. It wasn't just the sex, which was off the charts. There had been something between them that had been magical. He'd never experienced it since.

Before he could tell her that his memories of having her in his bed again hadn't lived up to the real thing, she'd said it was a mistake. That had put an instant end to the warm feelings he'd woken up with. She was right. It had been a mistake.

His phone buzzed, and he turned away, leaving her to cry her tears in private. "Yo," he said, at seeing Alex's name on the screen.

"How's Lauren doing?"

"Fine." The better question would have been how was he doing.

"Madison called her phone, but she didn't answer, so of course, my wife's worried about her. She planning on going to work today?"

"Yep." He glanced out at the balcony. Why was she crying, anyway? She hadn't moved, and he hated seeing her hurting even though she'd shut him out of her life.

Alex chuckled. "Damn, bro, you're chatty today."

"Go away, Alex." He disconnected. He made his favorite morning meal, scrambled eggs and bacon on buttered toast. Sandwiches made and orange juice poured, he called Lauren in.

"I'm not really hungry," she said, following him into the kitchen.

"You need to eat."

She eyed the two sandwiches on her plate. "I can't eat two of these."

"That better?" he said, taking one of them.

"You're going to eat three?"

"Growing boy." They ate in silence. Not happy with her at the moment, he didn't bother trying to start a conversation. Although she'd claimed not to be hungry, she ate all of hers. He put a half sandwich on her plate.

"Thanks. These are good."

"Welcome." He was glad to see she had an appetite, but he still didn't want to talk to her unless she decided it was time to trust him with her secrets.

"I guess I'll get ready to go to work," she said, pushing her plate away. "If Madison hasn't left yet, I'll catch a ride with her."

"I'll take you."

She made circles on the place mat with her finger. "Okay."

That lost little girl voice just about slayed him. Before he gave in and gathered her up in his arms, he picked up their plates, and loaded them in the dishwasher. When he was done, he leaned against the counter, crossing his arms over his chest.

"Why don't you tell me about your husband?" Maybe she could explain why she hadn't mentioned Stephan when they'd first met.

Her eyes shifted away. "I don't have a husband."

"But you did once. Seems like something you should have told me. That was pretty damn major, Lauren. Not like neglecting to tell me you'd stubbed your toe or overslept."

Her lips thinned in displeasure, but he didn't care. For years, he'd wondered what he'd done wrong. Turned out, it hadn't been him at all, if the assumptions he'd made so far were correct. He'd loved her and would have protected her if he'd only known she'd needed it. She'd taken away his chance to take care of her with her silence.

"That was the most beautiful week of my life. I didn't want to ruin it by bringing him into what we had between us."

Her voice was so soft that he had to strain to hear. Okay, he got that a little, but it still rubbed that she'd kept something that big from him. "Did you ever plan to tell me?"

"Yes." She lifted her gaze to his. "The next time I saw you."

"That didn't work out so well, did it?" Her bottom lip trembled, and he called himself an ass. But by keeping her secrets back then, she hadn't given them a chance, and she was still doing it with her refusal to tell him why she was so determined to run.

"Court—"

The doorbell rang, interrupting her. "Ignore it," he said when she glanced toward the door.

"Don't you want to see who it is?"

"Nope. It's one of my brothers. I'm hoping he'll go away." He guessed it was Alex, since Nate didn't know Lauren was here and would have let himself in. Whichever one it was, his timing sucked. Had she been about to finally open up?

CHAPTER NINE

The doorbell rang again. Lauren sat back, relieved at the interruption. She'd almost told him everything, which would have been a mistake. God only knew what Court would do if she'd told him why she'd refused to see him again.

"Still ignoring it," he said. "You were saying?"

She shook her head. "Just that at the time—" The bell rang again in three consecutive bursts. *Just that she would do the same thing again if it meant protecting him.*

Court sighed. "It was too much to wish for." He went to the door, looking through the peephole. "It's Nate."

Should she hide in the bedroom? She doubted Nate knew she was here. Deciding that was probably a good idea, she tried to disappear down the hallway, but as she ran past Court, he grabbed her hand.

"Going somewhere?"

"I think I should stay out of sight."

Without answering Lauren, he opened the door. "Go away," he said to Nate, and then he tried to slam the door shut, but Nate stuck his foot in the opening.

"We need to talk." Nate pushed past them, and as he walked by, he said, "Hello, Lauren."

He hadn't seemed at all surprised to find her in Court's condo. She had the feeling there wasn't much Nate didn't know. The man intimidated her, and she wished she'd been able to escape to her room. Court let go of her hand, following his brother into the living room. She reluctantly trailed behind them.

Court came to a halt. "Talk about what?"

"Several things. Stephan Kozlov for one. And why Lauren's staying with you." Nate walked to the glass doors, staring out.

The breath left her lungs as her legs gave out, her butt landing on the couch. What did he know?

"Baby brother can't keep his mouth shut," Court grumbled, sitting on the opposite side of the sofa.

"He's worried about you. As am I." Nate turned from staring out the balcony door, his gaze zeroing in on her. "Your ex is a nasty piece of work based on the photos I saw of you taken in the hospital. Unfortunately, he's been a model prisoner, not doing anything to risk getting time added to his sentence. He also has his own bodyguards, other prisoners who protect him from various gangs."

"What photos?" Court's eyes locked on hers. "Why were you in the hospital?"

"You promised you wouldn't invade my privacy." *This isn't happening. He was never supposed to know.* She pressed her hands against her stomach as it took a sickening roll. *How does Nate have insider information on a prisoner? And why does Court have a cop at his beck and call who could run off Peter? Who are these people?*

"Court made that promise to you, not me," Nate said.

"Please, you have to forget what you think you know." Didn't he care about putting his brother in danger?

"What photos, Lauren?"

"These," Nate said, tossing the folder he held in his hand to Court.

Before she could snatch the photos away, Court stood, then walked to the dining room table. Oh, God, Nate had no idea what he'd just done. She'd suffered greatly to keep Court's name from Stephan. Nate had just made that all for naught.

She looked at Nate, her eyes burning with tears. "You shouldn't have done that."

"He needs to know," Nate said softly.

Was that pity or sympathy in his eyes? It didn't matter which. "You should have stayed out of it." He didn't answer. She glanced over at Court. He had the photos spread out on the table. What was he thinking? There was no expression on his face to give her a hint.

Finally, he looked up at her. "When was this, Lauren? Before or after we met?"

"After," she whispered.

"How soon after?"

"The day I got back home." There was no use not answering. Nate no doubt already knew the answer and would tell him if she didn't. So fast she hardly saw him move, Court reared up and put his fist through the wall. She startled, letting out a gasp. Nate didn't so much as twitch, almost as if he'd expected that reaction. Tears leaked out of her eyes. She'd never wanted Court to see those photos.

"How did you get those?" she asked Nate as her gaze followed Court. He walked to the glass door, his back to her as he stared out, his hands fisted at his sides.

"I have my ways." He looked over at Court. "Give him a few minutes to digest the sight of you beaten to a pulp."

She squeezed her eyes shut. Why was he being so cruel to Court, showing him those photos? She'd refused to look at the pictures the police had taken of her, but she'd asked a nurse to bring her a mirror.

The swollen and blackened eyes and the clear handprint on her neck from where Stephan had tried to squeeze the life out of her had haunted her dreams for years, sometimes still did. Her black-and-blue body had taken weeks to heal, her broken ribs much longer. For six weeks, she'd had to eat her meals through a straw because of her broken jaw.

"If you loved him, you wouldn't have showed him what Stephan did to me."

His black eyes, so much like Court's, softened. "It's because I love him that I did. I always knew someone had hurt him. I just didn't know she had a good reason until now. So I'll say it again. He needed to know why you did what you did."

"You're wrong. He was better off not knowing."

"Stop talking about me as if I'm not here," Court said, turning to her. "How do you think it makes me feel that you didn't trust me enough to tell me?"

She didn't have an answer, had hoped she'd never be asked that question. It had never been about not trusting him. Avoiding Court's piercing stare, she kept her eyes on Nate. "You said Stephan's been a model prisoner. What do you know about him? A better question, how do you know?"

"We'll get to your last question shortly. As for what I know, even the guards speak highly of Stephan Kozlov. I suspect a few of them are on his payroll."

Court returned to the couch, surprising her by sitting so closely that their legs were touching. He still showed nothing on his face, not what he was thinking and not how much he must hate her for lying to him. It unnerved her.

"I'll ask again. How do you know all this?" All she could do was keep asking her questions so that she didn't fall apart in front of both of them.

Nate and Court shared a look, a message passing between them. She was missing something, and that didn't sit well. This was her life they were talking about, and she had the right to know.

"I promise we'll tell you," Nate said, moving to a chair. "First, I want to know the history behind you two, and don't try to deny there is one."

Not sure what Court would want him to know, she stayed silent. Would he tell his brother that he'd fallen in love with a girl he'd known barely a week? But had he really fallen in love, or had it been lust that he'd interpreted as love? For her it had been the real thing. She knew that because she had willingly sacrificed her happiness and almost her life for him.

Someone knocked on the door. "That's Alex," Nate said. "He needs to hear everything, too."

"Should've sent out invitations," Court muttered as he headed for the door.

"Got coffee?" Alex said, heading straight for the kitchen without waiting for an answer.

She snuck a look at Court as he sat down beside her again. He was staring at her as if he didn't know her at all. What worried her, though, was that his expression hadn't changed. He'd completely closed himself off to her.

Alex walked into the living room, a cup of coffee in his hand. To try to stop worrying about what Court was thinking, she studied the brothers. Seeing them all together, she was struck by how much they looked alike. There was no question Nate was the oldest and Alex the youngest, yet if not for the way each wore his hair—Nate's in a ponytail, Court's as a short buzz cut, and Alex's curling around his collar—someone who didn't know them would have trouble telling them apart.

As hot as all three were, it was Court who made her ache with longing. It would have been easier if he hadn't come back into her life. She'd gotten used to missing him, and she wasn't sure if she'd be able to manage it again.

"So where were we?" Alex asked, taking a seat in the last empty chair. His gaze shifted to the hole in the wall, but he didn't comment.

"Court was about to tell us how he and Lauren met." Nate eyed her with interest. "Unless you'd rather tell the story."

She vigorously shook her head. There was no way she could tell it without crying.

After a slight pause, Court said, "I met Lauren during spring break my senior year. I thought we had something, but when I called her a few days after I got back to school, she . . ."

He glanced at her, and the sadness in those dark eyes sent an all too familiar regret straight to her heart. She'd put that hurt there, and now she questioned every decision she'd made back then.

"Said she didn't want to see me anymore." He paused, his gaze still locked on hers. "Which I now know was a lie."

Lauren sucked in a breath. She dared to steal a glance at Nate to see his reaction. He stared at her as if he'd mentally climbed into her mind and was dissecting her brain. It was unnerving.

"Freaks me out, too, when he does that," Alex said, breaking the hypnotic hold Nate had on her.

Lauren gave her head a slight shake, trying to clear it. There was something off about these three, but she couldn't put her finger on it. She and Court hadn't talked about their personal lives much back then. Although she knew she'd have to tell him about Stephan at some point, she hadn't wanted to taint those magical first days with her family history. Because she didn't want to share personal stories, she hadn't encouraged Court to talk about his life before her either.

"You thought you were protecting him," Nate said. "Admirable but foolish."

She glared at him. Let him walk in her shoes before he judged her. "And I'd do it all over again if it meant keeping him safe." A hint of warmth flashed in his eyes, as if she'd pleased him somehow.

"I'm right here, people," Court said. "I had a right to know, Lauren. You gave it to me when you said you loved me." His eyes shifted to the dining room table, where the pictures were still spread out. "You should have told me what he did to you."

"I didn't want you in Stephan's sights. I still don't."

"That's my decision to make. Respect me enough to believe that I can keep both of us safe."

Maybe he could now, but then? He'd still been a boy, a college student. Although she regretted her lie, because it had taken him from her, it also meant she didn't have to live with the regret—that he'd been hurt or, God forbid, worse. The mere thought of what Stephan might do to him still terrified her.

She noticed that Alex was watching them with fascination, and her cheeks heated. This conversation was one she would have preferred to have with Court in private. "Well, my plan is to disappear. I'm thinking New Orleans. It should be easy to get lost there." She glanced at Alex. "I have a letter I want you to give Madison, turning over my share of the bookstore to her." Had Court actually just growled?

"You're not going anywhere," he said. "Not after I've seen what he's capable of."

"What did I miss?" Alex asked.

Nate waved a hand toward the table. "Take a look at the photos over there."

"We have some talking to do," Court said quietly while Alex flipped through the pictures.

The only thing she wanted to hear from him was how soon she could disappear. Her fear that Stephan would go after Court now extended to his brothers.

"Jesus," Alex said, staring at the picture he held in his hand. "The wall's lucky you only put one hole in it, bro." His eyes shifted to her. "We need to teach the bastard who did this to you a lesson."

"I plan to, believe me." Court stood, went to the table, collected all the photos, and put them back into the folder. He returned to the sofa. "Tell us everything you know about the Kozlov brothers."

Although she wanted to refuse, three men, each with a commanding presence, outnumbered her. She had the feeling they would sit here all day giving her their hard stares until she broke, confessing all. She gave up trying to keep her secrets.

"I met Stephan the day my mother died." She told them how she'd met him at the hospital, how he'd stayed by her side, helping her and her dad and sister get through the days that followed. "We got married six months later. He hit me for the first time on our wedding night because . . ." She couldn't do this. It was too personal and too embarrassing to share with these men, two of whom she barely knew.

"Because?" Court said, putting his hand over hers. "You need to tell us, G.G."

Maybe it was his hand, strong and warm on hers, or maybe it was how soft his pet name for her sounded that had her complying. She took a deep breath. "Because I didn't bleed, he accused me of lying to him about being a virgin." She lifted her eyes to Court. "But I was, I swear it."

He squeezed her hand. "I believe you."

"And even if you had lied to him, that was no excuse to hit you," Nate said.

"I should have left him that night, but as soon as it happened, he apologized, saying he was sorry, and it would never happen again. He said it was just because he loved me so much that the thought of another man touching me made him crazy."

"How long before he hit you again?" Alex asked.

"Six months, but even before then it didn't seem like I could do anything right. And he had this way of making me feel so stupid. Things would get really bad if he had an off night on the ice, like it was my fault. He also demanded I quit school, but that was the one thing I stood up to him about. Finally, I was so miserable that I told him I wanted a separation, except I didn't really mean it. I'd hoped that if he thought I would actually leave him that he would change back to the man I thought I'd married. That was when he hit me for the second time. He told me if I tried to leave him, he would kill me, that if he couldn't have me, no one could. That was when I truly became afraid of him."

"Did you ever call the cops?" Nate asked.

"No, he had friends who were cops. He'd get them tickets to the games, have them over for parties. I didn't know who I could trust. But my fear of him wasn't the only reason I stayed. I was raised in a very religious family. I don't expect you to understand, but I was taught that divorce was a sin. Once married in the eyes of God, it was forever. I thought if I could just learn how to be the perfect wife, everything would be okay."

Court frowned. "Your father approved of you staying with a man who abused you?"

"He didn't know. I was too ashamed to tell him what was going on in my marriage."

"We get that more than you know," Alex said, sharing a look with his brothers, making her wonder what that was all about. "When did you finally decide to leave and file for divorce?"

"When he said it was time to have a baby, a boy to be exact. A future star hockey player like his father."

Tears streamed down her cheeks as she looked at Court. "I couldn't bear the thought of my child having him for a father. Would he hit him, tell him how stupid he was if it turned out his son didn't want to play hockey? And what if we had a girl? Nothing but a son would be acceptable to him. That was when I knew I had to leave. I waited until he had an away game and walked out with only a few clothes and a diamond necklace he'd given me. I left the other jewelry, but I decided I'd earned that necklace. I sold it so I'd have some money. Then I hid at a woman's shelter. They referred me to an attorney and he filed for the divorce."

"You should have taken all the fucking jewelry," Court said. "Did you get any alimony or a settlement?"

"I just asked for a hundred thousand dollars." She glanced at Alex. "While I was waiting for my divorce to finalize, Madison and I started talking about opening the bookstore after we graduated. Since I didn't own anything, didn't even have a bank account, I needed the money to make it happen. Honestly, I didn't want to take that."

Court shook his head. "Don't apologize. You should have demanded more than that. He was worth millions."

"That's what my attorney said. Stephan fought the divorce, fought giving me a penny of his money, even hired a private investigator to try to find me, but finally I got my divorce. Three days later, I left for spring break." Where she'd met a beautiful young man, and for six days, she'd known how love should really be.

Court squeezed her hand again. "If I'd known about all this, I never would have let you go back."

If. There were so many *ifs*, but she might as well cry in her beer for all the good it would do her. There was nothing she could do to change the decisions she'd made.

"What can you tell us about Peter?" Nate asked.

"Stephan's house was huge, practically a mansion, so even though Peter also lived there, he mostly stayed out of sight in his own wing, except to join us for dinner sometimes. If Stephan wanted to talk to him or Peter needed to see Stephan, they always met in Peter's side of the house. Sometimes men would come over for a meeting, and I'd be sent to the bedroom."

"Was Stephan ever jealous of any attention Peter or other men gave you?" Alex asked.

She didn't miss Court tensing at the question. "Stephan insisted I dress sexy when we were out together. He liked seeing other men covet what he had. I think it fed his ego. At the same time, if one dared to outright flirt with me, he'd go ballistic."

She lowered her gaze to her and Court's joined hands, embarrassed about her next words. "Except for Peter. Stephan said several times that he'd share me with his brother if I were so inclined." She lifted her eyes, meeting Court's. "I wasn't," she said fiercely.

Court's eyes shimmered with rage as he held her gaze. Rage for her. "He's going to pay," Court said, and although his brothers were listening, she knew the words were meant for her.

"No, that's why I'm leaving. No one's getting hurt on my account."

Ignoring her, Court shifted his focus to Nate. "You thinking what I'm thinking?"

CHAPTER TEN

"Put you in the crosshairs?" Nate said.

"Exactly." Court couldn't get the photos of a severely beaten Lauren out of his head. The man needed to pay. It would be his greatest pleasure to teach the Kozlovs what happened to men who hurt or threatened women.

"No!" Lauren turned pleading eyes on him. "Absolutely not. I'll get on a plane, or a bus, or a bicycle if I have to, and leave right now before I'll let you do this."

If she said she was leaving one more time, Court was going to lose it. Hell, he was already a thin thread away from breaking into Stephan's prison and beating the man senseless. See how he liked being on the receiving end of someone's fists.

When she tried to stand, he hooked a finger into her waistband, pulling her back down. Listening to her talk about her marriage had sent a rage through him such as he'd never felt before. He'd been too young and helpless when he'd witnessed his father beat on his mother. That was no longer the case.

It took all his willpower to maintain an outward calmness that he was far from feeling. His walls *were* lucky they didn't have more holes. Thank God she'd found the courage to get away, although she'd ended up paying dearly for it. It wasn't just the beating she'd received that infuriated him, but that he'd lost her because of it. After spending so long trying to forget her, he didn't want to like having her here, but he did.

Although he hadn't planned it, he'd spent the night loving her, relearning all the places on her body where his touch made her sigh with pleasure. He'd woken up disappointed that she wasn't still in bed. Then she'd said it was all a mistake, so he'd walked away before he could say something he couldn't take back. For now, he'd concentrate on dealing with her scumbag ex-husband so she'd stop talking about fucking leaving. After that, maybe there was a future for them, or maybe not.

"It's the only way to end this, Lauren," he said.

"You can't seriously consider making yourself a target." She shot up, slapping his hand away. "You don't know Stephan. He's sly. Sneaky. He'll strike when you least expect it." She moved until her knees were almost touching Nate's, fury radiating off her in waves. "I won't allow it. You started this by showing him those photos, so you put a stop to it."

The last thing Court expected to be doing right now was smiling, but he was. Never mind that Nate was an intimidating son of a bitch. Lauren looked ready to take him on. Arousal stirred. Another minute of seeing all that fire in her eyes and he was going to embarrass her in front of his brothers by throwing her over his shoulder and carrying her to his bed.

"You got it bad, bro," Alex said, laughter in his voice.

Court glared at his baby brother. "Shut it."

"I know you deal with tough guys at the biker bar, but Stephan's different. He doesn't play fair." She stepped back, glancing at him, then turned back to Nate. "I'll disappear before I'll put any of you at risk, especially Court."

There she went again, threatening to disappear to protect him. He'd handcuff her to his bed before he'd allow her to do that. But he couldn't help admiring her determination to do what she thought was right.

He reached over and grabbed her hand, pulling her back down on the sofa. "You're not going anywhere. Not today, anyway."

"We'll put round-the-clock surveillance on him from the moment he takes his first step through the gate, but our goal needs to be sending him right back to a cell," Nate said. "The only way to do that is to bring him to us, and letting him know you're with Court will make that happen."

"Put surveillance on him? Send him back to a cell? Who the hell are you people?"

"You haven't told her?" Nate raised a brow.

Court shook his head. Before today, he hadn't trusted her enough to tell her they were FBI.

"Told me what?"

Nate slipped a thin black case from his back pocket, flipped it open, and showed her his FBI badge. "Special Agent Nate Gentry."

Her eyes widened.

Next, Alex held out his badge. "Special Agent Alex Gentry."

If her eyes went any wider, her eyeballs were going to pop out. She looked at him. "You, too?"

Not bothering to show her his badge, he said, "Special Agent Court Gentry."

"I'm dreaming. I must be. This is just too surreal." She pinched herself. "Nope, not dreaming. I don't even know what to say. Does Madison know?"

"Of course. She's my wife," Alex said.

"Why didn't she tell me? We talk to each other about everything."

Court shrugged. "Because she was asked not to. Aces and Eights is a cover for covert operations, Lauren. We're entrusting you with this information, but you can't tell anyone."

"Who would I tell? Other than Madison . . . well, I don't have much in my life except for her and the bookstore." She eyed each of their faces, as if seeing them for the first time. "So, you're all FBI agents. I guess that means you're trained to deal with psychos? I still don't like the idea of involving any of you."

"And I don't like the idea of you disappearing, whether it's in New Orleans or any other place." Somewhere along the way, she'd screw up and Stephan would find her.

She pressed her fingers against the bridge of her nose. "Okay. Let's say I go along with whatever you guys cook up. Exactly what would that be?"

Court already had a plan. "You're going to introduce me as your fiancé to Peter. That should get your ex's attention."

The blood drained from her face. "There must be a better way."

He hated making her worry about him. When would she understand that he was capable of not only protecting her but also keeping himself safe? Stephan Kozlov was an amateur compared to some of the bad guys they'd taken down. Bring the sonofabitch on.

"It's done, Lauren." It wasn't open for discussion. "Has Peter ever hurt you?" Peter better hope she said no.

She shook her head. "No, but he covers up for Stephan. He was Stephan's manager, and as far as he's concerned, it's my fault that Stephan's in prison. When Stephan lost his position with the Thunder, they both lost their income, so he hates me."

Nate leaned forward, resting his elbows on his knees. "Did you ever hear anything that led you to suspect either brother was involved with the Russian mafia?"

"Nothing specific, but sometimes men . . . You know, the kind with cold eyes and hard stares? Anyway, they would come to see Stephan and Peter. Why do you ask?"

"I turned up some red flags when I was checking out Peter," Court said. "Links to known Russian mafia members, money flowing into the brothers' bank accounts even though Stephan no longer has an income—those kinds of things. It's not unusual for the Russian mafia to have some kind of involvement with their country's hockey players."

Nate stood, picking up the folder he'd brought in with him. Court wanted to tear the file out of his brother's hand and burn it to ashes. Those photos of her beaten body were branded into his brain. If he ever . . . No, *when* he got his hands on the man, Stephan Kozlov was going to know how it felt to be on the receiving end. That was his promise to her.

Nate slapped the folder against his leg. "I've got a meeting with Rothmire to bring him up to speed. It should be enough to open a file on the Kozlovs."

"And I need to do some more research and finesse our plan," Court said. He glanced at Lauren. He'd told her he would take her to work, but he needed some time away from her to think. "Alex will take you to the bookstore. One of us will pick you up around lunchtime."

Her eyes narrowed. "I don't remember you being this bossy."

"He's been bossing me around ever since I was in diapers," Alex said. He winked. "If you can figure out how to make him stop, I'll be your friend forever."

Court wished that smile she gave Alex was directed at him. And that fire in her eyes when she was annoyed? It didn't have the effect she intended. He wanted to bury his nose against her neck and breathe in her earthy scent. He wanted to spend hours tasting every inch of her skin. All he wanted to do was kick his brothers out, and then take her straight to his bed, see just how bright he could make that fire burn.

Before he did just that, he stood. "We're done here." He knew that where Lauren was concerned his emotions were all over the place. If there ended up being an official investigation into the Russians, and if he could convince the powers that be that he should head it up, then he'd better get his act together.

"I'll be back in a few to take you to work," Alex said to Lauren.

After his brothers were gone, Court glanced at Lauren. She had curled up on the sofa, staring out the glass doors, but he knew she wasn't seeing or appreciating the view. She looked so lost and alone, and his heart took a tumble he didn't like. How had one slip of a girl managed to scatter his brain to the four corners where she was concerned?

He perched on the coffee table. "I know you feel like you've lost control—"

"No kidding." Her eyes shifted to his. "Please don't do this, Court. I couldn't bear it if something happened to you."

At the tears pooling in her eyes, he gave up the fight. Moving next to her, he wrapped his arms around her, pulling her against him. "Nothing's going to happen to me. I promise." He kissed the top of her head as he gave in and inhaled her familiar scent into his lungs. She buried her face in his chest, her tears wetting his shirt.

"I-I'm sorry."

"For what?"

"For lying to you when you called." Lauren lifted her head, meeting his gaze. "I never forgot about you. I just want you to know that." She could have bitten her tongue off when he stiffened.

He disentangled them. "For six years, I've done my best to forget you."

She flinched, his words shooting an arrow straight through her heart. Suddenly, he was gone, disappearing down the hallway. Then he was back, staring down at her, the warmth gone from his eyes.

"What about the men you've been with since?"

"What about the women you've been with?"

At that, respect shimmered in his eyes. "Touché." He glanced away for a few seconds before returning his gaze to her. "I guess we both have some hard thinking to do. Right now, though, you need to get ready for work."

"Okay." She definitely had some thinking to do. As she got dressed, Lauren asked herself what she wanted. Aside from turning back the clock, giving her a chance to do things differently, there was only one answer to her question. She wanted Court, but that wasn't going to happen. She would be leaving in a few days.

"Why didn't you tell me they were FBI?" Lauren asked as soon as she had a moment alone with Madison. They were taking a little break in their office.

"I couldn't. Their lives depend on that staying a secret, and it wasn't my secret to tell. Not even to you."

"Okay, yeah, I understand. I'm sorry. It wasn't fair to ask you that, but it makes sense now why you wanted me to tell Court about Stephan."

"See, you should always listen to me." Madison stirred the tower of whipped cream into her mocha coffee. "My mom's going to bankrupt us with how much of this stuff she puts in everyone's coffee."

"Leave Angelina alone. It makes her happy to overdose us all with whipped cream." Madison's mother was a godsend. Since coming to work for them, she'd made every customer who came into High Tea and Black Cat Books fall in love with her and her coffees, bringing them repeat business.

Madison's gaze settled on her mother. "I'm just happy to see her smiling again after all she's gone through."

"You went through it with her, Maddie." She squeezed her friend's hand. "As bad as it was, it brought Alex into your life. You can't regret that."

"I don't for a minute." Madison's eyes sparkled with love at the mention of her husband, and Lauren tried not to be envious. "I can't imagine how shocked you must have been at seeing Court again after so many years. It's obvious you still have feelings for him. I see the way you look at him."

"Seriously? Shock seems like too mild a word for how I felt." She dipped a finger into her whipped cream, then licked it off as she thought of how to explain her feelings for Court. "I was crazy in love with him six years ago, so he'll always own a part of my heart. In some ways, he's the same man I loved, but in a lot of ways, he's different. Harder, bossier, and God help me, sexier."

"Are you still in love with him?"

"God, Maddie, I don't know. There's just so much going on right now, that I can't even think straight. The chemistry between us is still there, though." That was one thing she couldn't deny, but another worry had added itself to all the others crammed into her head after learning Court was an FBI agent.

She'd experienced violence up close and personal and had promised herself once she'd gotten away from Stephan that her life would be nothing but peaceful. An FBI agent's life was far from peaceful, not to mention dangerous. She wasn't sure she could deal with it, worrying about the day his brothers showed up at her door to tell her he was never coming home again.

"Want to know what I think?"

Lauren rolled her eyes. "No, but I'm sure you're going to tell me anyway."

"Of course I am. I think you both still have a thing for each other, even if neither of you are willing to admit it. Considering you still have the hots for each other after all these years, don't you think you should give it a chance, see where it goes?"

"I don't know." She was going to leave him, but she wouldn't tell her friend that. "And stop looking at me like that. Whatever you're cooking up, the answer is no."

Madison grinned. "You know me so well. I was only thinking about how things are different from our mothers' time when they waited by the phone for a guy to call. We have as much right to go after what we want as men do."

"Meaning?"

"Go after him. You made him fall in love with you once. You can do it again."

If only it were that easy. "What's between me and Court isn't a game. I hurt him, and I don't know if he can get past that." And what if she did stay only to learn she couldn't deal with who he was? That wouldn't be fair to either one of them. She stirred the rest of the whipped cream into her coffee. "How did my life get so messed up?"

Madison blew a strand of hair from her cheek. "You're not to blame for Stephan's actions."

"I know, but I keep asking myself if I missed signs of the true Stephan. How could he have been one man before we got married, then a totally different one the day he put a wedding ring on my finger?"

"There was nothing to clue you in? No outburst of temper, something like that?"

"No. Stephan Kozlov was everything a boyfriend should be. Considerate, loving, supportive, all that jazz. I even loved that he was Russian. To a girl who'd been as sheltered as I had been, he seemed worldly. Add the fact that he was a professional hockey player, a totally hot one . . . Honestly, I kept asking myself how I'd gotten so lucky."

"Men like that are clever at hiding their true selves. You're not the first to fall for a snake in the grass, and you won't be the last."

That only made her sad for other women like her who'd fallen for a man they should have run from instead.

Madison tilted her head, studying her. "I could never figure out why you always ended things with a guy when he started getting serious. It was because you were still in love with Court, and, by the way, I'm still irked with you that you never told me about him."

"What are you, Dr. Phil now?" Madison wasn't wrong, though. No man had been able to replace Court in her heart.

"Ha-ha, but my rates are cheaper." Madison gave her a hug, then stood. "Guess I better get back to work before Mom comes looking for me. Alex said you're going to take a few days off to spend with Court."

"You sure that's okay?" She lowered her gaze, staring at the bottom of her empty coffee cup, hiding the tears stinging her eyes. This was the last time she'd share a coffee break with the best friend she'd ever had. In a few days, she'd be in a strange city, and wouldn't be able to so much as call Madison just to say hi. Loneliness crashed through her like a tidal wave, and she wasn't even gone yet. *I'm going to miss you so much, Maddie.*

"I think it's great. You two need some time together to get to know each other again."

"Thanks." Madison had visions of a fairy-tale ending for them, but a happily ever after wasn't in their future. She swallowed past the lump in her throat, then lifted her eyes. "I love you, you know."

Madison paused at the door, shooting her a grin. "I know."

There were a few more things she wanted to get from her apartment, so she headed upstairs. Halfway up, Hemingway ran past her.

"Hey, good looking, what's your hurry?" She followed him into her bedroom, frowning when he growled and the hair on his spine rose. "You're scaring me, Hemingway."

Still growling, he stalked around the room, his belly almost touching the floor. The closet door was open, and she was positive she hadn't left it like that. She backed out of her bedroom, and when she got to the hallway, she turned, racing downstairs.

"Madison!" she called out, seeing her friend talking to Angelina. As she hurried toward them, she glanced out the display window and saw a police car slowly cruising down the street. She made an abrupt turn, running outside, waving her hands, yelling for him to stop. When she reached his door, she recognized the cop Court had talked to the night Peter had shown up.

"Someone's been in my room," she said, gasping for breath. He pulled over, parking in a loading zone.

"Are you Court Gentry's friend?" he asked after exiting the car.

She nodded, wondering how he knew that. "My cat growled, and my closet door's open." God, that sounded so lame.

"Show me," he said.

Grateful that he didn't think she was a crazy woman, she grabbed his hand. "Come with me."

Madison ran out the door. "What's going on?"

"Someone's been in my room. Hemingway's growling."

"Hemingway never growls," Madison said, jogging alongside her.

"Tell him that." Lauren kept her hold on the cop's hand, pulling him up the stairs with her. She prayed she was wrong, that her imagination was working overtime.

When they reached her room, she glanced at the officer. "I'm Lauren." She nodded at Madison. "That's my friend, Madison. I swear I didn't leave my closet door open."

"I'm David Markham. You two stay here while I check out the apartment."

"Oh my God, he really is growling," Madison said, her gaze on a still prowling Hemingway.

"Told you."

David Markham returned a few minutes later. "Whoever was here is gone. The window in the second bedroom was jimmied open. Take a look around, tell me if there's anything you're missing."

Thank God he believed her. She went to her closet, skimming her fingers across the tops of the hangers. "These aren't straight. Someone riffled through my clothes."

"I'm calling Alex." Madison pulled her phone from her pocket as she walked into the hallway.

"I don't see anything missing in here, but look." She touched the shoebox holding the photos of her and Court during spring break. "It's crooked. I would've never put it away like that."

A chill raced down her spine. There was only one person she could think of who would have a reason to go through her things, but what had he been looking for?

CHAPTER ELEVEN

Court gripped the iron rail of his balcony, his gaze locked on the horizon. Maybe he should buy a boat and sail away. Get lost on some Caribbean island, drink rum cocktails, own nothing more than his boat and a pair of shorts and flip-flops, and do nothing more than watch his skin turn leathery under a blazing island sun. Someplace he could forget about a woman with pink-tipped spiked hair. She'd left him once and seemed determined to do it again.

That was what women did. They left without a word of explanation, be they mothers or lovers. His mother had walked down a dusty road one day without a backward glance, without giving her three young sons a reason for leaving them in the hands of a mean drunk.

He knew why, though. She'd been pregnant with another man's baby. Had she gone to meet the man? Was she living with him all this time, loving her new family? Her sons forgotten about?

It had only been because he'd been hiding behind the living room couch that he'd heard the fight between his parents the morning she left. Even all these years later, he could still remember it word for word.

He'd torn his jeans when he'd caught the fabric on a nail while doing his chores. He knew he was in trouble. His father was going to be furious. Money didn't grow on trees. Hadn't the old man said that a billion times? And when their father was angry, it meant a beating. So he was delaying the inevitable, hiding for as long as he could get away with it.

"That baby's not mine, Wanda. Who you been fucking?"

The word didn't shock Court. His father used it all the time. What did shock him was that his mother was going to have another baby. They didn't have enough food as it was, so another mouth to feed would mean less for him, Nate, and Alex. He hated the new baby already.

"It is yours. You know it is."

"I don't know no such thing. Women cain't be trusted. Who's the daddy? You better tell me if you know what's good for you."

That made Court mad. His mother could too be trusted.

"You, Gordon. You're the daddy. When would I have met someone? I never go anywhere, and you know it."

Now she was crying. Court wished he were bigger so he could make his father leave her alone.

"I told you we weren't having any more brats. I've been careful, always wearing a rubber. That baby in your belly ain't mine."

At the sound of his father's fist hitting her—a sound he and his brothers knew all too well—Court put his hands over his ears, squeezing his eyes shut against the stinging tears.

"We ain't having no more brats I have to feed."

As his father beat on his mother, Court bit down on his bottom lip to keep from yelling at his old man to stop hurting her. If his father knew he was behind the couch, he'd make sure Court was sorry for not only tearing his pants, but also hiding like a coward.

"Stop it, Gordon. You're going to kill the baby. Not my stomach. God, please stop."

"I aim to kill it right out of you."

"You're . . . you're right. It's not yours. Stop and I'll tell you."

"I knew it. You disgust me, wife. You're a fucking whore. I can't stand to look at you right now, but this ain't finished."

At hearing his father's footsteps recede, and then his father's truck start up and tear off down the road, Court felt like he could breathe again. Maybe he could hide his torn pants and the old man would never know.

"I can't let him kill the baby," she said, the pain he heard in her voice making him want to cover his ears.

At first, he thought she was talking to him, but then he realized she was talking to herself. It also sank in that she'd admitted the baby was another man's. He knew how babies got in a mother's stomach. The walls in their two-bedroom house were thin, and they could hear their father's grunts and the bed hitting the wall at night. Sometimes, when the old man was drunk—which was more often than not—he didn't even bother shutting the door.

Court didn't want his mother to be a whore, but he'd heard her admit that the baby had a different daddy. As he stayed hidden, waiting for her to leave the room, he thought about all that he'd heard and what he was going to do about it. What could he do? He was only nine, not old enough or big enough to take on his father. But for the first time in his short life, he sided with the old man. One thing he'd never do was tell Nate and Alex what he'd heard. Nope. It was bad enough he knew the truth. He didn't want his brothers to know their mother was having another man's baby. It would stay his secret.

As soon as she left the living room, he scrambled out of his hiding place, ran to the room he shared with his brothers, and changed his pants. Thirty minutes later, his world was turned upside down again when his mother gathered her sons together, told them she loved them, and then walked down the dirt road, out of their lives forever, carrying her meager belongings in a garbage bag. Even then, he'd kept his secret.

He'd refused to think of that day throughout his life. Remembering it now, he had the sickening feeling his nine-year-old self had gotten it all wrong. Had she said the baby was some other man's just to get his father to stop hitting her? So she wouldn't miscarry?

Until the day he'd overheard the fight between his mother and father, he'd thought of her as a good person. She'd protected them as best she could, had seen that they were fed and clothed with what little money her husband had given her. Hell, she barely ate so there would be more food for her boys. That he remembered. And she'd spoken the truth when she'd said she never left the piece of dirt they called home because their father never allowed her to unless he was with her.

All these years, he'd thought the worst of her, and he'd been wrong. So damn wrong. As a grown man, he could see it now. She'd tried to protect the baby the only way she knew how. As he stared out at the ocean, he apologized to his mother for allowing himself to believe his father's lies.

Where was she now? What about the baby? Did she have it? Lose it after the beating? What if she didn't have any money and was living on welfare? She had three sons in a position to take care of her. Shame on them if that were the case and they'd not done their best to locate her.

Although as a boy he'd resented her for leaving them to the volatile whims of their father, still did a little, he understood now that she'd left to protect the life of her baby. Did they have a sister or brother out there somewhere?

Anytime the subject of their mother came up, Nate would shut it down, refusing to talk about her. Why was that? It could be as simple as he, too, resented her for leaving, or it was possible Nate knew more than he'd ever told him and Alex.

What Court *did* know was that he hadn't a clue what to do about Lauren. He had been wrong not only about his mother, but apparently about Lauren, too. If he hadn't been so hurt, he would have questioned her abrupt change of heart when she broke off their relationship.

He hadn't fought for her, and he should have. Ever since she'd walked back into his life, he'd vacillated from wanting her to not wanting her from one minute to the next. That wasn't quite true. He always wanted her—he just didn't like that he did.

She was adamant about leaving, though, and he just couldn't go there again. If that was what she was determined to do, he'd keep his promise, teach her what he could in the few days they had, and then put her on a damn plane.

"Why aren't you answering your phone?"

He glanced back at Alex. "Didn't hear it. I think it's on the coffee table."

"It was." Alex tossed it to him. "Someone broke into Lauren's apartment."

The hell? "Is she there?" he asked as he headed for the door.

Alex jogged alongside him. "Yeah. Madison and David Markham are with her. I'll drive."

He shouldn't have let her leave his side. If anything had happened to her—

"Stop blaming yourself, bro. She's fine."

"It had to have been Peter. I should have considered the possibility he'd do something like this."

"We all should have."

Maybe true, but she was his responsibility to protect. Driving fast, Alex had them at the bookstore in ten minutes. Court took the stairs to her apartment two at a time. As soon as he walked into the room, Lauren stepped next to him, as if she needed to be close to him. He wrapped his arm around her shoulder, pulling her next to his side.

"You okay?" he asked. A shudder passed through her body, one he could feel. If he found out it was Peter who'd broken into her apartment, he'd make the man sorry, that was for damn sure.

"It's so creepy knowing someone went through my things."

"I'm just glad you didn't walk in on him." He glanced at David. "We'll take it from here." The last thing they needed was the police department getting involved.

"I'll report that it was a false alarm. Your favors are adding up, dude."

"Add it to my tab."

David snorted. "Trust me, I will."

After David left, Court glanced at his brother. "Why don't you and Madison wait for us downstairs. Oh, and call for a team to come dust for fingerprints. Maybe we'll get lucky." Probably not, but it was worth a try.

"Do you think it was Peter?" Lauren asked when they were alone.

He let go of her and perched on the edge of the bed. "Do you?"

"Who else would it be?" She looked around. "I don't think I can sleep in this room again, knowing someone was in here going through my things. But then I guess that doesn't matter since I'm leaving in a few days."

That remained to be seen. "Why don't you go through everything, make sure nothing's missing." He watched her check her dresser drawers, and then she went to the closet. She bent over, and his eyes were immediately drawn to her ass. If ever a woman was made to wear skinny jeans, it was Lauren, with her long legs and perfectly curved bottom. Even her feet were sexy, and he smiled at the combination of blue toenail polish and sparkly flip-flops.

"Stop staring at my butt." She stood, glancing over her shoulder.

"That's not possible. It's one of my favorite things to look at." He grinned. "How'd you know what I was looking at?"

"I can feel you doing it. I've always been aware of your attention on me."

He held her gaze, wondering if she realized what she'd just admitted. How could she even consider leaving, walking away from what they had? As if coming out of a trance, she gave a little shake of her head. Resuming her search of the closet, she pulled down a shoebox from the shelf. She opened the lid, frowning as she stared at the contents.

"What's wrong?"

Her gaze still on the box, she sat next to him. "There's a picture missing."

"How do you know?"

"I just do."

He glanced into the box, stilling when he saw photos of the two of them during spring break. "You kept all these?" He picked one up. It was one he remembered taking of her.

They were going out to dinner their last night together and had walked down to the beach to watch the sun set. She'd worn a white sundress, looking like an angel as the breeze blew the skirt around her knees. There was such joy on her face as she smiled for the camera.

"Love you," she'd said, right before he snapped the picture.

He'd looked into those golden-brown eyes, his heart beating crazily in his chest. It was the moment he'd known. *Her, she's the one,* his heart, his body, his soul had said. There hadn't been a sliver of doubt as he closed the distance between them, pulled her into his arms, and said, "You own me, Gorgeous Girl," before claiming her mouth in a kiss that had almost brought him to his knees.

"You should have told me," he said, still angry that she hadn't trusted him enough to believe he could have protected her.

"I thought I was doing the right thing."

At least she hadn't pretended not to understand. "It's not like we ever made a promise that we'd see each other again. You know, said love words and all that." He tilted his head as he eyed her. "Oh wait, we *did* do all that, didn't we? If you'd really loved me, you would have trusted me."

The woman made him crazy. His brain was the equivalent of scrambled eggs around her. He swiped a hand through his hair. "I can't even think straight anymore. Do you have any idea how it makes me feel to know that you let a man beat you within an inch of your life just to protect me?"

CHAPTER TWELVE

"Get over it." Lauren stood, backing away from him. He was starting to sound like a record stuck on the same words, over and over and over. Why couldn't he understand she had as much right to protect him as he did to protect her? Stephan had hurt her horribly that day, but she'd been proud—still was—that she'd not once uttered Court's name during her ex-husband's assault. She refused to let Court take that away from her.

"Get over it?" He stalked toward her. "I'll have nightmares until the day I die after seeing those photos of you beaten so badly I could hardly recognize you. Because of me, Lauren. You tell me. How am I supposed to get over that?"

She didn't have an answer.

"Nothing to say?" Using his body, he backed her up against the wall.

"You want me to say something? How about this? Go to hell, Court." Black eyes glittered with fury as they snared hers. She'd poked the tiger, and now the tiger was pissed. She didn't care. She'd done what she had believed was the right thing, and she'd do it again under the same circumstances. If he couldn't accept that, it was his problem.

"You don't have a clue, do you G.G.?"

Somehow, she'd lost the thread of the conversation. "A clue?" The way he was looking at her—heat simmering in those beautiful black eyes—turned her knees to jelly. She pressed her back hard against the wall to stay upright.

"Yeah. It's just this." He put his hands on the wall, caging her, staring down at her. "Send me to hell all you want, but I'll always fight my way back to you." He put his mouth next to her ear. "You're a witch, Lauren, casting your magic spells on me until I don't know up from down. But you're my witch. Don't ever forget that."

"Does that mean you're mine?" He wasn't the only one confused, considering the number he was doing on her.

"I've always been yours. How do you not know that?"

She'd known it for six glorious days, until he couldn't be hers anymore. But nothing had changed. She was still leaving.

He tsked. "Not going to answer? Fine, I don't feel like talking either." He covered her mouth with his.

God help her, she couldn't resist him. She wrapped her arms around his neck, moaning when he pressed against her. His answering moan brought her to her senses. Another few minutes, and she'd agree to anything he asked.

"Stop." She put her hands on his chest. "Stop, Court."

He lifted his head. "I'd rather kiss you. Look me in the eyes and tell me you don't like kissing me. Tell me you don't feel the connection between us. Look at me and say the words, Lauren."

She couldn't. "This is a ridiculous conversation."

"Only because you're making it ridiculous." He returned to the bed and sat. Picking up the shoebox, he flipped through the photos. "I remember every moment that each of these were taken. Do you?"

"Please don't do this," she whispered. He was killing her. How could she possibly forget one minute with him?

"Why not? Do you wish you'd never met me?" Not giving her time to answer, he said, "Where's the selfie we took right before I kissed you good-bye the morning you left?"

He remembered that? "Gone. It was on top."

"Are you sure?" He flipped through the photos again.

"I had them out not long ago. That was the last one I put back. It was my favorite." They'd been so happy then, never dreaming how much time would pass before they saw each other again.

He peered up at her. "Why were you looking at them?"

"I don't know." She sat next to him. "I've been thinking about that week a lot lately."

"Me, too," he said softly. "I'm curious about something. The first time I saw you, there was a sparkle in your eyes. You were happy. I would think that most people coming out of a bad marriage would struggle—"

"To find happiness again?" He nodded. "I was married to a man I grew to hate for the two most miserable years of my life. I promised myself the day my divorce was final that he would no longer steal my joy. Going to spring break had been a spur-of-the moment decision. I was finally free, and I wanted to go have fun."

He stared at the photo he held, the one of her he'd taken their last night together when they'd walked down to the beach to watch the sun set. "You were the last thing I expected. I hadn't planned on staying more than two or three days, but then there you were in that sexy green bikini, laughing as you spit sand out of your mouth." He captured her gaze. "I was a goner right then. Knew it and didn't care."

"Court . . ."

"You crushed me, G.G., tore my heart out without a word of explanation. For six years, I thought it'd all been a game to you, and I hated you for it." He put the photo back into the box.

"I'm sorry. I—"

"I get why you thought you were doing the right thing." He stood, stared down at her for a moment, and then moved away. "It wasn't, but it's done." Her window faced Collins Avenue, and he leaned against the frame, putting his back to her as he stared down at the street.

"It was the right thing to do. I have to believe that, otherwise I lost you for nothing." She swiped at the tears running down her cheeks. "You had school, finals coming up. You lived what? Five hundred miles away in Tallahassee? It wasn't like you could just pop in from next door and save me. He wanted your name, but I refused to give it to him because I knew what he was capable of. I loved you too much to make you a target."

He turned then, his eyes shimmering with anger. "I saw the photos of what he did to you. You almost died because of me, because you didn't trust that I could protect you. Even worse, you still don't think so or you wouldn't keep talking about doing a disappearing act. How do you think that makes me feel?"

She had no answer for that. At least not one he'd want to hear. He would never understand that nothing was more important to her back then than knowing he was safe. Not even her own happiness. Today, because of his job and his brothers, she did believe he was capable of going up against Stephan. But there were no guarantees that he wouldn't be hurt, and that was still her fear.

"Nothing to say?"

"I've told you I was sorry. I am, Court. If nothing else, believe that."

The anger in his eyes faded. "So am I. But know this. I'm not going to hide from Stephan Kozlov. And more importantly, I'll never let him touch you again."

"I don't even understand why he's focusing on me. Except for one letter shortly after he went to prison, I haven't heard a word from him."

He returned to sit beside her. "Do you still have the letter?"

She shook her head. "I shredded it without opening it. After that, I heard nothing from him until Peter showed up saying Stephan expected me to be at home when he arrived. Like that would ever happen."

"I think he was being cagey, letting you think you weren't on his radar so you wouldn't take off. But Peter showing up tells me they've kept tabs on you all this time."

She shivered. "That's creeping me out." When he put his arm around her shoulders, she let herself lean into him. Everything was so confusing. It wasn't fair to him that she was bringing her troubles to his door, but he was so big and strong, so very confident of his abilities. The thought of leaving, taking off on her own, made her both sad and scared.

"Let's go get some lunch, then we'll head back to my place, talk about what we're going to do."

"Okay. Let me pack up a few things." She was ready to be out of this room. The clutch she'd been using was too small to carry her Kindle, so she changed purses.

Court grinned. "It's fascinating, the stuff women haul around with them," he said as she put her wallet, hairbrush, lipstick, a mirror, pens, a notepad, a sunglasses case, tissues, her phone, her Kindle, and a charger into the bigger purse.

She grinned back. "How do men exist with only a wallet in their pockets?"

"The fingerprint tech's here," Alex said, stopping in the doorway. "They'll need to print you, Lauren, so they can eliminate yours from the ones they find."

After getting her fingers inked, she went to find Madison. "I guess I'll see you in the evenings since I won't be back to the store this week." She still felt guilty for not telling her friend that she might never be back. And when had she put a *might* in front of her plan to leave?

Madison gave her a hug. "Just trust Court and his brothers, and everything will be okay."

"Whatever's going to happen, I want it over and done with." Maybe then she could return to the life she'd created for herself.

"Why don't the four of us grab an early dinner tonight?" Alex asked, walking up to them.

"Can't," Court said. "I've got a meeting with Nate before he goes to the bar. How about picking up Lauren and taking her to dinner with you and Madison."

Alex smiled at her. "That okay with you?"

"I don't want to be a bother." It was funny how his smile was so much like Court's, yet Alex's didn't make her stomach twitchy.

"Don't be silly," Madison said. "I'll call you when we're on the way."

"Okay. Catch you later." She followed Court to his car. "I don't have a problem staying in and making a sandwich or something. I don't like everyone feeling like they have to take care of me."

He opened the passenger door, but put his hand on her arm, stopping her from getting in. "No one thinks that. Alex and Madison are your friends. They care about you. The invitation wasn't because they feel obligated, so stop overthinking it, okay?"

Something behind her caught his attention, but before she could glance back to see what, he cupped her jaw, lifted her face, and then kissed her. He'd caught her by surprise, and her mind said he wasn't kissing her because he'd suddenly felt like it. When he deepened the kiss, though, the thought evaporated.

Through hooded eyes, Court watched Peter Kozlov. The man stood on the corner, making no effort to stay out of sight. How long had he been watching the bookstore? Court didn't doubt that it was Peter who had broken into Lauren's apartment, probably sometime last night.

To give Kozlov something to take back to his brother, Court dropped the suitcase Lauren had packed and wrapped his arms around her, pulling her against him.

"Court?" she whispered.

"Hmm?" He leaned back, staring down at her.

114

"Why are you kissing me?"

"It just seemed like something I needed to do." He didn't want her to see Peter. She was upset enough already. "Get in the car before I decide I need to do it again." And although he'd done it to taunt Stephan, since he was sure Peter would tell him, he really had wanted to kiss her.

After closing her door, he walked around the back of his car, giving Peter a smirk when their eyes met. The man showed no emotion, only stared back. Court hummed with satisfaction. The hook had been baited, the first step in his plan to catch a big fish or two.

It was something of a surprise that Peter didn't try to follow them, but he only stood on the sidewalk, watching as they pulled away. Did he have someone else tracking them? Court made a few turns until he was certain they didn't have a tail.

He glanced at Lauren. She was looking out the window, and he wondered what she was thinking. When she trailed a finger over her kiss-swollen bottom lip, unconsciously signaling her thoughts, he smiled to himself.

Kissing Lauren Montgomery was what he imagined it would be like to shoot crack straight into his veins. Instant addiction. He could spend a lifetime having her mouth available to kiss anytime he wanted. Did he still want that?

There'd been a time, however briefly, that he'd thought he had a future with her. He glanced at her again. Whatever it was about her that called to him was still there. No matter how much he might wish otherwise, he couldn't deny that. All he could do for now was continue with his plan and see how things played out.

"Remind me to give you a key when we get home in case I'm not there when you get back from dinner." As he turned into his complex, he made a mental note to show her his safe room should the time come when she needed to hide.

"I've been thinking," she said, finally looking at him.

He comically widened his eyes. "Uh-oh."

"Yeah, scary."

It was good to see her smiling. "Why don't you hold that thought until we get upstairs? Then we'll talk."

Once upstairs, he said, "We have a few hours before Alex and Madison pick you up for dinner. Let's sit out on the balcony. Beer?" he asked, heading for the kitchen.

"No, I'm just going to have some water."

He grabbed a glass from the cabinet, and handed it to her, then got a beer from the fridge. After getting ice, she went to the sink, filling the glass with water. His gaze roamed over her from the back of her neck down.

If he'd met her for the first time today, he would be just as attracted, even though she wasn't wearing a sexy green bikini. He smiled as he eyed her pink-tipped spiky hair—for some strange reason a close second to her ass on his list of favorite things about her. And that was before he got to all the other parts of her that were damn near amazing. Even her sassy mouth—a new development—was a turn-on.

He walked up behind her, set his beer down, and then put his hands on the counter, trapping her. "I don't know what to do about you, Gorgeous Girl. One minute I'm so angry with you that I wish we'd never met." He nuzzled her neck. "The next, I want to handcuff you to my side and never let you go. Why do you think that is? I'd really like an answer because I sure as hell don't know."

She shook her head. "I don't have an answer for you."

"This is what you do to me." He rocked his hips against her, letting her feel his erection. "All I have to do is think about you, and I get hard. I smell your scent and I want to bury my nose against your skin and inhale you." He pressed his nose into her hair, breathing her in. "You walk into the room and all I want to do is strip you naked and spend hours exploring every inch of you."

A shiver rippled through her, one he could feel as it traveled down her spine. "Don't try to tell me it's not the same for you."

"You know it is, but . . ." She bowed her head. "I don't know what to do."

"Not the right answer." Why did he keep hoping that she'd decide he was worth fighting for? He got that she was afraid, both for him and herself, but if she really wanted him, she wouldn't run. Obviously, even after learning who and what he was, she still didn't believe he could protect her.

He picked up his beer, then headed for the balcony. What had he been expecting? That she'd declare her undying love? She was a runner. She'd done it once, and she'd do it again. Until she was willing to stand and fight, he wasn't going to put his heart out there for her to trample on again. Yet, like a whipped dog, he kept coming back for more.

The sea was calm today. He preferred it angry and crashing onshore. It would match his mood. Putting his feet on the railing, he balanced his chair on the back two legs. He drank his beer, breathing in the salty air as he watched the ocean. It usually brought him peace, sitting out here, but not today. He snorted. Peace and Lauren in the same sentence was laughable. Except he wasn't laughing.

He'd always been a decisive man, so this vacillating between thinking the best thing he could do for his peace of mind was to let her go and wanting to never let go of her was damn irritating. Did he still love her? When he'd told her that he belonged to her, that hadn't been a lie, even though he'd spent six years trying to rid his system of her. He'd believed he had, at least until the night he'd waited for Madison's roommate to arrive and in had walked his Gorgeous Girl. Life was a real bitch sometimes.

The glass door opened behind him, and Lauren stepped in front of him. "I'm sorry."

"For?"

"Everything."

"I guess that about covers it all." She flinched. Yeah, he was being a jerk, but he couldn't seem to help himself. Her eyes were red and swollen, which added guilt to his assholeness.

He lowered his chair, removing his feet from the railing so she could pass by. "Have a seat." Once she was settled, he resumed his position of feet on the railing and chair tilted back. "That's the last time I want to hear you say you're sorry. What's done is done."

"I just wanted you to know that."

"And now I do." He swallowed the last of his beer, then peered over at her. "Even though I disagree with your decision, I get why you thought you had to cut me out of your life six years ago. What I don't understand is why you're so anxious to do it again." He held up a hand when she started to respond. "And don't say it's to protect me because that just pisses me off."

Her mouth snapped closed. "Thought so," he said. He sighed, turning his attention back to the ocean. "One of the things I adored about you was your love of life. You let him take that away from you then, and you're willing to let him do it again by running."

"I don't want to run, but every time I think of what he might do to you . . . I couldn't bear it, Court, if you were hurt, or worse, because of me."

"Since you don't have faith that I can protect you, I guess that means I'll put you on a plane as promised." He shouldn't be disappointed. It was what he'd expected from her.

"No."

Surprised, he looked at her. "No?"

CHAPTER THIRTEEN

"No," Lauren answered. The decision to stay and stand up to Stephan once and for all had been brewing ever since the Gentry brothers had told her they were FBI agents. When Court had walked away from her in the kitchen, she'd understood that he was giving her a choice. Get on that plane and lose any chance she had with him. Trust him and maybe they could find their way to each other again. If she had the right to risk her life for him, how could she deny him the same?

She knew she'd hurt him badly and that she was gambling on an unsure thing, but she had to try. If she didn't, she would regret it for the rest of her life, and she was tired of regrets. And he was right. It was time to stand up to Stephan no matter what would or wouldn't happen between her and Court.

"If I disappear, leaving my family, my friends, and the bookstore, he wins."

"He does."

"You have to promise me one thing, though." She moved to the edge of her seat and reached for his hand. "You won't let him hurt you."

That was a stupid promise to ask for. He couldn't guarantee it, but she still needed to hear him say it.

"Trust me, Lauren. He's the one who needs to worry about getting hurt." He turned his hand palm up, lacing their fingers. "I'll admit, you just surprised me, but it's the right thing to do."

She stared at their joined hands, loving the feel of her skin pressed against his. Although Court seemed to think otherwise, she'd only been intimate with one man since him. That had been Nelson Lopez and look at how that had turned out. Not so good when the FBI, which she now understood had been the Gentry brothers, had arrested him along with Madison's uncle. It was all just too weird. People should have to wear a sign identifying themselves. Something like, "Bad guy here" or "Good guy here."

She'd once been a simple girl, sheltered by her religious parents. Then she'd had an accidental meeting with a pro hockey star, and nothing had been the same since. As much as she might regret walking into that waiting room where Stephan sat, it had, in a way, led her to Court.

"I know we have work to do if I'm going to face Stephan, but how much would it surprise you if I said I want you to make love to me before I have to start worrying about him?"

He squeezed her hand, his eyes turning as black as a midnight sky. "I've suddenly decided I like surprises."

Before she could reply, he scooped her up in his arms, carrying her to his bedroom. This close to him, she could smell his spicy scent, could feel his body heat, and desire spread through her like warm syrup, soft and thick.

Stopping next to his bed, he let go of her legs, letting her slide down his body. When she reached for the hem of her T-shirt he brushed her hands away.

"Let me."

She saluted him. "Yes, sir."

"I sense a bit of sarcasm there, Ms. Montgomery. Careful or I might have to punish you." He froze. "I'm sorry. I shouldn't have said that, not after what happened to you. I swear, I was only playing with you."

"You're not him." She put her hand on his cheek. "You're not him," she said again, whispering the words.

"No, I'm not. I'd never hurt you, G.G. Not intentionally."

"I know." She sat on the bed, leaned back on her elbows, and then smiled at him the way she had six years ago. "Take my clothes off."

His heart tripped over itself. "I can absolutely do that." When all that was left were her matching pink panties and bra, he stilled, staring down at her. "A man could forget his name at the sight of you all pretty in pink."

Lord, the heat in his eyes could start a bonfire. That or melt her on the spot. "Have you forgotten your name then?"

"I have a name?" he asked as he shed his clothes with astonishing speed. He grabbed a condom out of the drawer, dropped it on the nightstand, then grinned as he toppled over her, catching himself on his elbows. "You really are a witch, Lauren Montgomery. I should lock you up for casting spells on a federal agent."

She wished she could cast spells. If so, she'd take them back six years and do everything differently, beginning with telling him the truth. But as she looked into his eyes, the pupils dilated and darkened to the deepest black with desire, she knew that wasn't true. She'd do everything the same if it meant keeping him safe.

"Love me, Court." She wasn't sure exactly what she was asking— for Court to make love to her or for him to love her? Both, if she was honest with herself. She scraped her fingers over the bristles of a beard trying to grow back. He was a man who needed to shave twice a day if he wanted his face to stay smooth. She loved him both ways, scruffy and clean-shaven.

"Do you want me to tell you how it's done?" She gave him her best smirk in an attempt to get back to the lighthearted mood from moments ago. "I mean, there's more to sex than just you being sprawled on top of me, not moving."

Amusement returned to his eyes. "Oh, I'll definitely show you some moves."

There was something different about him. When they'd made love in the dark hours of the night, it had been dreamlike—as if they'd both pretended it wasn't really happening. This time, his eyes were clear and focused. She felt wanted. That was it, the difference.

She moaned in pleasure when he buried his face against her neck, nuzzling and then nipping at her skin. He was an amazing lover. There was no denying that, she thought, as he explored every inch of her body with his mouth and hands. His touch was reverent, almost as if he still loved her.

That was wishful thinking, but she wished it nevertheless. He worked his way down, kissing, sucking, licking. And, oh, God, he had the cleverest mouth in the world. Her body was going to float away, and there was nothing she could do to stop it if he kept doing that. But he was relentless. She fisted the sheets, trying to anchor herself to the bed. The pleasure he was creating in her built until she was chanting his name over and over.

"G.G.?" he said a while later, climbing up her body and lowering his talented mouth down on hers.

"Hmm?" She tasted herself on his lips when their mouths melded together.

He lifted his face, staring down at her. "Have I ever told you how much I love the sounds you make when you come?"

"Don't make sounds," she said while trying to catch her breath.

He laughed. "You so do."

She put her hands on his cheeks and stared into his eyes. "That was . . . That was . . ." She struggled to form a coherent thought after the best climax of her life.

"Awesome? Mind-blowing? Stupefying? Staggering?"

She punched him on the arm. "Arrogant man. All of those things."

"Arrogant I'll give you, if I can make you agree to all those words, Gorgeous Girl." He rolled over her, taking her with him.

Now covering him like a blanket, she peered down at him. "Just don't let it go to your head."

He laughed. "Oh, we're not done yet. Let's see if we can add some more stupendous words to my repertoire."

"I doubt that's possible," she said, issuing a challenge. She loved hearing his laughter. He'd laughed often during their time together in Panama City. The man he'd become rarely did, and she missed that.

He spanked her butt. "Put the damn condom on me."

"Bossy," she said, grabbing the foil pack.

"That a turn-on for you?"

"I'd never admit it even if it were. You'd just go into turbo-bossy."

"Is turbo-bossy even a thing?" His lips curved into a wicked smile, as if he were considering the possibility.

"Don't even think it."

"Can't promise that." He put his hands on her hips after he was sheathed. "Ride me, G.G. Let's see what moves you've got."

"Hold on, then." She loved watching him when they made love. He had a way of snaring her with his eyes, their focus never leaving her face. She could get lost in those smoldering eyes, not caring if she found her way back.

"Take my hands," he said, holding them up to her.

With their palms pressed together, him supporting her, helping her move, she made love to the man who'd owned her heart since the day she'd noticed him watching her play volleyball with the intensity of a man on a mission. Turned out his mission had been her. *I love you.* The words danced on the tip of her tongue, begging to be said. But not yet. He wasn't ready to hear them again. Didn't quite trust her. It hurt but she understood. She prayed the day would come when he would want to hear them again.

"Christ, G.G., close." The cords on his neck thickened. His lips parted. "Come with me."

"Now?" She'd been ready, had only been trying to hold out, waiting for him.

"Yes." He flipped them, sliding his arms under her, bringing them chest to chest. "Yes, now," he whispered into her ear, his warm breath tickling her skin.

She shattered in his arms.

"LaurenLaurenLauren," he chanted. Then, once their breathing had slowed, he hummed the Bruno Mars song "Just the Way You Are."

That had been their song for six glorious days because he'd claimed she was perfect just the way she was. Tears burning her eyes, she buried her face in his neck, breathing in his essence. She'd done her best to keep him in her past, but had never figured out how to make that happen. Now, he was back in her life, loving her to completion, and if she lost him again, she wasn't sure she'd ever be the same.

"I'll admit you got the moves, Gorgeous Girl." He curled his fingers into her hair, pulling her face to his, giving her a long, leisurely kiss. When he was done kissing her, he rolled them until they were side by side, facing each other.

He trailed a finger down the valley of her breasts. "I don't want to leave this bed, but duty calls. If I don't head upstairs, Nate will come looking for me. Then I'd have to kill him for seeing you naked." After a quick kiss, he sat up, swinging his legs over the side. "And you're having dinner with Alex and Madison, so you need to get dressed, too."

"Or I could stay right here and wait for you to come back." She waggled her eyebrows.

"Better yet, go with them, get something to eat, then we'll pick up where we left off. Sound like a plan?"

She liked her plan better. "Want me to bring you something back?"

"Sure. Alex knows what I like."

For some reason that made her sad. She should know all the foods he liked. Damn Stephan to hell.

Court wasn't sure what put the sadness back in her eyes. He didn't like it, but he didn't have time to find out. "After my meeting, I'll meet you back here. A little later, I'll have to head over to Aces and Eights." He thought he should mind feeling like he had to give her his itinerary. Strangely, he didn't, although he'd never seen the need to do so with any other woman. But then, Lauren wasn't any other woman.

After a shower, he shaved and dressed. With thirty minutes to spare before he had to go up to Nate's, he went looking for Lauren, expecting to find her out on the balcony. Alex had once said that from the time he'd met Madison, being with her soothed him. Court found that interesting because Lauren didn't soothe a single bone in his body. She made him restless and needy, made him anxious when she wasn't in sight. Not just from concern for her welfare, but from something deep inside him he couldn't name that demanded he keep her by his side. Maybe it was a lingering fear that she would run after all.

He found her in the living room, standing in front of his lone bookshelf as she flipped through a book.

"How come you don't have pictures of your parents anywhere?" she said without glancing back at him. "None that I've seen, anyway."

Although he hadn't made a sound, she'd known he was in the room. The same thing happened to him—this knowing she was near without seeing or hearing her. That was not soothing.

He walked in front of her and saw she held Goosebumps, the only thing he had left of his mother. Resisting the urge to snatch it away, he said, "Why would I have a picture of a man I hated and the woman who left us in the bastard's care?"

She frowned. "I guess I just assumed you had a happy childhood."

Puzzled, he said, "Why would you assume that?"

"It's obvious you and your brothers respect and love each other. The three of you seem well-adjusted. I mean, jeez, all three of you are

FBI agents. That's saying something. Then there're the words from your mother inside the cover. I could feel her love for you in what she wrote in the front."

He took the book from her, opened it to the front, and read his mother's words.

Happy birthday, my sweet son. You are growing into a wonderful young man, and I'm so proud of you.
Love always,
Mommy

It had been years since he'd read the inscription, but he remembered it word for word. He'd treasured his birthday gift, even knowing she'd gotten it secondhand at a thrift shop. Until the day she'd left, he'd never doubted she loved him and his brothers. Then she'd walked away, and for years, he'd hated her for it.

He handed the book back to Lauren, and then stuck his hands in his pockets, turning to stare out the balcony door. He didn't like talking about his past—that had been one of their problems when they'd first met. If they'd shared what was going on with each other, he would have been there for her when all her shit went down. She'd finally told him about her life, and he supposed she deserved to know about his.

"If that's what you think, you'd be wrong. About having a normal childhood, at least. Did my mother love us? I didn't used to think so, but I recently had a revelation that changed my mind."

She came up behind him, pressed herself against his back, and wrapped her arms around his waist. "Tell me about your life as a boy."

How about that? Her body wrapped around his *was* soothing. He leaned into her touch, and told her about his bastard of a father, about his mother leaving, and how Nate had raised him and Alex. Throughout it all, she didn't say a word, but her tears wet his T-shirt. He knew they were tears for him, and he accepted that she was slipping back into his heart.

"I liked my story better, that you had a wonderful childhood," she said when he finished.

He turned, staying in the embrace of her arms. "Sorry to disappoint, but all you can do is make the best of what you got, you know?" He'd never given much thought to how easy it would have been for any one or all of the Gentry brothers to go down the wrong road. They'd been handed all the excuses in the world for that to happen—their bastard of an old man, a mother who'd abandoned them, the squalor they'd called home. He could go on and on as the list was endless.

But they hadn't turned into thieving punks, and they had their mother to thank for that. She'd believed in them, had taught them the importance of an education. Before she'd left, no matter how tired they were from the chores their father had assigned them, even on school days, no matter how beaten down and worn out his mother must have been, she'd sat her three sons down at their scarred kitchen table, books open in front of them.

Although she'd never finished high school, she'd worked with them on their homework, somehow making it fun. Looking back on it now, he realized she'd been learning right along with them. She'd often said that she wanted her sons to grow into men she would be proud of. What she'd never said was, "Don't turn into your father." But that sentiment was there, shimmering under her words.

Wherever you are, Mom, I think you'd be proud of us. I just wish you'd stuck around to see that for yourself.

He would like her to know that Nate had stepped into the role of mother and father. She would be especially proud of her oldest son for his fierce determination in continuing their studies, following her nightly study tradition. It wasn't right that she didn't know how he'd walked a straight path, ignoring the temptation to take the easy way out, while dragging his two younger brothers—sometimes kicking and screaming—along with him. More than anything else, he wanted her to know that.

"You've gone real quiet. Penny for your thoughts."

Court let go of the memories crowding his mind. "Just thinking it's time we looked for our mother." Before she could respond, he stepped away, done with tripping down memory lane. But he was ready to have a conversation with his brothers. It was time to put the past to rest.

At the sound of the doorbell he said, "That will be Alex and Madison."

She grabbed her purse, then waved her fingers at him. "Wish you could come."

"Sorry. Duty calls." He wanted to send her on her way with a kiss, but he didn't. As soon as they left for dinner, he headed up to Nate's condo for his meeting with his brother and their fellow agent Taylor Collins. Nate was bringing her in on their investigation into the Russian mafia. An investigation he'd kept from Lauren, even though it involved her. He pushed aside his guilt about that as he walked into Nate's condo.

Taylor was already there, and she and Nate stopped talking as soon as he entered. Strange. He had the impression that their conversation was personal. Alex suspected there was something going on between them, but Court wasn't so sure. His big brother wouldn't fool around with a colleague. But what did he know?

Taylor Collins was a beautiful woman. Blonde hair cut in a sleek style that came to just below her ears, eyes as blue as the sky, and a creamy complexion. She was also an ace agent and as smart as a whip. A good match for Nate if that was the way the wind blew.

They spent an hour reviewing what they knew and what they still needed to learn about the Kozlov brothers. After refining the plan to bring down Stephan and Peter, Court pushed away from the table.

"I'm going to tell Lauren everything we know and plan to do," he said.

Nate eyed him. "You trust her that much?"

"Yes." He realized he truly did. She'd almost sacrificed her own life for his. If that wasn't proof he could trust her, he didn't know what was.

"I'll walk out with you," Taylor said when they finished.

"Sure." He'd half expected her to stay behind. Maybe there wasn't anything going on between her and his brother. "I want to go down to the lobby, show our doorman photos of the Kozlovs so he knows what to watch for," he said, punching the down arrow.

"Good idea," Taylor said as they waited for the elevator. "I heard Anatoly Gorelovea has his first court date next week."

"Yeah. The prosecutors have filed a motion that will allow Alex to testify in disguise, but the man's lawyers are fighting it. There's precedence for it, so hopefully the judge will agree. The defense wants his name, though, and if that happens, Alex is a marked man. That alone should be the deciding factor as far as I'm concerned. You and I both know that even from prison, Gorelovea's influence is far-reaching."

Alex had taken Gorelovea, aka Mr. X, aka The Ghost, down a few months ago, along with Madison's uncle, who'd been a major drug lord. Court had to admit he was a little jealous of his baby brother for capturing Gorelovea, a man wanted by half the countries in the world. Without even trying, Alex had become a legend among his fellow agents.

They stepped into the elevator. "Nate will go ballistic if the judge agrees to identify Alex, and I'll be right there with him." The thought of his baby brother getting hurt again made him want to punch something. Alex had been shot and had nearly died during the arrest of Madison's uncle and cousin. Court had never felt such rage and hopelessness in his entire life, not even when his mother or Lauren had left him.

Taylor shook her head. "I refuse to believe any judge would willingly hand over Alex's name to one of the biggest criminals on the planet. No matter what, we won't let anything happen to him."

She hugged him. He recognized and appreciated that it was a comfort hug and returned it. The elevator doors opened, and he glanced up to see Lauren and Madison standing there. Lauren backed up as if struck. Well, this was awkward.

"Ladies," he said, dropping his arm from Taylor's shoulder as they stepped out.

CHAPTER FOURTEEN

"Hi, Madison. Hi, Lauren," Taylor said, smiling.

"Hi, Taylor," Madison said, grabbing Lauren's hand and pulling her into the elevator after Court and Taylor exited.

Court glanced over his shoulder, his eyes meeting hers. "I'll be up in a minute."

The door closed, saving Lauren from having to answer. She'd met Taylor at Madison and Alex's wedding, but why was she here with Court? And that hadn't been an innocent hug. He'd had his eyes closed, his chin resting on top of the woman's head, and his arm around her.

Lauren's stomach took a sickening roll as the elevator rose. Court had said he was meeting his brother. Had that been a lie? But he wouldn't have spent the afternoon making love to her only to go meet another woman, would he?

"Stop it," Madison said, punching her arm. "It's not what you're thinking."

"She's gorgeous. It would be amazing if he wasn't attracted to her." She briefly considered stomping on the ham and cheese on sourdough in the to-go bag she carried.

See how Court liked a smashed sandwich.

"He's not, I promise you. She's an FBI agent."

"Really? I never would have guessed that." She glanced at Madison. "Are you sure? You know that there's nothing—"

"Yep. Actually, Alex thinks there's something going on between her and Nate."

She smiled, suddenly happy again. Court's sandwich was safe. "They'd make a striking couple." It was true, Nate with his dark features and long black hair, and Taylor, all blonde and creamy.

"I hope something comes of it. Nate needs someone like her who can stand up to him."

"He is intimidating." Big bad wolf intimidating.

"Why don't you come down after Court leaves? We'll have some wine and watch a sappy movie on the Hallmark Channel."

"I'd like that." It was nice having her friend close again. If a miracle happened and she and Court stayed together, they could visit during the nights their guys were working. But if you wished too hard for something, it wouldn't happen, so she tried not to think about it.

She dug the key to Court's condo out of her pocket as she walked down the hallway. As she slid the key into the door, movement at the end of the corridor caught her attention, and she glanced over. She squinted at the man walking toward her.

Peter? She fumbled the key, dropping it. A jackhammer took control of her heart, pounding against her chest as if it wanted to break through her skin. She scrambled for the key, got it in her trembling fingers, and finally inserted it into the lock. When she glanced back as she pushed her way inside, the man had stopped in front of a door down the hall, but he was watching her.

Was it Peter? He was too far away for her to see his features, and a ball cap covered his hair, so she couldn't tell if he was blond like Peter. The man's size and build were similar to her former brother-in-law's, though.

She slammed the door behind her, locking the knob, and then she slid the dead bolt closed. Leaning against the wood, she put her hand to her chest, taking several deep breaths. When she was calmer, she put her eye to the peephole, keeping it there for a minute, but no one approached the door.

But she'd be damned if she was taking any chances. Dropping her purse and Court's sandwich on the dining room table, she went to the guest room and dug through her tote bag until she found her gun. For five or so minutes, she paced the confines of the living room, unable to sit. Had that been Peter watching her?

At the sound of the door locks being turned, she backed up against the wall, holding up the gun. If it was him could she shoot him? She didn't know. If he advanced on her and she couldn't pull the trigger, then having a gun would only make the situation worse if he took it from her. She lowered the gun because she really didn't think she could shoot anyone, even Peter. The door opened, and by a nervous reflex, she lifted her weapon.

"Whoa!" Court said, coming to a stop in the doorway and putting his hands out to his sides, palms out. "Easy, G.G."

"Thank God it's you," she said, dropping the gun onto the dining room table. Her heart still beating as if she'd just crossed the finish line of a marathon, she ran into Court's arms. He held her against him, and all she could think was that she was safe.

He kicked the door closed, then picked her up, and she wrapped her legs around his hips as he carried her into the living room. "Did you lock the door?"

"It locks automatically," he said as he lowered them to the sofa, her across his lap. "Talk to me, Lauren. What happened?"

"I thought I saw Peter . . . in the corridor after I came back from dinner, but now I'm not sure. He was at the other end of the hall, too far away to see clearly, and had on a ball cap." She chewed on her bottom lip, starting to feel embarrassed because she'd probably overreacted.

Before panicking, why hadn't she stopped to think about whether Court's building was secure?

Court picked her up by the waist and set her on her feet. "Come with me."

She followed him to a closed door that she'd thought was a linen closet. He took her index finger, running it down the side of the wood molding framing the door. "Feel the button?"

"Yeah. It's like a little bump in the wood."

"Press down on it."

When she did, the door swung open. "Wow. That's cool."

"And once inside, there's a dead bolt you can lock behind you so if anyone on the other side discovers the button you just pushed, they *still* can't get in."

She walked into the windowless room that was *not* a linen closet, not even close. Spinning in a circle, her jaw dropped. "Whoa," she murmured. "Now I know where to come when the zombie apocalypse happens."

On the wall in front of her was a cache of weapons, handguns, rifles, and even what she thought was an assault rifle. A shelf held a small supply of bottles of water and boxes of protein bars, along with a first aid kit. The bank of monitors on a third wall caught her attention, and she walked over to them.

There were five monitors, each showing scenes from around the building, but the one that interested her showed the hallway outside his front door. "Can you back the tape up?"

"Where did you see him?"

"At the opposite end from here."

He touched the screen of the one she was looking at, and it switched to a different camera. "In that area?"

She looked at him in amazement. "Yes. Do you have cameras all over the place?" At his nod, she laughed. Couldn't help it. "Unbelievable. James Bond has nothing on you."

"Each of my brothers has a room like this. It's a safe room, bul-letproof door and all that. I'll show you some other things in a minute. First, let's find your dude."

"He's not my dude."

"Roger that. About what time did you see him?"

She thought about it. "Maybe ten minutes before you got home."

"Okay. Let's take a look."

A few seconds later, he had the man on the screen. They both leaned their faces closer to the monitor. She shook her head, really embarrassed now. "It's not him."

"No, it isn't, but he's also not one of my neighbors, and I don't like that he's watching you."

She didn't either. "You know what all your neighbors look like?"

"I know the face of every resident in the building." He straightened, glancing at her. "In my line of work, you want to know who belongs in these hallways and who doesn't."

"And he doesn't?" *In his line of work.* Another reminder of the kind of life he led.

"Don't know. He could be visiting. I'll call down to Jorge in a minute, see if the dude signed in." He pulled a rolling chair out and sat, and then his fingers flew over the keyboard. The man's face zoomed larger, boxed in by lines.

"What are you doing?"

"Running a facial recognition program."

Wow, it really was like being in a room with James Bond and his toys. The printer fired up, spitting out three sheets faster than her printer could even think about turning itself on.

She picked up one. "I've never seen him before, but he does remind me a little of Stephan and Peter. He has the same blue eyes they do."

"If he's in a database somewhere, we'll find out who he is. While we wait to see if we get a hit, let me show you some things." He pointed to the smaller monitors. "These are always on, and will switch every ten seconds to a different view in and around the building. If you're ever here alone and something like this happens again, come in here." He moved the mouse, hovering it over one of the squares showing a camera view. "If you want to keep it on a particular view, just click on it and the camera will stay there."

When he lifted his hand, she put hers on the mouse, bringing up different areas of the building. "You're just full of surprises," she said.

"My front door and the door to this room are solid steel, impossible to shoot through."

"Really? They look like wood."

"Yes, really." He smiled as if pleased with himself. "It took some experimenting to achieve the grain effect. The same for both Nate and Alex's doors. A bullet won't penetrate them."

"That's definitely good to know."

"Now to impress you."

As if he hadn't already. She followed him to the built-in shelves holding supplies, where he showed her a light switch. "Flip it on and off three times, pause long enough to take two breaths, then back on."

No light came on when she did it, but at the end of the sequence, the shelves moved aside. Lauren yelped, jumping back. When Court laughed, she punched him. "You could have warned me."

"More fun watching your reaction. This was originally a closet, but now it's an escape hatch. Go down to get to Alex's condo, and up to Nate's." A light had come on automatically, and he pointed to a buzzer. "Before you descend or scale the ladder, push this twice. It'll let my brothers know that you're on the move. If you don't warn them, either one will probably shoot you when your head or feet poke through."

"Good God, all this is kind of freaking me out. You really are afraid the day will come when someone will come for one of you."

Although she was already worried about his being a federal agent, she'd not understood until now how dangerous his job was. Yet even though her mind was terrified by the risks he took, her girly parts thought he was the hottest thing on planet Earth and were humming their mating song.

Considering he and his brothers went after the worst of the worst, Court thought there was a high probability that the day would come when someone would seek revenge against the Gentry brothers. The thought of his brothers being the target of some dude or gang wanting vengeance had kept him up nights. He'd come up with the idea of an escape hatch for all of them, and had then expanded on that idea with the safe rooms they each now had.

Not wanting her any more scared than she already was, he only shrugged. "Not really afraid, just playing it safe." He grinned. "More like it was fun to, as you accused me of, play James Bond. He was a cool dude."

She eyed the ladder. "So after pushing the buzzer twice, I just climb down or up and, poof, after going through a hatch, I'm in either Alex's or Nate's condo?"

She lifted her eyes to meet his. "Is it weird that all this is kind of turning me on?"

Well, if he'd known *that*, he would have shown her his *James Bond room* long before now. "Is it weird that all this turning you on is turning me on?" He trailed a finger down her spine. "I mean seriously getting me hot." The way the gold flecks in her whiskey-brown eyes shimmered as she stared up at him sent all his blood south.

"Court."

It was the way she whispered his name, as if it meant something special to her, that had him backing her up to the wall in the damn closet. "Lauren," he answered, pushing his body against hers, aligning them so that his erection settled into the vee of her sex. "Tell me to stop before I take you right here."

She stayed silent, but her eyes shimmered with a challenge. *Do it,* they said.

"So be it," he murmured as he covered her mouth with his. From the first day he'd laid eyes on her, he'd wanted her. He'd had her and then he'd lost her. She had ruined him. He couldn't enjoy any other woman, and during the past six years, that had fucking pissed him off. But here she was, back in his life, and he both wanted to punish her and tenderly love her. How did one go about achieving both those goals?

"Sometimes you make me crazy, G.G.," he said as he expertly stripped her of her T-shirt, jeans, panties, and bra in the confines of his closet.

"Bad crazy or the good kind?"

"I'm still working on figuring that out." Christ, she was the sexiest thing he'd ever seen. "I'm going to worship every inch of you."

She tugged at his shirt. "Not fair. I want to see you."

Since he'd always thought of himself as a fair man, he pulled a condom out of his wallet before shedding his clothes, dropping each piece carelessly onto the floor as they came off.

"Much better," she said as she wrapped her hand around him.

"Ah," he muttered. He slid a finger inside her, stroking her. "You're ready for me, Gorgeous Girl. This isn't going to be pretty. No finesse. I'm too desperate for you." And there was anger fueling him—that the man in the hallway might have been stalking her.

"I don't want pretty. It's not what I need right now." She grabbed his face, pulling it down to hers.

They were in agreement then. Their tongues dueled, and when her fingers dug into his hair, he broke away. "Give me a minute," he said when she tried to meld their mouths again. He ripped the condom open with his teeth, then rolled it on. He trailed his hands down to her bottom, lifting her against the wall. She wrapped her legs around him, gasping when he slid home.

"Yes," she said.

The word came out breathless, flowing through his veins like a drug whose side effect was to steal any control he might have had. She was so hot and tight he couldn't hold back.

"Like that," she said as he urgently thrust into her. She clamped her teeth down on his shoulder.

He jerked at the sting of her bite as lust crashed through him with the force of a tsunami. She'd turned him into some kind of primitive barbarian who had to claim his woman right here, right now.

A low moan began in the back of her throat, growing deeper as she tightened her core muscles around him. His climax hit at the same time as hers, and she clung to him as she shattered.

The air left his lungs, and he couldn't get it back. He slid to the floor with her landing on his lap, both their chests heaving as they struggled to breathe. "That was . . ." What? He couldn't think of a word strong enough to adequately describe what had just happened.

"The best sex ever?"

He leaned his forehead against hers. "Yeah, that." They'd lost six years, but damn if he was going to let anyone tear them apart, not this time. Unless she did the tearing apart by deciding to run after all. But she'd said she was ready to stand and fight, so he let her have a little piece of his heart again. Not all of it. He wasn't ready for that yet.

"What are you thinking?" she asked, snuggling her face into his neck.

"My brain is mush right now. No thinking going on." He didn't know how to explain his fear that she would leave him again. The computer dinged, telling him the program had found a hit on the man in the hallway.

"As much as I'd like to relocate to my bed and spend the night continuing this, I'm going to have to go clean up and get ready to head to the bar." He lifted her to her feet, then pushed himself up. "I'll be back in a minute. Looks like the computer identified our mystery man."

CHAPTER FIFTEEN

Lauren glanced at the monitor, but no name was scrawled across the screen. She scrambled into her jeans and T-shirt, while keeping a wary eye on the computer.

"Please let it be someone who was just visiting one of Court's neighbors," she said to the machine. It was surreal. One minute she was luxuriating in the afterglow of the most incredible sex of her life and the next she was pacing in a safe room, waiting for Court to tell her the man's name.

Her life was out of control. That was all there was to it. She'd let this happen by sticking her head in the sand, assuming Stephan would forget about her. Considering she'd heard nothing since that first letter shortly after he'd gone to prison, she supposed it was a reasonable assumption. It'd been a stupid one, though. The day he'd be free again had seemed eons away. When had time started moving so fast?

"Let's see who our man is," Court said, coming back into the room.

She moved behind him, her hand on his shoulder, as he sat in front of the computer. The man's face came up on the screen, along with his name and background information. Her heart dropped to her stomach at reading the name.

"Vadim Popov," Court read aloud. "You ever hear that name?"

"No, but if he's Russian, that doesn't bode well, does it?"

"I don't believe in coincidences. I need to go, but I'll take a closer look at him after I get to Aces and Eights."

She didn't want him to leave, wanted to tell him that she only felt safe with him, but she was afraid he'd think she was a big baby.

"Why don't you come with me," he said, as if reading her mind. "Bring a book. You can hang out in the office."

"I was supposed to go down to Madison's, but I'd really like to go with you. We need to tell her to be careful if she leaves her condo."

"Give her a call. See if she wants to come. You can keep each other company. Can you be ready to go in twenty minutes?" At her nod, he said, "I'm going to eat the sandwich you brought me. If Madison wants to go with us, tell her we'll come down and get her."

"Court," she said as he reached the door, "thank you."

He stopped, strode back to her, put his hand around the back of her neck, and covered her mouth with his. After a lingering kiss, he lifted his head. "Everything will be all right, G.G., I promise."

She put her fingers on her tingling lips as she watched him walk away. She'd known all those years ago that he was a good man, but she hadn't known then just how amazing he was.

As she and Court rode down in the elevator to collect Madison, who'd definitely wanted to go, she let her gaze roam over Court's mighty fine body. He wore black jeans and a black T-shirt with an Aces & Eights logo on it. On the pocket was the king of clubs card. She'd noticed already that each brother's Aces & Eights T-shirt had a different logo. Alex had the jack of hearts on his, and Nate had the ace of spades.

"You need a queen of diamonds," she said. "You know, you each have your own card on your shirts. Who's the queen?"

"The bar's the queen and a bitch queen she is."

"You don't like Aces and Eights? I think it's really cool. You know, that the people who come there have no idea you and your brothers are FBI agents. It's kind of surreal, if you think about it."

"I like it most days. Other times, I think it's the worst idea Nate ever had." He knocked on Madison's door. "Soon enough someone's going to connect the dots, and it'll be time to move on."

"You'd leave the FBI?"

He looked at her as if she'd lost her mind. "Never. Why? Does it bother you that I'm a federal agent?"

"I think it's hot that you are." Except that his job was dangerous, so it did bother her. It scared her to think of why he had to carry a gun every day. She bumped her shoulder against his upper arm. "Although I've yet to see your handcuffs."

He put his mouth next to her ear. "G.G., one more word and I'll have to use those handcuffs on *you* for getting me all hot and bothered when my sweet sister-in-law's about to open her door."

"Promise?"

"Yes, and that was a word."

"Hey," Madison said, swinging her door open.

"And just so you know, she's not all that sweet," Lauren said.

Madison pulled the door closed behind her as she stepped out into the hallway. "Who's not sweet?"

Lauren smirked at her friend. "You."

"Am, too." She leaned around Lauren to look at Court. "Ask Alex. He'll tell you I am."

"So not going there," Court said. "Ladies, after you."

She linked arms with Madison, managing not to jump when Court, walking behind them, squeezed her butt.

"He was watching you?" Madison said after Lauren told her about the man in the hallway.

"Maybe. I don't know." Her attention was on the wall monitor showing the bar area of Aces & Eights. She and Madison had been watching the goings on for a little over an hour. "Court doesn't believe it's a coincidence, considering the guy's Russian. I don't want to think about it right now. It gives me the creeps."

She pointed to the screen. "Do they break up fights like that every night?" Nate and Alex were pulling apart two of the biggest men she'd ever seen. Not minutes before, they'd seemed to be best friends, until they'd decided to arm wrestle. Now they were circling each other, each accusing the other of cheating.

Madison laughed. "Pretty much, and they love every minute of it. Don't let them tell you any different."

"Nate wasn't very happy to see us show up."

"Ah, Nate. I secretly call him Grouchy Bear. But what he doesn't want you to know is that he has a soft heart, especially for Alex and Court. By extension, that includes us since his brothers love us."

"For you maybe, but he knows Court doesn't love me. Nate only tolerates me right now."

"Pfft. Take your blinders off, and you'll see how Court looks at you. Maybe he doesn't realize it yet, but he's feeling it."

Is he? If so, she was pretty sure he wasn't happy about it. Even though they were sharing a bed, she couldn't help but believe his feelings for her went no deeper than the sexual chemistry that had always existed between them.

"I think my situation with Stephan needs to be resolved before I can worry about what is or isn't between Court and me." She wanted a final confrontation with her ex-husband, while at the same time, she wanted to do her disappearing act. She still wasn't convinced that dropping out of sight wasn't the best option.

A large group of the scariest-looking men she'd ever seen walked in . . . More like *swaggered in*, as if they owned the place. Her gaze darted to the bottom left of the screen, where Court leaned on the bar, talking to a small wizened man, one of the few who wasn't wearing a leather vest claiming his colors to any club. She'd learned about motorcycle clubs and their colors on her first visit to Aces & Eights, back when Madison was dating Alex.

At seeing the men enter, Court pushed away from the bar, his body stiffening. Like cats on silent feet, his two brothers appeared out of nowhere, coming to stand behind him, presenting a united front. Lauren didn't know what was happening, but she wished she could go stand with them, help them protect Court.

"Who is that?" she asked when one of the men, the biggest one, stepped up to Court. The man's face looked as if it was set in stone, no expression at all. *Menacing* was the word that popped into her mind. His friends—she did a quick head count—fifteen of them, crowded around him as if forming a defensive wall.

Madison leaned forward, peering intently at the monitor. "I don't know."

"I don't like this," she said, standing.

"Me either, but don't even think about going out there. You'll just make it worse."

The air deflated from her lungs as she sank back onto the leather couch. Of course, she'd only make things worse, but she'd allowed a man to beat her to protect Court. She'd kept his name a secret to make sure he stayed safe. It was hard to let go of that mind-set.

"Aren't you worried?" she asked. "I mean, it's sixteen against three."

"No it isn't. Watch."

Even as Madison spoke, others in the bar—the bartender, their cook, the little man Court had been talking to, as well as other patrons—formed their own wall behind the brothers.

Lauren's heart rate spiked when the man who seemed to be the leader of the newcomers suddenly had a wicked-looking knife in his hand. "Oh, God," she whispered.

Court had expected Dragon to show up once he'd posted bail. Dragon might consider it was conceivable that Court wasn't the snitch who'd ratted on them, but he'd want to make sure. Thus, the showdown about to happen.

As his brothers, their employees, members of the Cubanos, who'd been playing pool until they realized some fun shit was about to go down, and Spider, who didn't have enough sense to disappear at the hint of trouble, surrounded him, he eyed the brass-knuckled bowie knife with the badass curved blade that Dragon held up.

"You get a new toy there, Dragon, my man?" he asked. Dragon slid his thumb over the blade, and Court supposed the blood now dripping down the man's hand was supposed to intimidate him. "Ouch. Bet that hurt."

"Nothing like how bad you're gonna be hurtin' I find out you're a fucking narc for the feds."

"I got no use for the feds, dude. You were there. I got hauled away in handcuffs just like you." Court let his gaze roam over Dragon's club, the Satan's Minions. "If it wasn't me and it wasn't you, you might want to take a look in your own house."

The club members crowded in closer, the tension in the air so thick it was almost visible. "You better shut your trap," said Stroke, one of Dragon's men.

Court crossed his arms over his chest. "Or what?" The worst thing he could do with these dudes was back down or show any weakness.

"Or I'm going to beat the shit out of you. I resent your insinuation that we'd rat on our own."

"Insinuation, huh? I'm impressed, Stroke. That's a big word." Stroke had at least fifty pounds on him, but that didn't worry Court, nor did the knife Dragon still brandished. "You want to take me on?" he said, eyeing Stroke as the man bounced on the balls of his feet. Court held out his hands, bracing his legs. "Bring it on, dude."

Like a charging bull, Stroke came at him, a chain suddenly appearing in his hand. *Idiot.* Court sighed and rolled his eyes. His brothers had his back, but they'd stay out of it unless Dragon's club decided to gang up on him. The Gentrys were also busy keeping the Cubanos out of it, for the time being anyway.

Stroke swung the chain at Court's feet, while at the same time lowering his head, aiming for Court's stomach. Although Court enjoyed playing with the dude, he knew Lauren was watching them on the monitor. The last thing he wanted was for her to worry that he'd be hurt. With the intention of putting a quick end to this nonsense, he leaped, twisted his body, and kicked back, planting the heel of his boot hard on Stroke's nose. The man fell to his knees, crying like a baby as he flattened his hand to hold his bloody face.

Court scooped up the chain Stroke had dropped and wrapped a length of it around his fist. Ignoring Stroke and the other members of the club, he leveled his gaze on Dragon. "You still want to call me a snitch?"

"No, we're good, man." He slid the knife back into its leather holster. "Unless I find out different."

"Same here." Court tossed the chain to Dragon. "You know the rules, dude. No weapons. That includes knives, guns, and chains. Leave them on your bikes or check them at the door. This is the only pass you'll get. And get Stroke out of here. He's bleeding all over my floor."

Dragon glanced at his man, disgust on his face. "Stop your whining." He lifted his chin to the club member closest to Stroke. "Get him out of here."

As Stroke was dragged away, Court didn't miss the glare coming his way. He'd made an enemy of the man, embarrassing him in front of his club. Too bad. Dragon would be able to keep him in line. Hopefully.

"Show's over," Nate said, dispersing the crowd, most of them grumbling about not being allowed to join in the fun as they wandered away.

Court glanced up at one of the cameras and winked.

After the bar was closed and everyone had ridden off on their motorcycles, Lauren and Madison came out of the office. Lauren came straight at him, and Court braced himself for a lecture on fighting.

"You were amazing!" She beamed at his brothers. "Wasn't he amazing? I've never seen anything like it."

There she went again, surprising him.

"I could've taken the dude down in half that time," Alex said, shooting him an evil grin.

Lauren shook her head. "No way you could be faster. If I'd blinked, I would have missed it."

"Well, shit," Court muttered at seeing the gleam in Alex's eyes just before his brother put him on the floor. He looked up at Lauren. "Do me a favor, G.G. Don't ever challenge him like that again."

"Wow," she said, transferring her admiration to Alex. She glanced at Nate. "Are you some kind of ninja, too?"

"I leave the play to my baby brothers." He walked to the bar, grabbed a beer, then went to a back table.

"That's just sad," Lauren murmured.

Court had always thought so. Even sadder in his opinion, that because of all the responsibilities dumped on Nate's shoulders at a young age, he'd never learned how to have fun, yet he'd made sure his two brothers had playtime. Or maybe it was just that the old man had beat all the fun out of his big brother. Nate never talked about it, but both Court and Alex knew that Nate had protected them as much as he could, taking the brunt of their father's punishments. But those were memories he didn't want to revisit.

He pushed up. "I'm going to go wash my hands." Who knew what was on the floor? "Join Nate." He gave Lauren a quick kiss. "I'll be there in a sec, and we'll have a talk about just which brother you should be admiring."

"The one who just got his butt put on the floor?" She patted his ass as he walked by.

"That would be the very one." He glanced over his shoulder and winked, smiling at the grin appearing on her face. There had always been a sense of play between them, something he'd never experienced with another woman. She made him happy. That scared him.

CHAPTER SIXTEEN

Sitting at the table next to Court, Lauren half listened to the conversation between the brothers. She twirled the beer Alex had brought her, watching the condensation drip down the bottle. What was the deal with Court? Between the time he had left to wash his hands and returning, something had changed. One minute he'd been smiling and winking at her, and the next, he was practically ignoring her. Even his brothers were giving him odd looks.

"Madison told me someone was hanging around your hallway, watching Lauren?" Alex said.

"Yeah, a man by the name of Vadim Popov, Stephan and Peter's cousin."

Lauren tuned back in to the conversation. "He is?" That wasn't something she wanted to hear.

For the first time since he'd returned from the restroom, Court looked at her. "Yeah. And you never met him or heard his name mentioned?"

"No. But Peter's side of the house had a separate entrance, so it's entirely possible he visited."

"Not while you were still living there. Popov's only been in the US for six months. He is staying at Stephan's house now."

"What do you know so far?" Nate asked.

Court leaned back in his chair. "Lauren can probably fill in any missing blanks, but my sense is that Stephan Kozlov was used to getting what he wanted without having to work very hard at it. He was a naturally gifted athlete, a hockey stick put in his hands at the age of two by his father, and then a professional hockey player on a Russian team. I'm guessing he was coddled by his family and coaches."

"Stephan used to brag that he'd been a star player on every team he'd been associated with, from Russia's Youth Hockey League on." When they were dating, she'd been impressed, too naïve to see it as conceit. "He led his Russian team to a gold medal in the Olympics, and as he often told me, he returned home to a hero's welcome."

"That got him noticed by the Thunder," Court said. "They signed him to an eight-year, eighty-six-million-dollar contract. Blond, blue-eyed, and rich, Stephan Kozlov had no trouble attracting the ladies. I found numerous photos of the man with different women on his arm, including some celebrities." Court glanced at her. "Sorry."

"Don't be. They can have him." Too bad Stephan hadn't zeroed in on one of them instead of her.

"Anyway, he was a player until he met Lauren. After that, it seems he never looked at another woman." He took out his phone, brought up some pictures, and held it out to his brothers. "Scroll through them. Tell me if you see what I do."

Alex leaned over, watching as Nate brought up each photo. When he finished, Nate's eyes landed on her. "He always has his hand on the back of your neck, as if he's controlling you. It wasn't a soft touch, was it?"

"No," she whispered, even now, years later, almost feeling Stephan's painful hold. She pushed her beer away, her stomach rebelling at the little bit of alcohol in it. Stephan's touch had never been gentle, not like Court's.

Madison reached across the table, taking Lauren's hand. "He'll never hurt you again." She eyed each of the brothers. "Right?"

"Right," Alex and Nate said at the same time.

"Fucking right," Court said.

Lauren squeezed her eyes shut against the tears trying to fall down her cheeks. She'd been alone for so long, not even telling Madison the half of it. It was hard to believe she now had these men at her back. She didn't have the words to tell them how much this meant to her.

"Open your eyes, G.G.," Court said, putting his hand in the same position as Stephan always had. The difference . . . Oh, God, the difference in his touch, so gentle compared to the fingers Stephan used to dig into her skin. Did Court even know that he was replacing bad memories with good ones?

She opened her eyes, meeting his. "What?" she asked. The air seemed to sizzle between them, and forgetting about the cold shoulder he'd been giving her, she leaned against him. He tensed for a moment, then put his arm around her, drawing her close. The gesture eased her worry, but only a little. There was definitely something on his mind.

"Do you want to wait in the office while I finish telling my brothers what I've learned?"

It was tempting, but no. "I need to hear it all, and like you said, I might be able to fill in any blanks."

His eyes softened as he nodded. "Then let's get this done. It seems Peter lived in his brother's shadow. Although older than Stephan by four years, it was Stephan's star the family had orbited around. I assume Peter didn't show a talent for the game because there was very little to be found on him as a boy. His particular talent seemed to be making the right connections and managing his brother's career. Their mother died—"

"Four years before I met him," she said. "That was why he was so understanding of what I was going through, losing mine."

"It was an act, Lauren." Court took his phone back, brought something up on the screen, and then handed it to her. "Read this interview in a Russian newspaper shortly after she died."

"He said his mother was the biggest bitch to have ever lived, and as far as he was concerned, good riddance?" she asked, after reading it. Stephan's understanding and comfort during her own mother's death was the only good memory she had of him, and even that had been a lie. After everything else he'd done, that shouldn't hurt, but it did.

"It's been translated into English, so there might have been something lost in the translation, but it's close enough to the original to know what he thought of her."

"He played me from day one," she said.

Court nodded, sympathy in his eyes.

How could she have been so stupid? And why her? She'd like to ask him that right before she punched him in the nose. Better yet, she was going to do everything in her power to help Court send him right back to prison, hopefully for a long time. And if she had the opportunity, she still might punch him in the nose.

"I can see the wheels turning. What's going through that mind of yours?" Court asked, taking his phone back.

"Whatever it takes to send him right back to prison, I'll do." Court stared at her for a long moment, and she held his gaze, letting him see her resolve to follow this through.

"This is the first time I think you really mean it." He reached under the table, took her hand, and squeezed.

Had that been the reason for his running hot and cold? That he'd believed she would end up taking off? She turned her palm up, lacing her fingers around his. Why wouldn't he think that if she'd done it once she'd do it again? Disappearing had still been in the back of her mind if she'd thought for one minute he'd be hurt because of her, and she was sure Court had sensed that. But no more. She was done with running.

"I trust that you"—she met Nate's eyes, and then Alex's—"and your brothers can take Stephan and Peter down." She looked at Court. "I know you can." And she meant it.

He let out a breath. "Finally."

She leaned her head on his shoulder. "Yeah, finally. Just don't arrest me if I decide to do him bodily harm, given the chance."

"We'll hold him down for you," Alex said. "Take all the punches you want."

She laughed. "I'll hold you to that."

The smile faded from Alex's face. "How much has Court told you about our father?"

Both Court and Nate jerked their gazes to their youngest brother. She shrugged. "Just that he wasn't a nice man."

Alex snorted. "Understatement of the year. He beat us black and blue almost every day of his life." He glanced at Nate. "Especially Nate."

Nate's eyes hardened. "And your point is?"

The tension around the table stretched, making her uncomfortable as everyone waited for Alex to respond. She exchanged a glance with Madison, who gave her a little shrug.

Seemingly unfazed by Nate's glare, Alex smiled at her. "My point is, Lauren, that we have a deep-seated aversion to bullies, ingrained in us from an early age. There aren't three other men on this planet who understand better than we do what you went through. And you won't find three men more dedicated to stopping men like Stephan Kozlov."

"Amen," Court said.

Nate settled back in his seat, his brooding eyes on Alex. "Truth," he said quietly, then shifted his attention to Court. "You were saying, before baby brother decided it was true confession time?"

The more she was around these men, the more she grew to like and respect them, and although no one shared anything specific about the abuse they'd suffered, she gathered it was pretty horrific. She'd played no part in the men they had become, but she was proud to claim them as friends.

Court straightened in his seat. "Right, back to Stephan. He only played out four years of his contract with the Thunder before he decided it would be a good idea"—he glanced at her, compassion in his eyes—"to beat his ex-wife to a bloody pulp."

Madison gasped. "Jesus, Court."

"No, he's right. I don't want to sugarcoat anything Stephan did, especially to me." She got why he'd worded it that way. He was reminding them how much of a bastard Stephan was.

"Good girl," Court said. "This isn't a situation that calls for blinders. As for Vadim Popov, he's a known member of the Bratva—"

"What's that?" she said.

"The Russian mafia. I have Peter's phone records, and the two were in close contact even before Vadim arrived here. I've just started investigating Peter. There's much more to learn, but if the Russian mafia is involved, we're looking at extortion, blackmail, ransom, things like that."

Even things like murder? A shudder passed through her. Had she been that close to the kind of men who had no qualms about hurting people, even murdering them? The world was collapsing on her head, or at least, that was how it felt. Her religious parents appeared naïve in hindsight. In their eyes, people were intrinsically good. If they'd gone astray, all that was needed was God's forgiveness. Nowhere in her life before meeting Stephan had she been taught that there was true evil walking among them.

"You also need to look for ties to any of the Russian hockey players," Nate said.

Court nodded. "Doing it."

"Why?" Lauren asked.

"The Russian mafia targets professional Russian hockey players," Court said. "They've been known to kidnap a family member living in Russia, holding them for ransom. And sometimes, the players here pay protection money to keep their families in Russia safe."

"That's awful. If anyone had told me when I was dating Stephan that he was involved in such things, I would have laughed. He was just so sweet. I feel like such a fool."

Nate turned that intense gaze of his on her. "Men like Stephan and Peter are masters at hiding their true selves right up until they want you to see them for the monsters they are."

It struck her that what he'd just said was also true of the Gentry brothers, except their reveal had shown them to be knights in shining armor. That was pretty damn awesome.

Court picked up their bottles. "It's late, and I am wanting my bed." He glanced at her. "In the morning, you'll need to call Peter and set up a meeting."

"And so it will begin," she murmured. Ice-cold dread traveled down her spine. They were going to put a target on Court's back, and everything she'd done to protect him would be for naught.

"I so don't want to do this," Lauren told her reflection in the mirror. In a fit of rebellion, she'd dyed her hair purple, her favorite color. When she'd been planning her wedding, she'd wanted purple dresses for her bridesmaids. Stephan had talked her into yellow and green—his team colors—instead. She'd bought the purple hair dye a while back, on a whim, but had never used it. Spying it in the bathroom cabinet this morning, she hadn't been able to resist. It was a temporary dye and would rinse out when she washed her hair tonight. She nodded in satisfaction with just how purple the color was.

Let Peter take that back to Stephan. When she and Stephan had married, her blonde hair had reached almost to her waist. The first time she'd mentioned wanting to cut it in a shorter style, he'd forbidden her to touch it.

Her first act the day her divorce was finalized had been to march herself into a hair salon. As she'd sat waiting for her appointment, she'd flipped through a book filled with various hairstyles. The photo showing a short, spiked hairdo had caught her attention. Stephan would hate that, she'd thought, which was why she'd chosen it. As it turned out, the short hair suited her face, so she'd kept it.

Peter had agreed to a meeting in the park at eleven, and Court had dropped her off earlier at her apartment to get ready. After an internal debate about what to wear to the meeting, she decided the question wasn't worth the time and worry she was putting into it. Her purple hair was enough of a statement. It said, "I don't care what you think anymore, Stephan." Jeans, a white button-down shirt with the sleeves rolled up, a black belt, and black flats would do.

At ten 'til eleven, she headed downstairs to find Court talking to Madison. He glanced over, and after a long look at her, a grin appeared on his face.

He stepped up to her, wrapping a strand of hair around his finger. "Interesting. Is this some kind of rebellion?"

"You get me," she said, making a joke, although it warmed her that he really did understand.

"I've always gotten you, G.G."

When he said things like that, he turned her insides to marshmallows, especially when he looked at her with heat shimmering in his eyes. If not for Madison clearing her throat, Lauren might have climbed on him right then and there.

"I'm dreading this," she said as they walked across the street.

He glanced at her. "I know, but it's always best to take charge of a situation."

"I know you're right. Doesn't mean I have to like it."

"I don't like you having to do this either. Before I forget, I have something for you." He pulled a ring from his pocket, handing it to her. "My fiancée should have a ring. And before you say I shouldn't have, it's only costume jewelry."

As she slipped it onto her finger, she swallowed past the lump in her throat and tried to ignore the sharp pain that felt like she'd taken a hard punch to her heart. The ring was beautiful, the stone maybe two carats, impossible to tell it wasn't real.

"Lauren."

He'd said her name so softly, so gently. The tears she'd been fighting pooled in her eyes, threatening to escape down her cheeks. She didn't want him to see her like this—vulnerable and hurting.

Court put his finger under her chin, lifting her face. She wished he hadn't done that. The last thing she wanted him to see were her tears. She tried to pull away, but he wouldn't let her go.

"I know what you're thinking, Gorgeous Girl. I'm thinking the same thing, and yes, it hurts. But we'll get to us as soon as we know you're safe. Okay?"

She nodded, even though his gentleness and the pain that she saw mirrored in his eyes was gut-wrenching. He wasn't unscathed either. Stephan had destroyed two lives, and neither she nor Court had deserved that.

"Okay." She lifted her shoulders and straightened her back. "Yeah, let's get this done." They stood at the edge of Lummus Park, and she saw Peter sitting on the stone wall, watching them. "He's here." God, she didn't want to talk to him.

"It's showtime, Lauren. You can do this," Court said. "I'm going to kiss you. Give him something to take back to his brother."

He slowly trailed his hands up her arms, and then his mouth covered hers. She forgot about Peter, forgot they were standing on a public sidewalk. When Court finally pulled away, she blinked, bringing the world back into focus. Her life was crumbling around her, but he had the ability to make her forget her troubles by the simple touch of his lips to hers.

"Ready?" he asked. At her nod, he took her hand, leading her toward Peter. "Remember to flash that ring so he sees it."

The ring that signified nothing more than a ruse, a prop in the game they were playing. But it was that very ring that made her the saddest. It also made her mad. It should have been real. Anger was what she needed to get through this, so she latched onto the fury over all that Stephan had stolen from her, what he was still trying to take from her.

When they reached Peter, Court squeezed her hand, and she understood everything he was saying by that small gesture. *I'm here for you. You can do this. Don't cower. Stand tall and strong.*

And, dammit, she could and would. She lifted her chin and met Peter's gaze straight on. "I asked to meet you because I don't think I made myself clear when you showed up at my bookstore, Peter. So, to make sure there is no misunderstanding, tell Stephan—"

"Do you think purple hair is attractive, Lauren? Perhaps on a twelve-year-old it would be cute. Stephan will be less than pleased that you cut your hair."

Next to her, Court tensed. It wasn't a visible thing, nothing that Peter could see, but she knew from the tightening of Court's hand around hers. He was like a cobra, coiled to strike. And Peter? He acted as if Court were invisible, a thing not worth his attention. She should have told Court that Peter liked to play head games, even more so than Stephan.

"I like it, so that's all that counts." She lifted her hand, making sure the stone on the ring was visible, and fingered a strand of hair. "What Stephan thinks is of no concern to me." She swallowed a smile of satisfaction as his gaze landed on the ring.

"I like it, too," Court said. "Says my woman's passionate and free-spirited."

His woman? She almost rolled her eyes. But this was a serious game they were playing, so she smiled adoringly up at him. "Only for you, my love." She held out her hand, catching the sun on the stone so that it sparkled. "See this? We're getting married. Tell Stephan that I have no desire to cause him trouble, but if he comes near me or Court, all bets are off."

"He owns a biker bar, Lauren. You're better than that."

So he'd already investigated Court. That scared her. "I don't care if he shovels shit. I love him. End of story."

"And I love her, Mr. Kozlov, meaning I won't take kindly to you or your brother coming anywhere near her." Court put his arm around her, tucking her into his side. "I protect what's mine."

Peter laughed. "The two of you are hopelessly naïve." He pushed off the wall. "You're nothing but trouble, Lauren. Stephan had the pick of the litter as you Americans would say, but he's obsessed with the runt. Why he's still determined to have you after your treachery is puzzling, but he is. So be it."

Rage burned so hot that it felt like flames were eating at her neck and cheeks. She stepped in front of Peter when he turned to leave. "You listen to me." She poked a trembling finger at his chest. "I'll never"—her voice was rising, drawing attention, but she didn't care—"ever return to Stephan. You tell him I'd rather die first."

Court pushed between them. "Mr. Kozlov, you're upsetting my fiancée. That upsets me. I strongly advise you and your brother to stay far away from her."

"If we're handing out advice, Mr. Gentry, mine would be for you to return to the hole you crawled out of and try not to play games you have no chance of winning. Good day." Peter turned his attention to Lauren. "If you care for this man at all, you should convince him to go back to his little biker bar and forget he knows you."

"Oh, God," she whispered after Peter walked away.

Sandra Owens

"Look at me, Gorgeous Girl." Court stepped in front of her and put his hands on her shoulders. "That went exactly as I'd hoped."

"How can you say that? You heard him. Add that to what we now know about them—they're not people you want to mess with."

"Believe me, I really do want to mess with them."

It wasn't fair. She wasn't a possession to be fought over, but they would come after her, and Court being in the way wouldn't stop them.

"They're going to kill you," she said, burying her face against his chest.

"They might try, but I'm a mean sonofabitch when the situation calls for it." He wrapped his arms around her, tucking her next to him. "No one's going to kill me. And I won't let them get near you."

"You can't know either of those things. If they can't find me—"

"Hush. You're *not* a coward."

CHAPTER SEVENTEEN

Court wanted to kill something, namely the Kozlov brothers. He got that Lauren was afraid for him, got that she still didn't understand the formidable force the Gentry brothers were when banded together. But Peter had played his mind games, and now she was talking about doing her disappearing act again.

He took her hand. "You're not going anywhere. I'm not going to die. It's lunchtime. Let's get something to eat."

She sputtered a laugh. "You're weird."

"I've been told that before."

"I don't think I can eat."

"Sure you can. I know just the place." He took her to The Front Porch Café in the Z Hotel because they had indoor and outdoor seating. Since everyone wanted to sit outside where they could watch the happenings in South Beach, he asked for a table inside where it would be quiet and they could talk.

"You really love your fish-and-chips," he said after she'd devoured half her lunch, choosing not to remind her that she'd thought she couldn't eat.

"One of my favorite foods."

He knew that. She'd eaten them every chance she could during spring break. "You're going to grow gills."

She lifted her eyes to his. "You used to tease me about that because I ate so much fish in Panama City."

She remembered. "Do you still have that green bikini?" He'd loved that bathing suit.

"God, no."

"Pity."

"So it was the bathing suit you fell for, not me?"

He shook his head. "It was you in that bathing suit I fell for."

Tears pooled in her eyes, and he wished he could take the words back.

"I'm sor—"

"Dammit, Lauren, don't you dare say it." He reached across the table, putting his hand over hers. "We both made mistakes. I should have known you wouldn't have blown me off like that without a good reason. Christ, I should have. I let pride get in the way of questioning why you refused to see me again. So do we just sit here and trade apologies?"

And with that said, all his lingering resentment toward her evaporated. It was true—he was just as responsible for what had happened between them because he hadn't trusted her the way he should have. He hadn't gone to her when she'd needed him the most, and for that, he needed to say *I'm sorry* a thousand times for each of her apologies.

She fiddled with her napkin. "I'd really like to start over, as if we'd never met before."

"That's actually not a bad idea, but first let's concentrate on eliminating the Kozlov brothers from your life."

"You mean like kill them?"

He laughed at her wide eyes. "As much as that appeals to me, no. Let's aim for putting them behind bars and keeping them there." He caught their waiter's attention. "Check," he said.

"I have faith in you." The soft smile that followed her words had him wanting to kiss her senseless, which he would before the night was over.

"We have some work to do to get ready." Stephan's release date was the following week. Aside from additional research on the brothers, he had to get Lauren mentally prepared for what was coming. And he had to spend some time kissing her.

Back at his condo, Lauren wanted to call her father. After a lingering kiss as soon as he closed the door behind them, Court reluctantly left her to her phone call and went into his home office. He'd been digging into Peter's business for an hour when his brothers walked in.

"Got tired of waiting to hear how the meet went," Alex said. "So we came to you."

Court leaned back in his chair. "About as expected. Peter told me I should crawl back into my hole and not play games I had no hope of winning."

"So it begins," Nate said. "Any luck finding proof he's tied to organized crime?"

"Look at this." He brought up a screen. "I hacked into Peter's emails. Problem is they're in Russian. Know anyone we can trust who can translate?"

"Taylor can," Nate said.

Court blinked. "Really?"

"Since when?" Alex said.

"Since she was a baby. Her mother was Russian."

Court stared at his big brother. "Didn't see that one coming, but cool if she can translate these. Does Rothmire know that?"

"That she's half Russian, yes. That she speaks the language? No, and she wants to keep it that way."

"They'd probably have her working at headquarters if they knew." And why had she trusted Nate with that secret? Maybe Alex was right about something going on between Nate and Taylor.

"That's one of the reasons she's not shared that little bit of info, so both of you keep your traps shut."

"I sure as hell don't blame her," Alex said. "I'd hate working at HQ."

Court agreed. All that political shit that went on both in the town and at headquarters would be a drag. There was one thing he could say about their bureau chief—Rothmire didn't play political games.

"Think she'd be willing to translate for us?"

"Probably. I'll call her," Nate said, fishing his phone from his pocket as he walked out.

"Why's he leaving the room to call her?" Court asked Alex.

"I'm telling you. There's something going on between them."

"If so, you got a problem with that?" He hoped not. Court didn't think there was a better match for Nate than Taylor. She'd keep his big brother on his toes, for sure.

"Nah. They'd be good together." Alex smirked. "As long as he doesn't screw up with her so badly that she decides to kill him."

"Knowing Taylor, I doubt we'd ever find his body."

"Truth. The lady's one smart cookie." Alex peeked around the doorway. "Lauren's asleep on your couch, so he probably went out on the balcony to talk to Taylor."

Court groaned. "I got so immersed in looking into Peter that I forgot to check on her."

"How'd she take him threatening you?"

"Not well. She started talking about disappearing again. I want to break something every time she says that."

Alex leaned against the wall. "Start teaching her how to defend herself so she feels like she has some power to deal with them if either one comes after her. I did that with Madison when her cousin was messing with her. Made a big difference in her confidence."

"I plan to. If she's not too tired, I'll start this afternoon before heading to the bar."

"Take tonight off. She shouldn't be alone after hearing Peter's threats."

"You'll need to be here tonight anyway," Nate said, walking back into the room. "Taylor will stop by around eight."

"Great. In the meantime, I'll keep digging. Right now, I'm trying to follow some money trails, but they're disappearing into Mother Russia. I'll get there, though."

"Whatever you learn, we'll have to find a way to legally get the evidence." Nate lifted his hand in a wave. "I'm heading to the bar. Call me if Taylor comes up with anything good."

Court nodded. "Will do."

"I'm off, too," Alex said. "Catch you later."

He followed them down the hallway, intending to check on Lauren. As he walked behind them, he was tempted to tug on Nate's ponytail and ask what the deal was with Taylor. But Nate was closemouthed when it came to something he didn't want to talk about, and there was nothing you could do to change that short of torture. Probably not even then.

Since Lauren was still asleep, he decided to take a quick shower. Ten minutes later, he walked into the living room with a towel wrapped around his waist.

"Hey, sleepyhead," he said, seeing her sitting up.

She yawned. "I didn't mean to fall asleep."

"That's okay." He stepped in front of her. "Are you rested up enough to have a lesson in self-defense?"

"With a naked man?" Mischief shimmered in her eyes just before she yanked off his towel. "That's an offer I can't refuse."

"Not exactly what I had in mind, but I can adapt." He scooped her up, carrying her to his room. "We'll start with wrestling, and for that, we need a good mat."

She giggled when he dropped her on the mattress. Grinning, he toppled onto her, catching his weight on his elbows. "Now, says the teacher to the student, let's see who can pin whom."

"You're going to be crying uncle real soon, Teach."

"Says you." When she tried to flip him over, he laughed at the determined expression on her face. Because it suited him to have her straddling him, he let her pin him. "I missed you, Gorgeous Girl," he said, meaning it with every fiber of his being.

"My heart hurt every day without you," she softly said.

"Good. Only fair mine wasn't the only one. Now take off your clothes."

Lauren assumed the shooter's stance that Court had taught her, aimed her Baby Glock at the chest of the paper bad guy, and pulled the trigger. She removed her ear protectors, leaned forward, and squinted at the target.

"Ouch," Court said with a laugh. "Poor guy will never sire children."

She giggled. "I swear I aimed for his chest."

"You keep shutting your eyes right before you fire, then you drop your hands." He gave her a soft smile. "You don't like the thought of shooting someone, which is why those beautiful eyes of yours keep closing."

"I don't know if I can, even if it's Stephan or Peter." She would have nightmares the rest of her life.

"Listen to me. If it's a choice between them or you, you don't stop to think about it. You shoot to kill." He curled his fingers over her gun hand, pointing it away, and then he wrapped his other arm around her, holding her close. "I hope it never comes to that, but you've got to get your mind in the right place on this. You have the right to protect yourself, and if the time comes and you need to and you don't, I'll be a real unhappy man."

"I know that in theory, but—"

"There are no *buts*, Lauren, not when your life is at stake." He kissed the top of her head. "Suppose you have to shoot someone to save *my* life. Could you do that?"

She didn't even have to think about it. "Yes. I wouldn't hesitate."

"Is your life worth less than mine then?"

"No. It's just that—"

"Stop it." He leaned away, peering down at her. "You have to know when you point a gun at someone that you'll follow through if it comes down to it. If you can't, then you've made a bad situation worse. At your hesitation, he'll shoot you first. If he doesn't already have a weapon, then you've supplied him with one, because if you don't use it he will."

"I know all that." It was the same thing she'd been telling herself ever since she'd bought the gun.

"Think about it another way. What if he does manage to get your gun away, kills you, then turns it on me? Because you couldn't pull the trigger, you got us both killed."

She had never imagined that scenario, and it chilled her to the bone to think she could be the reason they both died. She glanced at the gun in her hand. Its purpose was to kill, and she hated that she even owned one. But this wasn't a game Stephan and Peter were playing. It was real, and there wasn't a doubt in her mind that either one of them would harm her or Court if given half the chance. She couldn't envision Court allowing it to come to that, but if it did? A calm resolve settled in her mind.

She met Court's eyes. "I can pull the trigger if it becomes necessary." He must have heard the determination in her voice, seen it in her eyes, because he gave her a satisfied nod.

"Good girl." He put his hands on her shoulders, turning her to face the target. "Let's try something. Aim and keep firing until your clip is empty. I'm guessing you'll automatically close your eyes the first time you pull it, but I bet you'll open them as you keep shooting."

As he'd predicted, she did exactly what he'd said. Once she learned to keep her eyes open, he had her practice for another thirty minutes. "Yes!" she exclaimed when her last shot hit in the vicinity of the silhouette's chest.

"You did great," Court said. "We'll come back in the morning for some more practice."

"Okay, but before we leave, how about showing me what you got, Mr. Agent Man."

He smirked as he picked up the gun—bigger than hers—that he'd brought to the shooting range. "Watch and learn."

She stepped to the side as she put her ear protectors back on. The past three days had been spent at a gym, Court teaching her how to use her feet, knees, fingers, and hands to defend herself. Surprisingly, she'd loved her time on the mat. Some of the things he'd taught her, she knew in theory. It was learning how to put everything into practice that eased her fear somewhat.

Today had been her first day at a shooting range. Already she was more confident in handling her gun, but even more gratifying, between her self-defense and weapons training, she had a sense of power she'd never felt before.

She still prayed she'd never have to aim her gun at anyone and pull the trigger. If it meant her life or Court's, however, she would do what she had to do. That was the most important thing she'd learned today, and she owed it to the man putting on his ear protectors.

She watched as he spread his legs, lifted his weapon, and fired one shot after the other without pausing. Her gaze landed on the silhouette, where a quarter-sized hole appeared in the middle of the chest.

"Seriously?" she muttered. He'd told her his clip held fifteen bullets, and every single one had gone through the same hole. She shook her head in astonishment.

He glanced at her, an eyebrow cocked, and an arrogant grin on his face. "Are you duly impressed?"

She shrugged. "Not bad."

"Not bad the lady says," he muttered, looking up at the ceiling. He set his gun on the shelf, pulled off his ear protectors, and then prowled toward her, amusement lighting his eyes. "Maybe I can convince you to revise that opinion. You know, something like, Wow, Court, that was some amazing shooting."

"Oh, was it?" She backed up a step as he crowded her. "I mean, I have nothing to compare it to. How do I know Nate or Alex can't do better?" She backed up again, hitting the wall.

"Now where you gonna go?" He braced his hands on the wall. "Remember that little talk we had about which brother you're supposed to admire?"

"Nate?"

"Wrong answer."

"Alex?" She grinned. "Did you just growl?"

He tilted his head, lowered his mouth close to hers, and said, "I think you need to be taught a lesson, G.G."

"And you're just the man to do it?" She loved that he felt free to tease her the way he had when they'd first met. The last thing she wanted him to do was to feel like he had to walk on eggshells around her.

"I sure am." He brushed his lips over hers. "By the time I'm through with you, you won't be uttering any name but mine."

She didn't doubt it. "Hmm, that's a pretty bold statement. I don't know if you're up to the task."

"Oh ye of little faith."

The man was driving her crazy. He felt good pressed against her, he smelled delicious, and if he didn't kiss her right now—He kissed her. She put her hands on the sides of his waist as she opened her mouth in invitation.

His phone buzzed, and he stilled. She moaned in disappointment. When he stepped back, she blinked, looking around. Unbelievable. She'd forgotten they were in a public building. No one seemed to be paying them any attention, at least.

After a short conversation, Court stuck his phone back into his pocket. "That was Taylor. She's got some of Peter's emails translated. She'll meet us at my place in an hour."

"I guess we should go then."

He trailed his finger over her bottom lip. "We'll finish your lesson later, Ms. Montgomery."

She patted his ass. "I'm counting on it."

CHAPTER EIGHTEEN

"You got through more than I expected," Court said, flipping through the stack of translated emails Taylor handed him. She'd only had the printouts for three days, and it looked like about a hundred pages in the folder.

"I tried to hurry and get them back to you, so I didn't take the time to think much about what I was translating."

"No problem. I'd want to read them myself, anyway."

Sitting at the dining room table with him and Lauren, Taylor glanced between them. "Nate explained to you that, as far as you know, I don't speak Russian."

"Your secret's safe with us." He glanced at Lauren, who nodded. "We really appreciate it, Taylor."

She stood. "That's about half of what you gave me. I'll have the rest to you in two or three days."

"You're the best." He grinned. "But we already knew that."

"Thanks, Taylor," Lauren said. "If anything in those emails helps Court build a case, I'll owe you big-time."

"You don't owe me a thing. I have no use for men who can't take no for an answer."

"Tell me about it," Lauren muttered.

Taylor touched Lauren's shoulder. "You've got Court and his brothers on your side. You couldn't pick a better team."

"I'm finding that out," Lauren said, looking at him.

Court saw Taylor out, then walked into the kitchen. "Beer?"

"Sure. Taylor's nice."

He handed Lauren one of the bottles. "She is."

"She's also very pretty."

"She's that, too." He opened the folder containing the emails.

"Were you . . ."

At her pause, he looked up. "Ever involved with her?" Was she jealous? He kind of liked that.

"Or thought about it?"

"No and no. I can certainly appreciate that she's beautiful, but I've never seen her as more than a fellow agent."

From her pleased smile, he figured that satisfied her. "Do you have something to do while I go through these emails?" he asked.

He picked up the top one. It was to Peter, apparently from a friend in Russia bragging that his son had made the Olympic hockey team. Unless it was code for something else, there was nothing of use in it.

"Can I help?"

He almost said no, but this was her life, too. And actually, she could be helpful. "Yeah." He handed her some pages. "Since you know Peter better than me, you might catch something I wouldn't. Watch for anything that sounds odd or doesn't fit with the rest of the contents."

"Got it."

"If something does catch your eye, put it to the side."

They worked in silence for an hour, and with each email he read, he got a better sense of Peter. The man was arrogant, selfish, and an ass. He was also stupid for saving all these emails, never considering that anyone would hack into his computer. There had been firewalls and passwords, but they'd been at the level of an amateur. Court hadn't had any problem getting past them.

Lauren sat back in her chair and stretched. "You must be getting hungry. I know I am. How about I order a pizza?"

"Sounds great." He scrolled through his phone, then handed it to her. "Here's the number. I like anything but olives and anchovies."

"Mushrooms and Italian sausage sound good?"

"Making my mouth water."

While she was ordering the pizza, he picked up the next email, read it, and smiled. "Gotcha," he murmured.

Lauren handed him his phone. "Forty-five minutes. My eyes need a rest. I think I'll take a shower."

"'Kay," he said absently, flipping through the sheets, looking for one particular name on the *To* or *From* line. After he pulled out all those with the name he was looking for, he read them over again. The emails weren't enough to win a case against the Kozlovs, but he had more than enough leads to pursue now. Thanks to Peter's carelessness, they had solid proof that the Kozlov brothers were involved in extortion and kidnapping for ransom. Unsurprisingly, their targets were Russian pro hockey players. Court guessed that was only the tip of the iceberg.

"Both your asses are mine," he said. He closed the folder, then remembered he hadn't let Jorge know they were expecting a pizza. He called down to the lobby. Their doorman had taken it as a personal affront that Vadim Popov had managed to get past him, and was now giving every visitor the third degree.

"A shower was just what I needed," Lauren said, coming back to the table. "I'm all refreshed and ready to start again after I get something in my stomach."

He glanced at his watch. They still had fifteen minutes before the pizza arrived. "A shower sounds good. I think I'll take a quick one before we eat."

"You'll feel better for it."

"A kiss will make me feel even better." He pulled her chair in front of him so they were facing each other. "Bring those sexy lips over here," he said, leaning forward.

She put her mouth against his, then caught his bottom lip in a gentle bite. He groaned as desire shot straight through him. Cradling her cheek with his palm, he angled his head, deepening the kiss. She had the sweetest taste, one he could drown in.

Damn, he loved kissing her. He didn't want to stop, but another second and he'd forget about a shower and pizza. "Is it too late to cancel the pizza?" he said, forcing himself to let go of her lips.

"My stomach says yes." She took his hand, putting it over her sex. "This part of me says no." Grinning at him, she said, "Which will win?"

"Both. We'll eat and then take up where we left off. Win-win." He let go of her. "I'll only be a few minutes. Don't go anywhere."

"I'll be right here, waiting for you."

"You damn well better be. I have plans for you." He gave her one more quick kiss before heading for the shower.

Lauren admired his butt as he walked away, and then went back to reading the emails. How had she lived with Stephan for two years, only suspecting near the end of their marriage that he and his brother were involved in criminal activities? Okay, in her defense, once Stephan had showed his true self, she'd done her best to ignore anything to do with the two of them. Why hadn't she paid more attention?

She frowned as she read one of Taylor's translated emails between Peter and Vadim, dated almost seven months ago.

From Peter: He is obsessed with her. I do not know why. She is a dog compared to the women he could have picked. The only way he will agree to return to Russia is if she comes with him.

She was a dog? "Screw you, Peter." She read the next one.

From Vadim: Is she a fool? He is our greatest living hockey player. They will live as king and queen when they return.

From Peter: In my opinion he is the fool. When will you arrive? He wants her ready to go when he is released.

From Vadim: I will email you my flight details in a few days. Keep an eye on her.

Lauren put her hand on her chest, attempting to suck air back into her lungs. They planned to take her to Russia? Court needed to see these emails. She snatched them up, heading for the bathroom.

The doorbell rang. Dammit. The pizza delivery. She detoured to the kitchen counter where her purse was, dropped the emails on the counter, got her wallet, and pulled out a twenty and ten for the pizza and a tip. Even if it was too much, she didn't care. Whatever it took to get rid of the man so she could get to Court. She put her eye to the peephole. Yep, it was their pizza.

"Here," she said, thrusting the money at the man wearing a ball cap and holding a pizza box. She was too late recognizing Vadim. He slapped a cloth filled with something sickening smelling over her mouth and nose before she could scream.

"Did you kill him?"

Lauren recognized Peter's voice. She'd woken up a few minutes earlier when the car she was in went over a speed bump too fast, almost bouncing her off the backseat.

"I did not see him and did not take the time to look."

That had to be Vadim. They had planned to kill Court? Thank God he had been in the shower. Her hands and feet were tied, rendering her helpless for the moment. The best thing she could do was pretend to still be unconscious. Hopefully they would say where they were taking her.

What would Court think when he found her missing? That she'd left him again? No, she'd promised him she wouldn't do that, and she was sure he believed her. His security cameras! He would check them first. But would he be able to find her? If they were taking her to Stephan's house, yes. Were they that stupid, though?

She wiggled her hands, trying to loosen the plastic tie. It was tight, and there was no way she'd be able to get it off. *Think, Lauren.* A plan was what she needed, but her mind was still fuzzy. Had they used chloroform? She didn't know much about chemicals. How long could she get away with pretending she was still out of it?

Her hands were going numb, and she rubbed them over her butt, trying to get her circulation going. As she scraped them across the back pocket of her jeans, she stilled at feeling her phone. Her heart beat with excitement. Could Court trace her through her cell? Did it have to be activated?

They hadn't discovered it when they'd tied her up, but at some point they would. Somehow she had to hide it. She slid her fingers into her pocket, pulling it out, careful not to drop it. If only she could see the screen so she could call Court. With it behind her, though, that was impossible.

Where to hide it? There really wasn't a choice, as there was only one place she could reach. She pushed it inside her jeans, fumbling to get it inside her panties, and then she managed to slide it to her hip, praying there wouldn't be a visible outline.

How long had they been traveling? Since she didn't know how much time she'd been out, she had no way of telling. If they were going to Stephan's house, then they were headed for Coconut Grove, about a thirty-minute drive from South Beach. She prayed that was their destination. Court could find her there, and it was a place she was familiar with, making it easier to escape.

"She should be awake by now," Peter said.

The man she thought was Vadim said something in Russian, and a conversation ensued between the two men in their native language. Why couldn't they talk in English so she could understand them? She kept her eyes closed, hoping they would leave her be, giving her time to think. At least she had her phone. She just needed to find the privacy to use it.

One of them suddenly shook her, startling a scream out of her.

"You *are* awake," Peter said.

"No, I'm not." She was prone on the seat with her back to them, so he couldn't see the tears running down her cheeks. She squeezed her eyes shut, willing the tears to go away. It was important she not appear weak, if only to herself.

"It didn't have to be this way, Lauren."

"I'm not much up on the laws in Russia, but in America, kidnapping's a federal offense. You might want to think about that. If you stop here and let me out, I'll pretend this never happened." Not.

Peter laughed. "You always were amusing. Maybe that is what Stephan sees in you."

"If that's the reason, I promise to bore him to death."

The other man she assumed was Vadim said something in Russian, causing Peter to bark a laugh. She figured he'd just said something dirty. Why hadn't she tried to learn Russian when she was married?

"Where are we going?" It seemed like they should have been at Stephan's house by now. If that wasn't where they were headed, how would Court ever find her?

"Someplace no one will think to look for you."

Even when Stephan had beaten her, she'd never felt such despair. She squeezed her eyes shut, wishing she'd wake up to the morning sun shining through her window to find this was just one of her nightmares. Fear tightened its talons around her heart, squeezing so hard that it was difficult to breathe. She'd never felt so alone or so scared.

Breathe, Lauren, she mentally chanted. *In and out. In and out. See, you can do it.*

During her marriage, she'd lost herself until the day Stephan announced he wanted a son. Somehow she'd found the strength to leave, and dammit, she was strong enough to get through this new nightmare.

"Court," she whispered, needing to hear his name.

As if he'd heard her, his voice was there in her mind, repeating what he'd said during one of her self-defense lessons. "Always remember, G.G., you will have options." To keep from giving in to a total meltdown, she ticked off all his instructions.

She should pay attention to her surroundings. Always watch for a chance to escape, something she should do as soon as possible. "The longer you wait, the less chance you have," he'd said. And, "If there's the possibility of anyone hearing you, scream your head off."

After showing her ways to get away from her attacker, he'd put his fingers under her chin, lifting her face. "Your hands, the back of your head, your feet, your knees, are all weapons. You're not helpless, Lauren. Use whatever you can, but most of all, use your brain."

Her phone was her best hope. Beyond that, she needed to watch for any opportunity to get away. More than anything, though, she had to remember to believe in herself. She'd survived Stephan once. She would again. Miraculously, her breathing calmed, returning to normal once she realized that she possessed the tools to fight back. Stephan could play his stupid games, but she'd find a way to come out the winner.

The car slowed, and she strained to hear anything that would tell her where they were. All she heard was the engine and . . . What was that? A garage door opening? A minute later, the car stopped, the engine going quiet. It *had* been a garage door because it was now closing.

She was pulled out of the back, and Peter carried her inside a house she didn't recognize. *Remember to use your brain, Lauren.* When he set her down on a kitchen chair, she said, "If you don't take these damn ties off my hands and feet, I'm going to tell Stephan you two gang-raped me."

Peter snorted. "He will not believe you."

"You sure about that? He has a jealous streak that keeps him from thinking straight." And yes, it had been Vadim in the car. She glared at him. "Who the hell are you?"

"She has a mouth on her," Vadim said, ignoring her question. "She cannot escape. Cut the ties."

"Do you have a name?" They didn't know she knew who he was, but she feared she might blurt out his name at some point. That wouldn't be good if he hadn't told her.

"Vadim. I am family."

"Maybe you're Stephan and Peter's family, but you sure as hell aren't mine." Peter opened a drawer, removing a knife. Good to know where the knives were. After her ties were cut, she rubbed her tingling wrists. "Where's the bathroom?"

Peter went to an alarm box, punching in some numbers. "Down the hallway. Do not try to escape through any windows. They are all alarmed—we will know if you try."

That was discouraging. "Fine. Don't crawl through the window. Got it. When I get back, I want to know exactly what you plan to do with me." Although she was shaking inside, she was proud of herself for managing to give them attitude.

"Stephan will explain everything when he arrives tomorrow," Peter said.

Did Stephan really think he could get away with taking her to Russia? Well, she had news for him. Wasn't going to happen. In the bathroom, she shut the door and locked it. Thank God they hadn't discovered her phone. She pulled it out, her fingers trembling as she keyed in Court's number.

"Please answer the phone," she whispered as it rang.

CHAPTER NINETEEN

Court walked out, refreshed from the shower, ready to tackle the emails again as soon as they finished their pizza. Lauren wasn't at the table, and thinking she had gone out on the balcony, he checked there. He searched his entire condo, including his safe room.

He stood in the middle of his living room, fighting down panic. Had she decided to run after all? No, she wouldn't have taken off. She'd said she wouldn't, and he trusted her. The realization that he really did settled over him, but at the same time, his panic grew. He walked to the door. The dead bolt wasn't closed. Maybe she'd gone up to see Madison. That had to be it.

He grabbed his cell from the dining room table, and called Alex's home phone. Lauren was going to get an earful about taking off without letting him know. Right now, even the condo's hallways weren't safe. She knew that.

"Hey, Madison," he said when she answered. "Can you put Lauren on the phone?"

"She's not here. Is she supposed to be?"

The panic returned in full force. "Let me talk to Alex."

"He's at the bar. What's going on, Court?"

"Lauren's gone." He strode to his safe room.

"What do you mean she's gone?"

"I don't know. Listen, I'll call you back when I know something." He slid his hand down the side of the frame, unlocking the door.

"I'm coming up."

"No, stay put, Madison. I doubt anyone's hanging around, but we don't need to take any chances."

"Okay, but I'm calling Alex."

"Yeah, do." He disconnected, setting his phone on the desk. The first security camera he pulled up was the one outside his door. He backed it up until a man wearing a ball cap, the visor pulled low, and carrying a pizza box came into view. The dude kept his head down as he approached. When he rang the doorbell, he turned his face, giving the camera a full view.

"Fucking Vadim." Court wanted to stick his hands through the monitor and choke the bastard. "Don't open the door, Lauren," he said, knowing the warning was useless. "Please don't open it."

All she would have seen was what she expected, a man delivering pizza. As soon as she opened the door, Vadim slapped a cloth over her mouth and nose. Still holding the pizza box, he caught her with his free arm. A second man jogged up, and scooped her up in his arms.

"I'm going to kill you, Peter." That was a promise. Court watched helplessly as Peter carried her away, Vadim following them. How the hell had they gotten past Jorge? And how had they known pizza was being delivered?

His phone buzzed, Nate's name coming up. "What the hell's going on?" Nate asked as soon as Court answered.

"They got Lauren. I was in the shower. We were expecting a pizza delivery, so she opened the door, thinking it was the delivery guy. I have to find her, Nate."

"We will. Alex is on the way now. I'm closing the bar early, then I'll get over there. I doubt they'll take her to Stephan's house since that's the first place we'd look. Start doing your hacker thing and see if you can find someplace the Kozlovs might have bought or rented. Another house, a warehouse, storage shed. Anything like that."

"I'm going to kill them. Both of them."

"Just stay calm. And don't take off before I get there," Nate said, then disconnected.

Stay calm? He was ready to tear the town apart. He was not fucking calm.

How did they know about the pizza delivery? That bugged him. There was only one way he could think of. They had to be listening. He opened the bottom drawer of his desk, taking out a small, black debugger. By the time he'd scanned all of Lauren's possessions, he'd found three bugs, one in the larger purse she'd taken from her apartment, one in her backpack, and one under the cover of her Kindle. He left them alone for the time being.

While he waited for his brothers to arrive, he returned to his soundproof safe room, shutting the door. He reviewed all the security tapes for the last forty-five minutes. When he finished, he called Alex, since he was supposed to get back to the condo first.

"When you get here, let Jorge out of the office. He's tied up at the moment."

"Is he hurt?"

"No, but he looks pretty pissed. My condo's bugged, so don't talk when you get here."

"Just stay calm, bro. We'll find her."

People needed to stop telling him to stay calm. It was pissing him off. His next call was to his friend on the police force. "David, need another favor."

"That fishing trip to the Bahamas is going to come faster than I thought, dude, if the favors keep happening."

Court wasn't in the mood for jokes. "Sorry if I'm not laughing. My girlfriend's been kidnapped."

"Oh, shit, man. Tell me what you need."

"First, for you to keep your mouth shut about it. I don't want your department to get involved."

"You got it. What else?"

"I want you to scare the hell out of a pizza delivery man. He took money, looked like a hundred-dollar bill maybe, from the kidnappers, giving them the pizza to bring up to my place." Court gave David the name of the pizza joint, along with a description of the deliveryman.

David swore. "It'll be my pleasure to chew him a new one."

"I guess you should give him a reason for showing up." Court thought for a moment. "Tell him the woman he was delivering the pizza to had a restraining order against the man who bribed him."

"That'll work. I'll make sure he thinks twice before he does something like that again. I'm really sorry, Court. You'll find her. You guys are like superheroes with all your fancy toys. Keep in touch, and anything else I can do, I'm here for you."

"Thanks, man. Later."

As he set his phone down on the desk, he stared at it, then slapped his forehead. "Stupid." Did she have hers with her? He made a search, and not finding it, he resisted the urge to call her. What if she'd managed to keep it on her? If the ringtone wasn't cut off, then he would alert Peter that she had it.

He had to assume that she would have called him if she'd had the opportunity. If they hadn't discovered the phone and ditched it, he could track her. His fingers flew over the keyboard, so absorbed in connecting to her cell that he didn't hear the safe room's door open. When the sound of someone entering penetrated, he put his hand on his gun.

"Don't shoot, bro. It's just me." Alex walked in. "Whatcha got?"

"Close the door." Once he was sure they couldn't be overheard, he brought Alex up to speed.

"How long they been listening?"

Court had thought about that already. "Since she changed purses the day her apartment was broken into. Her backpack's in the guest room, and we're never in there. She only reads on her Kindle when I'm not around, so they wouldn't have heard anything there. As for her purse, she usually drops it on the kitchen counter. Most of the time, we sit out on the balcony to talk. Earlier tonight, though, we were reading a bunch of Peter's emails."

"Did you discuss what you were reading?"

"No, thankfully. We each took a stack to read. After a while, she said her eyes were tired and took time out for a shower. We ordered pizza, and while we were waiting, I took a shower. I should have waited."

Alex put his hand on Court's shoulder. "Stop beating yourself up. You couldn't have known."

He should have. Somehow he goddamn should have. He'd promised her that he would keep her safe. "Anyway, there were some things I learned from the emails that I wanted to talk to her about, but decided to wait until after we'd had our dinner."

"Did she find anything?"

"Don't know. Give me a few minutes here. I'm trying to trace her phone."

Alex wandered out, and Court returned to tracking down Lauren using a cell-site simulator that mimicked cell phone towers. Hopefully, the signals the program sent out would trick her cell phone into replying with a location.

Court not only liked his toys, he also believed in being prepared. In the back of his mind, he'd feared the day would come when a bad guy might decide it was a good idea to kidnap one of his brothers. If that ever happened, he wanted to have every resource at his fingertips that would help him find them.

If their bureau chief knew he had a cell-site simulator at home, there would be hell to pay since legally he needed a warrant to use it. Court didn't give a shit. If anyone had a problem with it, they could fire him. With a big antenna, it would work up to a hundred miles, but with the one he'd put on the roof of their building, Court estimated he could only go out at the most fifty. He didn't think they would have taken Lauren farther than that. If it didn't work, then he'd start looking for any properties the Kozlovs owned. That would be time consuming, though, so he was counting on the program working.

"Did you read these?" Alex said, walking back into the room, shutting the door behind him.

He glanced at the papers Alex held. "What are they?"

"Some of the emails. These were sitting on the counter, next to Lauren's purse."

"They must have been the ones she was reading. Something important on them?"

"More like something disturbing. According to these, Stephan plans to take Lauren back with him to Russia."

"The hell?" Court snatched the sheets away.

The door opened, hitting Alex in the back.

"Move your ass, baby brother," Nate said, walking in after Alex made room.

After reading the emails, Court handed them back to Alex. "He's a dead man."

"Bring me up to speed," Nate said, moving to stand behind Court. "What's that?" Nate asked, eyeing the simulator.

"Don't ask. Alex can fill you in. I'm busy. And close the door." Court half listened as Alex explained all that had happened. He patted the simulator. "Come on, baby, you can find her," he murmured.

His phone buzzed and, annoyed at being interrupted, he glanced at the screen. At seeing Lauren's name, he snatched up his cell. "Where are you?" he said, putting the call on speaker.

"Court, oh God. I don't know where I am. Peter and Vadim brought me to some house, but they drugged me and laid me down on the backseat, so I couldn't see anything."

She was whispering, which told him they were nearby. "Did you hear or see anything at all?"

"No. I don't know what to do."

It sounded like she was close to losing it. "I'll find you, Gorgeous Girl. I swear it."

"Tell her to keep her phone on her person," Nate said.

"Did you hear Nate? Keep your phone on you."

"I heard. I'm in the bathroom right now, but I have to go before one of them gets suspicious. I'm hiding my phone in my underwear, but I'm scared they'll find it."

Christ, he didn't want her to disconnect, but she couldn't get caught with the phone. "How long was the car ride?"

"I'm not sure. I can't tell how long I was drugged. Maybe thirty, forty-five minutes."

"Okay, that's something. You have to hang up, baby."

"I know, but I don't want to."

"Lauren, turn your ringer off," Nate said.

"Right. I-I should've thought of doing that."

She was crying now. "Listen to me, Lauren. Be smart. Be strong. I'm coming for you."

"I believe you. That's the only thing keeping me from falling apart. I-I'll be s-strong."

"Good girl. And Lauren?"

"Yeah?"

"I love you, Gorgeous Girl." It wasn't how he'd imagined telling her, but he knew better than anyone how easily things could go wrong. If nothing else, he wanted her to know that.

"I love you, too. So much. Someone's coming down the hall. I have to go."

And then she was gone. He slammed his fist down on the desk. "Fuck. Fuck. Fuck."

After turning off the ringtone, Lauren pushed the phone back into her panties, in the front this time. That was the least likely place they would notice it. She turned on the faucet, splashing cold water on her face.

Court had said he loved her. He couldn't know what those words meant to her. She could take strength from them. She *could* be strong. He was coming for her, but until then, it was up to her to keep herself safe.

"Unlock the door, Lauren," Peter said, pulling on the knob.

She squeezed her eyes shut, taking a deep breath. What would Court say in this situation? Something snarky. She inhaled air into her lungs one more time, and then opened the door. "Why? So you can watch me pee? Pervert." She marched past him, back to the kitchen, taking a seat at the small breakfast table.

And Court would say what now? He'd have another wiseass comment. "I'm hungry. What's for dinner? I was planning on pizza, but the two of you rudely nixed that idea. One of the rules of kidnapping someone is that you have to feed them."

Vadim said something in Russian, causing Peter to laugh. At Peter's reply, they both snorted a laugh.

"It's rude to say things I can't understand, you know? What's so funny?" Pretending to be Court was kind of amazing. She was able to say things Lauren Montgomery wouldn't dare.

It wasn't that she was afraid for her life. Not yet, anyway. Stephan wanted her back, and Peter wouldn't allow any harm to come to her. Her fear was Court not finding her or her not being able to escape and ending up on a plane to Russia. But she couldn't think about that now. She had to be smart.

"He says you talk too much. He does not understand Stephan's obsession with you. He believes his cousin is letting his"—Peter grabbed his crotch—"*пенис* do his thinking for him."

"You're disgusting, Peter." She eyed Vadim. "You both are."

"There is a Russian saying, *The tongue will bring the chatterer no good*," Peter said. "You should consider the wisdom of that."

She waved a dismissive hand. "Whatever." Somehow, pretending to be Court had let her be herself. Until Stephan made an appearance, anyway. Then she would go back to being very afraid. "Peter, for Stephan's sake, you need to put a stop to this. It's not going to end well. Does he think I'll just move back into his Coconut Grove mansion with him as if nothing happened? As if he hadn't almost killed me?"

"That is not the plan."

"Then what is"—she made air quotes—"*the plan?*" From reading the emails, she already knew, but she wanted to hear it straight from Peter.

"You will find out soon enough."

Jerk. She'd never been fond of her brother-in-law, and he wasn't improving her opinion of him with this stunt. She peered down at her toes, realizing for the first time that she was barefoot. At least she was wearing jeans and a T-shirt. The only reason she hadn't put on her favorite nightclothes—boxer shorts and a soft cotton camisole—was because they'd been expecting a pizza delivery.

She wiggled her toes. "You could have let me get some shoes at least before you hauled me off. Against my will, I might add."

The cousins had another conversation in Russian, which she assumed was more of the same, considering they were laughing as they stared at her. She didn't bother asking for a translation because who needed to see Peter grab his crotch again?

Peter's phone rang, interrupting their hilarity. He answered in English, listened a moment, then switched to Russian. Something he said seemed to get Vadim's attention, and he stared intently at Peter.

She understood one word. *Stephan.* Her heart picked up speed, the fear she'd managed to tamp down earlier returning full force. God, she wished she knew what they were saying. After what seemed an intense conversation, Peter put his phone back into his pocket, looked at her for a moment, then picked up the keys to the car from a hook on the wall next to the garage door.

"I have to leave for a while. Vadim will stay. The alarm will be on, Lauren. Do not try anything foolish. Vadim is not as nice as I am."

Lauren swallowed a snort. It was far from nice to kidnap a woman against her will. Even though she hated Peter more with each minute she spent in his company, there was a dangerous element to Vadim that she didn't detect in her former brother-in-law. She did not want to be alone with Vadim, not that either one cared for her wishes, so she stayed quiet. But what had the conversation been about, and where was Peter going?

Be smart. Be strong, Court's voice said in her head. He was trying to find her, and he might or he might not. One thing she knew, though, she wasn't going to sit by and idly wait. She needed to try to escape. How to do that? In a movie she'd seen years ago, a woman had thrown hot water into her kidnapper's face. Peter had only been gone for about ten minutes, but he could come back at any time, so if she was going to do it, it needed to be now.

"Is there any coffee in this damn house," she said, going to the cabinets, opening doors. "Well, lookie here." At seeing a can of instant coffee, she wrinkled her nose. Ugh. Who even drank that crap? She grabbed it and a cup. "You want some?" she asked, keeping her back to Vadim, afraid he'd see how much she wanted him to say yes.

"Yes, please."

She let out a quiet breath. This had to work. After heating water in a saucepan, she filled two cups, then added two spoons of the coffee into each. "There's not any cream or sugar. I hope you like it black."

She turned, a cup in each hand, and threw the hot liquid from both at Vadim, aiming for his face.

He bent over and clawed at his face as he yelled a slew of Russian words that didn't sound so nice, but Lauren didn't wait around for him to recover. She ran to the front door, and after fumbling with the locks, got it open. The alarm blared behind her as she ran down the street.

CHAPTER TWENTY

❋ ❋ ❋

"Got her," Court shouted. He pushed away from the desk, going to his weapons wall.

"Where is she?" Alex asked, choosing his own weapons from Court's collection.

"A house not thirty minutes from here. Where's Nate?" He filled a pouch with grenades, smoke bombs, and extra ammunition. Whether he'd need all that, he didn't know, but he believed in being prepared for every scenario.

"He got a phone call."

Nate walked back into the room. "Bad news. Stephan Kozlov was released a day early. A clerk anxious to start his vacation mistakenly put the wrong date on the paperwork."

Court whipped around. "Tell me you're joking."

"Wish I was," Nate said. "What's happening?"

"I found her."

Without asking more questions, Nate loaded up his body with weapons from Court's stash. Christ, he loved his brothers. They were going rogue, yet neither one hesitated or attempted to tell him he needed to call it in and get approval from their bureau chief.

"How long ago?" Court asked.

Nate grabbed three pairs of night vision goggles. "Less than an hour."

"We have to get to her before he does." Stephan Kozlov would go straight for her. If he put one finger on her, he was going to be sorry. Dead sorry.

The house was set back from the street in a middle-income neighborhood. Court estimated each home was on a half-acre lot. He stood with his brothers—each of them dressed in dark clothing—at the edge of the densely landscaped backyard. All the trees and bushes would aid in their approach.

"I wish I knew which room she was in, but we don't have time to reconnoiter," he said. He did, however, have a little device very few citizens were aware of; it was used by the FBI and a few police departments to detect movement on the other side of a wall. The Range-R radar wouldn't show a picture of what was happening inside, but it would tell them the placement of human bodies.

"Let's get a little closer, see what this thing tells us." He edged along the shrubberies, Nate and Alex following him. All the blinds were closed, but several rooms had lights showing at the edges of the windows. When they were within feet of the house, Court held up the Range-R.

"That can't be right," he said. "There's only one person inside." Did he have the wrong house?

Nate put his hand on Court's shoulder. "There'll be hell to pay if we crash in on a little old lady, scaring her into having a heart attack."

Dammit. Lauren should be here, but what if it was one of the houses on either side they wanted? They couldn't go around breaking into people's homes, as much as he wanted to.

"I'm going to go knock on the door," he said. "See what happens. Alex, keep an eye on the garage, make sure no one comes out there. Nate, you stay here, watch the back door."

He headed off, Alex following him. Alex took a position near the garage, and Court continued on. As he approached the entrance, he paused. "Front door's wide open," he said into his mic.

"That's not good," Nate responded. "Alex, back him up. I'm going to break into the back."

With Alex shadowing him—their guns drawn—Court eased up to the door. When they were about ten feet away, Vadim Popov came running out.

At seeing Court and Alex, he stumbled to a stop, his hand going to the back of his pants. As much as Court wanted to shoot the bastard, if he did, some neighbor would call the cops. That wouldn't make their bureau chief happy at all, so he tackled the man before Popov could draw his gun.

Popov fought like a wild animal, but it was two against one, and he and Alex had the man subdued within seconds, his weapon confiscated. As they pulled him up, a car with two men inside slowed in front of the house, then sped off, tires burning rubber.

"Dammit," Court said, watching the vehicle as it disappeared into the night. "That had to be the Kozlovs." Had Lauren been in the car? Their SUV was parked a block away, too far to go get it and try to chase the bastards down.

He pressed his gun to Popov's temple. "Where the hell is she?" Popov smirked. Court was rethinking his decision not to shoot the man when Nate walked out the front door.

"House is clear. Who's this?" He walked up, looked Popov up and down, then said, "Vadim Popov, I presume. What happened to your face?"

Court inspected Popov's face. It was red and blistering.

"The *cyka*, she throw the coffee at me. I need doctor."

"Who's *cyka*?" Was there a woman involved they didn't know about?

Nate chuckled. "I think it's a Russian curse word."

Alex whipped out his phone, a moment later saying, "Translator says it means *bitch*."

"Yes, the bitch did it." Popov gingerly touched his face, wincing. "I demand a doctor."

That's my girl. Had she managed to get away then, or did Stephan have her? There hadn't been anyone in the back of the car, unless they'd made her lie down on the backseat.

"Answer my question before I decide to just shoot you." Court pressed the barrel of his gun hard against Popov's head. "Where is Lauren Montgomery?" His phone buzzed. He shifted, putting his back to Alex. "See who that is."

Alex pulled the phone out of Court's back pocket. "It's Lauren." He held up the phone so Court could see her name on the screen.

"Take this scumbag." He grabbed his cell from Alex. "Lauren?"

"I got away, Court."

She was breathing heavily, as if she'd been running. "Where are you, baby?"

"I don't know. I threw coffee in Vadim's face and then I ran. I just kept running."

"Okay, take a deep breath. Do you see any street signs?"

"No, I'm hiding under a bush in someone's backyard. I think I ran for ten or so minutes."

"Okay, listen. Stay where you are. We're at the house and have Vadim in custody. But I think Peter and Stephan just drove by, so I don't want you wandering around. Can you see the street from where you are?"

"Yes. But Stephan doesn't get out until tomorrow."

"I'll explain after I find you, okay? I'm going to drive around until you see me. Do you know which direction you went?"

"Yes. Yes, I do. Toward the ocean."

"Good. Real good, Gorgeous Girl. That helps. Don't hang up." He glanced at his brothers. "You got this, right?"

"Go get your girl," Nate said. "Take her to my place. Alex and I will meet you there."

Alex grabbed his arm. "Get Madison on your way up to Nate's. I don't like her being alone right now."

"Will do." Anxious to find Lauren, he stepped away, then he stopped, turning back to Popov. "You better hope she's not hurt when I find her."

Vadim spouted off something in Russian. Just from the sound of it, Court wanted to put a hurt on the man.

"Go," Nate said, pulling Popov out of reach when Court stepped toward him. "You'll need these."

Court caught the car keys Nate tossed him. "What are you going to do with him, and how are you getting home?"

"Taylor or Rand," Nate said. "One or the other will come get us and this piece of shit."

That meant Rothmire would be hearing about this little situation before the night was over. "When you talk to the boss, try to talk him out of firing me." He ran to their SUV. "You there, G.G.?"

"I'm here. Someone let a dog out next door. I think he knows I'm here. He's barking like crazy."

He rolled all his windows down. "That's not a bad thing. Something for me to listen for. I have my hazard lights on. Don't come out for anyone else."

"I won't."

Since she'd said she thought she'd run for about ten minutes, he didn't waste time driving along the first several streets. "Lauren, I should be getting close. When you see a black SUV with hazard lights blinking, it's me."

"Please hurry. I think the dog is trying to dig under the fence."

Court heard the faint sound of a barking dog. "I'm close, baby. Watch the road." He'd been driving in a grid, but at another bark from a dog, he turned a block short of where he'd intended to turn onto the next street. The barking got louder.

"Lauren, I'm close. Remember, don't come out until you're sure it's me."

"I see you! Court, I see you."

He braked. "Did the car you see just stop?"

"Yes. Oh God, yes."

He shoved the SUV into park, then jumped out. Not sure where she was hiding, he stood in the middle of the road, his phone to his ear. "Come to me, baby."

Out of the darkness a form ran to him. He opened his arms while willing his knees not to buckle in relief at finding her. She flew at him, her aim more true than a heat-sensing missile.

"Christ," he murmured into her hair. "Christ, Lauren." Any other words were beyond his ability to speak.

When she tried to climb up him, he slipped his arms under her knees, helping her. With her plastered against him, he took her to the SUV, then buckled her safely in. As he walked around the hood, he came to a stop and looked up at the night sky. He didn't know if he believed there was a God. He hoped there was because his mother had, and he didn't want her to be wrong.

So, just in case there was a supreme being looking down on them, he wanted to make sure one thing was understood between them. *You take her away from me one more time, my response isn't going to be pretty. You got that, God?* God didn't answer, but he hadn't expected him to.

It took him thirty minutes—her holding his hand in a death grip as she stared out the window—to get back to his building. She didn't seem to want to talk, so he didn't pressure her. He had a lot of questions, though. Tons of them. But everything he needed to know could wait until she felt safe again. That was what he could do for her. That and keep her hand held securely in his.

Lauren wanted to tell Court to never let go of her hand. Ever. Something had happened to her as she'd curled into a fetal position under a bush, though, while a dog had done his best to tell the world where she'd been hiding. Now that she was safe, she couldn't speak. Couldn't tell him how afraid she had been that she would never see him again. That damn dog had stolen her voice. So she kept her hold on Court, and although she was looking out the window, her eyes weren't seeing anything.

"Wha . . ." She cleared her throat. "What did you mean that Stephan drove by?"

"A clerk made a mistake in his release papers, letting him out a day early."

She let out a shuddering breath. That was where Peter had gone, to pick up his brother. What if she hadn't gotten away? It didn't bear thinking of.

"I pretended to be you," she said after he'd parked in his space, her voice barely above a whisper.

He shifted to face her. "I don't understand."

"You told me to be smart. To be strong. But I was afraid, so I thought, what would Court do? What would he say?"

"Oh, baby." He leaned across the console, wrapped his arms around her, and held her. "I'm sorry. I should have waited for the pizza to be delivered."

"It wasn't your fault. It wasn't."

He pulled away, locking his eyes on hers. "I should probably warn you that I'm not letting you out of my sight."

"I'm good with that." At least until Stephan wasn't a threat anymore. She sure as hell wasn't opening any more doors unless she absolutely knew who was on the other side.

"Don't move," Court said before exiting the car.

She watched him jog around the hood, and after he opened her door, he scooped her up. "I can walk."

"I know, but I like you right where you are."

"If you insist." She buried her face against his neck, breathing him in, his familiar scent calming her.

Strong arms held her securely as they rode the elevator up. She wasn't a woman who wanted or needed a man's constant attention. Nor did she want a man who thought he should take care of her every need, hovering over her as if she couldn't do anything for herself. Not on most days. But tonight, she needed it, and somehow Court had known that.

She hadn't been paying attention to their progress until he stopped and knocked on a door. It flew open, and Madison grabbed them in a group hug.

"Are you okay? Are you hurt?" Her frantic eyes shifted to Court. "Is that why you're carrying her? Cause she's hurt?"

Lauren laughed, feeling like the filling in a sandwich with Court and Madison plastered against her. "I'm not hurt."

"Are you sure?" Madison said, apparently not believing her.

"Positive. I think he just needs to take care of me for a little while until he assures himself I'm safe."

Court grunted an agreement, then winked at her. "I might set you down in about a year."

"Alex called," Madison said. "I'm supposed to go up to Nate's with you two and wait for him. He's okay, right?"

Court nodded. "He's fine. He just doesn't want you to be alone right now."

They were going to Nate's place? She tamped down her disappointment that she and Court weren't going to be alone tonight. All she wanted was to take a shower, and then curl up in bed with him, have him hold her, and tell her again that he loved her.

"Can I at least shower? I feel like I have bugs crawling all over me." She held out her arm, showing them the angry red bites. "The ants didn't like me invading their space."

"I have some stuff that will help," Madison said. "Be right back."

While they waited, Court stared down at her with such intensity that she had to force herself not to squirm. "Aren't your arms getting tired of carrying me around? You really can put me down. I promise I'm capable of walking."

"No."

"No?" A laugh escaped, which was a miracle considering that less than an hour ago, she was crouched under a thorny rosebush, getting eaten by ants, and praying Court would find her before the barking dog managed to dig under the fence and out her.

"That's what I said." When Madison reappeared, he strode to the elevator, Madison jogging along behind them.

Lauren peeked at her friend over Court's shoulder and rolled her eyes. "He apparently thinks I've lost the use of my legs."

"He thinks you scared a year off his life when you disappeared," Court said, sounding grumpy. "He needs you in his arms."

Although she felt silly being carried around, she had to admit this caveman side of him was kind of sexy. Too bad Madison was with them. It would be interesting to find out what it was like to have a caveman in her bed.

CHAPTER
TWENTY-ONE

"Wow, this isn't what I'd expected Nate's place to look like," Lauren said, surveying his living room.

Court snorted. "Let me guess. You imagined something dark and gloomy to match his personality." It always amused him the first time someone saw Nate's condo. No one ever expected the beach décor, the pale mint-green walls, dark green leather couch, and various creamy yellow accessories.

"Yeah, I guess that's what I pictured," Lauren said.

Madison picked up a pale pink conch shell from the coffee table. "Surprised me, too, the first time I was here. I think Nate has had so much darkness in his life . . . still does, that he needed a calm place to come home to."

"It's calm all right." She took the large seashell from Madison. "This is beautiful."

Madison had nailed it. Nate had always found peace at the beach, and this was his big brother's refuge. It was why they'd bought condos on the ocean. Because it was where Nate needed to be. He still carried internal scars from their old man, some Court could only suspect based on the visible scars on his body.

Both he and Alex knew that Nate had taken the brunt of the son of a bitch's abuse to protect them. Then there was the job. They all three loved their work, but again, Nate was their self-appointed guardian, always worrying about them. He was technically their boss, a shield between them and Rothmire. If they screwed up, he took the blame, so they both did their best not to. After tonight's doings, though, Rothmire wasn't going to be very happy.

"Either of you want something to drink?" He glanced at Lauren as he asked the question. She'd refused to let him carry her up here, and he was still miffed about that. He hadn't been kidding when he'd said he needed to hold her. Her hair was still wet from her shower, and dressed in white shorts and a pale blue T-shirt, she looked downright edible. She also looked like she was about to fall on her face.

"Sit," he said.

"Have you noticed how bossy he is tonight?" Lauren said, taking a seat on the sofa.

Madison giggled. "I like it when Alex gets bossy, especially in bed."

"TMI," Court muttered, heading for the kitchen. He did not need to know about his brother's bedroom activities.

"Water for me," Lauren said. "Anything stronger, I'll fall asleep."

Madison joined Lauren on the couch. "I'll take a glass of wine."

He was carrying their drinks, along with a beer he held by the neck with two fingers when the door opened. Nate walked in, followed by Alex, followed by Rothmire. *Speak of the devil and he appears.* This was going to be interesting. Maybe with the girls here, he wouldn't get yelled at too badly.

"Where's Popov?" Court asked, handing Lauren and Madison their drinks.

Nate reached over and snatched the beer. "Stowed away for the night until we decide what to do with him."

"That was mine, dude."

"My house, my beer." Nate consumed half of it.

Nate wasn't a big drinker, so if he was guzzling it, it probably meant Rothmire had already chewed his ass for their going rogue. Whatever. He'd do it all over again where Lauren was concerned.

When Alex headed for the kitchen, Court followed him. "Rothmire pissed?" he asked quietly.

"Understatement, bro."

Court popped his head around the corner. "Rothmire, you want something?"

"You boys are going to be the death of me yet. Or drive me to drink. A scotch neat."

Ouch. Boss man definitely wasn't happy.

"Coming up." Although Nate never drank anything but beer, he kept wine for Madison and a bottle of Chivas Regal on hand for the rare times their boss was here.

"Should we slip a Valium into his drink?" Alex whispered.

"Two at least." If they actually had a bottle of Valium, he would be sorely tempted. The next few minutes weren't going to be pretty. Court grabbed another beer for himself, and returning to the living room, he handed Rothmire his scotch.

Their bureau chief was usually a calm man, except when he wasn't, like now. As he paced Nate's living room, drink in hand, Court studied the man who—after his brothers—he respected above all others. Tall, lean, skin the color of rich dark chocolate, strong-jawed, and opinionated as hell, he was also fair and protective of all his agents. No one in his field office doubted he had their back . . . even when they screwed up. That didn't mean he tolerated any shit from them. But he'd never once thrown one of his people under the bus with the higher-ups. Court was counting on that to stay true.

Rothmire swiped a hand through his close-cropped salt-and-pepper hair. "Madison, it's good to see you again."

"It's good to see you, too, Mr. Rothmire." She chuckled. "Someday we'll have to meet when it's not in the middle of a crisis."

"Doubtful. These boys swim in trouble."

Lauren scooted to the edge of the sofa. "Please don't blame them, Mr. Rothmire. I brought the trouble to their door."

"I'm responsible," Nate said, unsurprisingly. "I didn't call in."

Damn if anyone else was going to take the blame. "I would have gone for her with or without you, bro."

"He wouldn't have gone off without me," Alex said.

"Jesus," Rothmire said, staring up at the ceiling, as if looking for divine intervention. "Save me from these sacrificial lambs." His gaze zeroed in on Lauren. "Ms. Montgomery, I presume?"

She nodded. Thinking Rothmire was going to give her the third degree, Court stepped toward her, his protective instinct taking over. Nate put a hand on his arm, shaking his head. Nate was right. Whatever was about to happen between Lauren and Rothmire needed to play out. She'd been through hell tonight, but she was strong and perfectly capable of standing up for herself. Even more importantly, Rothmire would respect her for it.

"It is a pleasure to meet you, Ms. Montgomery."

"Lauren."

"Lauren then." He held out his hand, and when she put hers in his, he held it there. "Are you sure you know what you're getting into involving yourself with one of the Gentry brothers? If not, I have a headful of stories that might give you second thoughts."

Her eyes darted to him, and Court winked, his heart giving a thump in his chest at her soft smile.

Rothmire sighed. "I see you are a lost cause, Lauren, my dear, so the stories will stay in my head where they belong."

"Mr. Rothmire, do your best, but there's nothing you can say to convince me I shouldn't consider it an honor to have the Gentry brothers as friends."

"I like you, Miss Lauren." He let go of her hand. "Let's get down to business, people." He set down his empty glass, then seated himself in a chair. "Nate and Alex updated me earlier on tonight's events, and I've read Stephan Kozlov's original arrest report,"—he looked at Lauren—"seen the photos of you taken at the hospital. I want to start from the beginning, from the moment you met your ex-husband."

Court moved to the sofa, sitting between Lauren and Madison, and took Lauren's hand, cradling it in his. Alex perched on the arm, next to his wife, and Nate sat in the chair across from Rothmire. As Court listened to a story he'd already heard, the ever-simmering rage at Kozlov's treatment of Lauren returned full force. The only thing anchoring him to his seat was her touch.

Both his brothers' lips were pressed together in thin lines as Lauren spoke of a husband who'd treated a woman the way no man ever should. It was Rothmire's calm demeanor and soft voice as he asked questions, though, that Court suspected was the only reason Lauren was able to get through the retelling.

When she finished, Rothmire sat back in his chair. "He will pay, Lauren. You have my word on that. As for his plan to take you to Russia with him, that will happen over my dead body."

"Mine, too," Nate said.

Alex nodded. "And mine."

"I'll kill him first before I'll let him touch you," Court said, squeezing her hand.

"Thank you. All of you," Lauren whispered. She didn't know what else to say to express what was in her heart. Stupid tears pooled in her eyes. Each time she'd had to tell her story, it had seemed like she was living it again. She understood why she had to do it, but she hoped it was the last time. And she refused to agree to Court killing anyone on her behalf.

She lifted her face to Court's. "Let's just settle for either sending him right back to prison or deporting him back to Russia without a chance of ever returning."

"Although I hesitate to interrupt this intimate moment between the two of you, Court won't be killing anyone," Mr. Rothmire said.

Lauren swung her gaze to his. "I don't want him having that on his conscience. Not because of me." She ignored the sound Court made. He could growl all he wanted, but she knew him. Killing anyone, even Stephan, would come with regrets. He would forever wonder if there'd been some other way.

Mr. Rothmire smiled, as if he understood. Much like Nate, the man intimidated her when he turned those piercing black eyes on her. But as with Nate, she liked Rothmire. He didn't pull any punches. She found him fascinating, and couldn't wait to get Madison alone so she could find out more about him. She figured she probably shouldn't tell Court that. Madison would get it, though. There were men who got your attention that you weren't necessarily attracted to.

"Let's talk about his brother and what we know about him. Can we connect Peter Kozlov's activities to Stephan? What do you have on that so far, Court?" Mr. Rothmire asked.

Lauren leaned her back against the sofa, relieved the spotlight was off her. Court hadn't let go of her hand, for which she was thankful. She needed to touch him. As long as they were connected, she felt like she could keep breathing. What she hadn't said, because they wouldn't have understood, was she had memories of two different Stephans. The beautiful, kind man a young girl had fallen in love with, and then there was monster Stephan, his true self.

"Peter's connection with the Bratva is through Vadim Popov. I have some emails between him and Peter you need to read."

"I'm not going to ask how you got them since I haven't seen a request for a warrant cross my desk," Mr. Rothmire said. "I'm also not going to read them for the same reason. Give me reasons to pull a warrant the old-fashioned way. I put out a BOLO on Stephan and Peter Kozlov."

"That means *Be on the lookout*," Court told her before she could ask.

"It's getting late, and Lauren looks like she's about to fall asleep," Mr. Rothmire said, standing. "We'll continue this tomorrow. You boys try to stay out of trouble for the rest of the night."

Truthfully, she was past tired. It was considerate of him to notice. She gave him a grateful smile. "It was nice meeting you, Mr. Rothmire."

"The pleasure was all mine. If everything goes as planned, your troubles will be over soon. Very soon."

After he left, she said, "There's a plan?"

"We're working on one," Court said. "For now, you need to get some rest. Tomorrow, when your chin isn't nodding on your chest, we'll go over everything. You're staying with Alex and Madison tonight."

"Why?" She needed to be with him, even if all he did was hold her through the night. That was all she'd thought of since getting away from Peter and Vadim. Just her and Court, safe in his bed. She didn't think she could sleep without his arms wrapped around her.

"Nate and I have some things to do, and I'm not sure when I'll be back. I don't want you alone at my place."

"Come up when you're ready to go," Nate said, standing. He smiled at her. "You'll be safe here with Alex."

"Where are you going?" she asked Court. "Didn't your boss tell you to stay out of trouble tonight?"

Alex snorted. "Trust me, Rothmire knows that went in one ear and out the other."

Court took her hand, pulling her up. "We'll be out on the balcony for a few minutes," he said.

"Don't be long," Nate said as he walked out.

"What's going on?" Lauren asked after Court closed the balcony door behind them.

Instead of answering, he cradled her cheeks with his hands, lowered his face, and brushed a feathery kiss across her lips. He lifted his head, stared at her a moment, then said, "Have I told you how much I love kissing you?"

"No," she whispered.

"Then let me show you."

His kiss this time was possessive, demanding, and a little wild, as if he were afraid she'd disappear from his arms like a puff of smoke. Their tongues touched, explored, dueled for supremacy. She put her hand on his chest, feeling his heartbeat under her palm. He slid his hands down, resting them low on her back, pulling her tight against him.

His masculine scent—citrusy with a hint of leather—filled her lungs, heat from his hands warmed her skin, and his arousal pressed against her belly. She whimpered, and he answered with a growl deep in this throat.

"You make me crazy, Gorgeous Girl," he said, pulling away, chuckling when she tried to follow, wanting his mouth back on hers. "I don't want to go, believe me, but I have to."

Reality returned, and along with it, her questions. She took some deep breaths, trying to calm her heart. At least he was breathing as hard as she was. "Where are you going?" she asked when she could manage to get words out.

"Just a little reconnoitering." He put his finger over her lips when she opened her mouth. "Nothing dangerous, I swear. We'll talk tomorrow, okay?"

She wanted to protest, wanted to grab his hand and refuse to let go. He could say 'nothing dangerous' all he wanted, but she didn't believe a word of it. Was this what life would be like with him? Every time he walked out the door, her stomach turning sick and her mind imagining all the things that could happen to him. How did Madison stand it?

It was his job, and she understood that. She also knew he thrived on going after what he called *bad guys*. She would never ask him to quit, but could she live with that? It was a question for which she didn't have an answer, not when she was too tired to think clearly.

"Just promise to be careful, okay?" That was the best she could give him. If he wanted her approval, he wasn't going to get it. And at that thought, guilt slammed into her. He was the good guy. The kind of good guy the world needed. To resent him for what he did was wrong.

"I always am." He trailed the back of his knuckles down her cheek. "Don't worry about me. Big bad Nate would never let anything happen to me."

"I know." She smiled, then lifted onto her toes, and kissed him. "See you tomorrow."

"Alex and Madison will walk you down to my condo so you can get whatever you need for tonight."

"Okay."

He wrapped his arms around her again, until his body was flush against hers. "One more kiss," he said.

When he pulled away for the last time, she forced her hands to let him go. "I want to go see my father and sister tomorrow," she said as he opened the sliding glass door. Now that she wasn't running and Stephan was out and on the loose, he needed to know what was going on. She wouldn't put it past Stephan to show up at her father's house.

He paused, glancing back at her. "Sure. Just don't take off on your own. I'll go with you," he said, then walked away.

She had no intention of going anywhere on her own until Stephan was no longer a threat. Peter and Stephan had made her a prisoner, and she hated it. A misty rain was falling, but thunderstorms were forecasted for later. She stood under the overhang, wishing Court wasn't out in this weather.

"How do you stand it, knowing Alex faces danger every time he walks out the door?" she asked when Madison joined her.

Madison leaned on the railing next to her. "He promised to always come home to me. I decided to believe him."

If only it were that easy.

That night, she tossed and turned, punching her pillow in frustration when sleep refused to come. How was she supposed to sleep when Court was out there somewhere, doing who knew what, putting himself in danger?

As she drifted off, she smiled, remembering the first time Court had kissed her. He'd cradled her face with his big hands, stared at her for a moment, his black eyes warm and soft, and then had asked permission to kiss her. That he would ask did something funny to her heart.

She hadn't wanted to leave him when their week came to an end, but he'd promised he'd come to Miami soon. She returned home, walked into her apartment, already missing him and anxious to call him.

"That's a smile I haven't seen in a long time. Who put it on your face, Lauren?"

Ice flowed through her veins. *Run,* her brain had screamed. Why was Stephan in her apartment? She tried to run, but he'd somehow trapped her arms and legs.

"What's his name?" Stephan pointed to the corner.

She didn't want to look. God, she didn't, but her eyes followed Stephan's pointing finger. She gasped. "No, Stephan. Please no. He's no one. I swear."

Tears slipped from Court's eyes at her betrayal. He gave her a sad smile, then lowered his chin to his chest, not trying to escape the chair where Stephan had bound him. Stephan's hand turned into a gun. Smoke puffed from the barrel when he fired it.

"No!" Lauren shot up, her heart jackhammering in her chest. "No," she cried.

As she struggled to draw air into her lungs, she clutched the blanket in fisted hands. "It was just a dream," she whispered. "Only a dream."

CHAPTER TWENTY-TWO

"Because of the Kozlovs, you're on our radar now," Court said to Alexi Ivanov, the owner of Xander's Bar and Grill. The bar was a hangout for Russian nationals, but the bulk of Ivanov's income came from gambling. Court had made a list of everyone living in the area who'd had contact with Peter, Vadim, or Stephan through emails or phone conversations. He and Nate were paying each one they could find a visit with the intention of isolating Peter and Stephan.

Nate leaned on the bar, leveling a cold gaze on Ivanov. "It wouldn't be in your best interest to offer assistance if either of the Kozlovs should ask."

"I don't appreciate being threatened by the cops," Ivanov said as he wiped down the bar counter.

"Did you hear either of us say we were cops?" Court raised a brow at Nate.

Nate shrugged. "He didn't hear that from me."

"If not cops, what are you?" The rag in Ivanov's hand moved faster over the same spot he'd been cleaning since they'd started talking. The man was getting nervous. Good.

"It doesn't matter who we are. You'll never see us again as long as you don't get involved in something that's none of your business. Not your monkeys, not your circus, and all that."

Ivanov could think whatever he wanted as long as he didn't give aid to the enemy. Court and Nate hadn't blown their cover, hadn't once implied they were the law. They were dressed in jeans and black T-shirts, with chains hanging out of their pockets and heavy motorcycle boots adorning their feet. They'd both let their black leather jackets fall open, giving a glimpse of the guns tucked into shoulder holsters. If they weren't the law, Ivanov's next best guess would probably be that they were some kind of biker outlaws. No one wanted to mess with those dudes.

Court put his fist over Ivanov's hand. "You're going to wear the lacquer off in about a minute." He leaned toward the man. "Listen closely. You do talk to Stephan Kozlov, you give him a message from me. The girl is mine. He can't have her because I'm keeping her."

He'd delivered that same message on every visit they made that night, a dare for Stephan to come after him. Hopefully one of them would repeat his words to the bastard. The plan was to set a trap, herd the Kozlov brothers into a proverbial canyon with no way out. Rothmire had assigned agents to stake out Stephan's mansion and two more were keeping watch on the house where Peter had taken Lauren. There had been no sign of the brothers at either place.

There were no more houses or buildings in either of their names, but they were holed up somewhere. It was possible Stephan would decide Lauren wasn't worth the trouble coming down on them, but Court's gut said the man was still obsessed with her and would try to get to her.

Over his dead body.

After stopping at an all-night diner for an early breakfast, they headed home. As much as he wanted to curl up around Lauren and get some much-needed sleep, he didn't want to wake her. He shucked off his clothes and considered falling into bed, but he felt dirty. He detoured to the shower. Once clean, he did fall face-first onto his bed and was asleep as soon as his head hit the pillow.

Sometime later, he awoke to a warm body pressed up against his back. Not opening his eyes, he smiled. "I think Goldilocks found her way into the big bad bear's bed."

She giggled. "All the better to eat you with."

"Aren't you getting your fairy tales jumbled?"

"The bear didn't eat Goldilocks?"

"Mmm, now that you mention it, I think he did. And if he didn't, he should have." He flipped over, wrapped his arms around her, and stilled. He leaned his head away, grinning as his gaze slid down her body. "A very naked Goldilocks. I like this story much better."

"I thought you might." She put her palm on his cheek. "I was worried about you. You're okay?"

He leaned his face into her hand. "All in one piece. Tell me you didn't come home by yourself." *Home.* He hadn't realized how much he wanted his home to be hers until that had slipped out.

"Of course not. Alex played bodyguard and escorted me up."

"Good girl." He stroked a finger across her bottom lip. "Did you sleep okay?"

"No, I missed you."

"Did you?" He walked his fingers up her side to her breast, flicking his thumb over the nipple. "I think Goldilocks needs a little special attention."

"She does."

"You're beautiful," he said, and then lost himself in loving his gorgeous girl. Much later, he spooned his body behind hers. She'd wanted to hear the ocean, so he'd cracked the window. He trailed the palm of his hand down her side, to her thighs, and then back up, loving how soft and silky she felt.

Her body relaxed under his hand as she slipped into sleep, and he whispered, "I love you, Lauren Montgomery."

Suddenly, she was facing him. "You do?"

So much for her being asleep. "I told you I did."

"I thought . . . The only time you said it was on the phone when you were worried about me. I thought it was just something you said to make me feel better. You know, to keep my spirits up."

"I'm an idiot," he said, then kissed her. "I love you, and I hope that makes you feel better, but it's not why I'm saying it." She sniffled, and he slid a thumb across her cheek, collecting tears. "That's not supposed to make you cry."

"I don't . . ."

"You don't what?"

"Nothing. They're happy tears." She pushed a leg between his, nestling into him. "I love you so much, Court. So damn much. They were going to cart me off to Russia, and I didn't know if I'd ever see you again."

"Hush, G.G. I'd never let that happen." He kissed away her tears, but the hesitation in her voice floated above him like a black cloud promising a coming storm.

Court was nervous. He'd never met a parent of a woman he was interested in before, and that he was in love with the one who walked up the sidewalk next to him made it even worse. Would her father think he wasn't worthy of his daughter?

He and his brothers had risen above their environment, made something of themselves in spite of all the obstacles against them. But for the first time in years, he felt like the little boy who'd been shunned by his classmates because he was poor and always had dirt under his fingernails. He gave his head a slight shake. He wasn't that kid anymore. He reminded himself that it was normal to be nervous meeting a girl's parents for the first time, no matter your background.

"Is there anything I should know about your father?"

"I told you he was a minister, right?"

He nodded.

"Just don't say shit, damn, or worse, and you'll be okay."

He laughed, his nerves suddenly calm. "Got it." Her father could like him or not, and he hoped the man did, but it wouldn't make a damn . . . a darn bit of difference. Lauren was his gorgeous girl, and no one and nothing was going to change that.

Before they reached the door, it opened, and a girl with the same golden-brown eyes as Lauren walked out. "I thought you'd disowned us."

"You know better than that. It's just been kind of crazy lately," Lauren said.

That was putting it mildly. He stood by as the sisters hugged. The girl eyed him over Lauren's shoulder, and he smiled.

"Who's he?"

Lauren took his hand, pulling him next to her. "This is Court Gentry, my boyfriend. Court, my sister, Julie."

"A pleasure to meet you," he said. The girl was very pretty, and he wondered what Lauren had looked like at that age. Other than their eyes, there wasn't much resemblance. Julie's wheat-blonde hair almost reached her waist, and she was already taller than Lauren.

"Where did you guys meet? How long have you known each other? You haven't said a word about having a boyfriend, Lore. You don't tell me anything anymore. He looks like a movie star." She eyed Court. "Are you? A movie star? That would be so cool."

"Julie! Hush." Lauren shook her head, smiling at Court. "I guess I should have warned you that she likes to talk."

"Isn't that what people are supposed to do? Talk?" Julie said, sounding serious.

Court grinned. He bet the girl was a handful. "I've always thought so. And no, I'm not a movie star. Sorry to disappoint."

"Well, you're as gorgeous as Nick Jonas, so I guess it's okay if you're not famous."

"Thank you, I think." He had no idea who Nick Jonas was, but apparently it was high praise.

"Julie, leave the poor man alone," a man said from the doorway.

Lauren hopped up the steps. "Hi, Daddy."

More hugs followed, and Court watched, fascinated by Lauren's closeness to her father. There had never been any hope that he'd have any kind of normal relationship with his father, and he'd settled that in his mind a long time ago. But what about his mother? If she'd stayed, would they be close today? Impossible to know, but as soon as he made sure Lauren was safe, he planned to talk to Alex. It was time to look for her, whether Nate liked it or not.

"Court, this is my dad, William Montgomery. Dad, Court Gentry."

"Mr. Montgomery, it's a pleasure to meet you." He held out his hand. As they shook, Court noted that although Lauren's father wasn't sending him a death glare, his eyes weren't shining with warmth either. Who could blame him for being leery after the way his daughter had been treated by Stephan Kozlov?

"Come inside," Mr. Montgomery said.

Court followed the family, expecting they'd go into the living room, sit around, and have an uncomfortable chat. As soon as he could reasonably suggest it was time to go, the ordeal would be over. He could handle that. Instead, they ended up in the kitchen, sitting on stools arranged around an island.

"Would you like something to drink?" Lauren's father asked him. "I have tea, coffee, and orange soda."

"Water will be fine, sir."

"So, if you're not an actor, what do you do? I know, you're a model," Julie cried before he could answer her question.

"Guess again," he said, glancing at Lauren. He should have asked her how he should answer questions about himself. A bar owner likely would not be someone a minister would want his daughter dating. Court was willing to trust Lauren's father with the fact he was FBI, but Julie was another matter altogether. She was young and excitable, and he doubted she could keep from whispering that secret to her friends.

"He owns a biker bar," Lauren said, shocking them all, including him.

Especially him. Court wished he had a pin he could drop to see if it really was true that one could hear it when there wasn't another sound in the room. He swallowed uncomfortably, clueless as to what to say.

"Like a motorcycle bar?" Julie screeched.

Did she not know any other way to talk? "Ah . . ."

"That is so cool."

It really wasn't.

She hopped off her barstool. "Can I go see it? I mean, I know I can't go there when it's open. I'm only sixteen." She slyly eyed him. "But could you take me there when it's closed? My friends won't believe I got to go to an honest-to-goodness biker bar. Oh, please, please, please?"

Court glanced helplessly at Lauren, narrowing his eyes at her smirk. When they got home, he was going to spank her for being so amused at his expense.

Mr. Montgomery peered at his watch. "Julie, have you forgotten you're supposed to be at the Haymores' in fifteen minutes to babysit?" Lauren's father said while looking at Court, finally sending him the death glare that he'd been expecting.

Lauren was torn between feeling sorry for Court and being amused by his discomfort. He'd borne up well so far in the face of Julie's never-ending chatter and her father's wariness toward him. She hadn't meant to blurt out that he owned a bar, but sometimes being around Julie dulled her brain, as if Julie's peculiar brightness dimmed hers. She loved Julie to the moon and back and didn't resent that. It was just the way it always had been ever since her sister had arrived in this world.

She poked Julie's arm. "No, you cannot visit his bar. Go babysit."

Julie danced her way around the island to Court. "Never fear. I'll get to see your bar," she said in a stage whisper, then twirled her way out of the room.

"Never fear? That girl scares me to death," Court muttered, then gulped down half his water, wishing it was something stronger.

Her dad stared at Julie as she merrily danced away. "You should be scared. I know I am."

That a teenage girl had reduced the two men Lauren loved most in the world to whining babies struck her as hilarious, and she couldn't hold in her laughter.

"So not funny," Court said, glaring at her.

"How do you think I feel? I'm the father of that one," her father said.

Court clicked his glass against her father's. "You have my sympathy."

"You two are total wimps. She's harmless, just a happy girl." Although if she were Julie's father, she'd be quaking in her boots, too, but she wasn't about to tell them that.

"So you own a biker bar?"

At her father's question, the room went silent again. She couldn't bear her dad thinking badly of the man she loved. He could be trusted with the truth, and that was one reason she'd wanted to come home. So her father could meet Court and learn who he was. She also needed to warn him about Stephan, which she was dreading.

"Court has something to tell you, but you can't tell Julie, okay? You and I both know she can't keep a secret," she said.

Her father looked from her to Court. "Tell me what?"

"It's like this, sir. I do own a biker bar with my two brothers. The bar, Aces and Eights, is a cover, though. All three of us are FBI agents."

Curious about her father's reaction, she kept her eyes on him, and almost laughed at the shock on his face. "Didn't expect that, did you?"

"No, I didn't, but I have to admit that I'm relieved there is more to you than being a barkeep." He studied them for a moment. "How long have you known each other?"

It was time her father knew her history with Court, and so she told him about meeting Court at spring break and why she'd broken up with him. Then she explained what was going on with Stephan.

"I knew his release date was nearing, but I naïvely believed he'd moved on." Her dad lowered his head and closed his eyes as if in prayer; then he lifted his tear-filled gaze to her. "How were we so wrong about him? Every day I live with the regret that I didn't recognize what he was capable of. I'm your father. I should have protected you."

Tears stung her own eyes as she put her hand over his. "You didn't know until the end of our marriage. By then it was too late. I should have told you he was abusing me when it first started."

"Men like Stephan Kozlov are very good at hiding their true nature until they have full control of their victim," Court said. "You wouldn't have seen him for what he truly was until he was ready for you to, so your guilt is misplaced."

Her father steepled his hands. "I understand what you're saying, but she's my daughter, and I—"

"He's right, Daddy. The only one to blame is Stephan. Besides, we can't change the past . . . as much as we'd like to."

"You'll keep her safe?" he said, eyeing Court.

"I swear that I will. If you hear from him, which is entirely possible if he decides you're the only way to get to her, tell him that you've had a falling out and haven't seen Lauren in months, and then you call me." Court fished his wallet out of his pocket, took out a business card, and handed it to her father. "My cell number's on this."

"I don't believe in lying." Her father stuck the card into his shirt pocket. "But I'm sure this is one time God will forgive me."

Court stood. "We need to get going, Lauren."

"Would you give me a few minutes alone with my daughter?"

"Of course. I'll be outside. Although it should have happened six years ago, it was good to finally meet you, sir."

"'To every thing there is a season, and a time to every purpose under the heaven.' That's from Ecclesiastes." Her father gave Court the smile she'd always thought of as his benevolent one, bestowed on those he believed needed his prayers. "We may wish things happened differently, but they happen according to God's plan for us. It was good to finally meet you, too, son."

Court's eyes widened, then softened as he smiled at her father. "You, too, sir." He touched her shoulder, then walked away.

"Did you notice his reaction when I called him son?" her father asked once they were alone. "Why was that?"

"His father was apparently a mean drunk. Maybe he's not used to a man using the word affectionately. You did mean it that way?"

"I did. I'll include him in my prayers, but are you sure he's right for you? I don't mean that he'll hurt you the way Stephan did." With a worried expression on his face, he glanced out the window to where Court stood by the car, reading something on his phone. "Can you live with him walking out the door every day, not knowing if he'll return home in one piece . . . or at all?"

She shifted on the stool, looking out the window. "I don't know." She turned troubled eyes back to her father. "I love him, but I don't know."

CHAPTER
TWENTY-THREE

On their drive home, Court had been on the phone with his brothers. As soon as they'd arrived back at his condo, he'd gone into his safe room to work and had stayed in there until he'd wandered out a few hours later, saying his stomach was growling.

Something was bothering him. He'd been quiet all through dinner, except to thank her for cooking. The kitchen wasn't her favorite room, but there were a few meals she had mastered. When she'd started to get hungry, she'd searched through his pantry and freezer, finding the ingredients to make chicken fettuccine.

They'd cleaned up the kitchen together, and then had brewed a pot of coffee, and now sat out on his balcony. She'd stayed quiet, hoping he would tell her what was on his mind, but he seemed content to sit there and stare out into the night.

"What has you so deep in thought?" she asked, when she finally couldn't stand it anymore.

Court glanced over at her. "Your father." He sat in silence a bit longer. "I like him," he finally said.

"He liked you, too." She smiled, happy that she could truthfully say that.

"He doesn't think I'm good enough for you, and he's probably right." His gaze shifted back to the view of the ocean.

She supposed she shouldn't be surprised that he'd judge himself by his past, but she'd never thought of him as lacking in any way. Not even after she'd learned about his childhood.

"I don't know why you'd say that." She shifted in her chair so she could face him. "If it's because of the way you grew up, you've put that behind you. You're one of the good guys, doing your part to make the world a better place. So don't give me that 'Poor me, I'm no good' speech."

"Yeah, I guess that was kind of sappy." He shrugged. "You can't deny he has a problem with me, though."

"He asked if I could live with what you do, considering your job is dangerous."

"And?"

"I told him I didn't know." She wouldn't lie to him. "I asked Madison how she dealt with it. She said Alex promised her that nothing would happen to him, but that's not something he can promise. I don't know if I could handle losing you, Court." And if they had kids? Having to tell their children their father was never coming home was too devastating to even think about.

He went to the railing, and looked out over the ocean. As he stood there, her eyes roamed over him. There wasn't a thing about him that she didn't love, but was it enough? Her dream had unsettled her. Would the day come when she couldn't watch him walk out the door one more time, not knowing if he'd come home?

She never wanted to resent Court. Nor would she ever ask him to give up his job. He loved what he did, and if she made that a condition, he'd end up resenting her for it.

"When did you turn into a coward?" he said softly, keeping his back to her.

She dug her fingers into the arms of her chair. Before she said something she couldn't take back, she closed her eyes, taking several deep breaths. His words angered her, but she had to wonder. Was she being a coward? She stood and joined him at the railing.

"Last night, I dreamed you were killed." She didn't share that the monster who'd shot him in her dream was Stephan. That had nothing to do with what she wanted him to understand. She was also afraid to say it out loud, as if speaking it would somehow make it come true.

"I fell asleep worried about you, which is probably why I had the dream. It . . . It just really shook me up."

He shifted to face her, put his arms around her, and pulled her against him. "I think we're both on edge with this shit Stephan's trying to pull. I'm sorry you dreamed that, but that's all it was. A dream."

He kissed the top of her head. "I love you, G.G. But maybe that's not enough right now. It might be best if we take a step back until your ex-husband is out of your life for good. Then we can take the time to get to know each other again. Or not. It will be your choice."

Tears stung her eyes. She wanted to take back everything she'd said, but the words wouldn't come. Until she came to terms with the danger he faced on a regular basis—if she could learn to live with it—she wouldn't make promises she couldn't keep.

Yet the arms he'd wrapped around her were strong, and lately, close to him was the only place she felt safe. She buried her face in his chest, swallowing hard against the burning in her throat.

"I'm sorry," she whispered.

"Hush." He tightened his hold on her. "You have no reason to be sorry. We just need to get through this, and then we'll figure out if there's an us." He sighed. "It's getting late, and I have some more work to do."

Even though he still held her, she sensed he was withdrawing. Forcing herself to do the opposite of what she wanted to do, she stepped back. "Yeah, I'm tired. I'm going to call it a night."

When he didn't make a move to come inside with her, she walked to the balcony door. Before she stepped through, she paused. "I do love you."

He gave her a weary smile. "Just not enough."

The tears she'd been holding back pooled in her eyes, and before she lost it in front of him, she hurried to the guest room. In bed, she pulled her pillow over her head and cried. Was he right? Was she a coward who didn't love him enough?

Court stayed out on the balcony after Lauren left. When would he ever learn? Women left, even when they claimed they loved you. He gripped the railing as he stared at the ocean. The night was overcast, the moon hidden behind thick clouds. The only visible evidence that there was an ocean out there were the whitecaps of the waves as they came onshore. Lightning flashed in the distance, followed by the low rumble of thunder. It was a dreary night, and it matched his mood.

Never again would he fall in love. It sucked, this ache in his heart. Below him, he heard Alex and Madison come out onto their balcony. Madison's laughter floated up to him. He hated being jealous of what his brother had, but it was there. He'd get over it, though. All he had to do was harden his heart. He'd done it before, and he could do it again.

He watched the approaching storm a few minutes longer, then went inside. The door to the guest bedroom was closed, a barricade between him and Lauren. He paused, staring at the slab of wood that separated them. Could he give up his job for her? Should he have to? There wasn't anything he'd ask her to give up if it defined who she was. Did she not get that?

Alex had somehow found a woman who loved him without reservation, was there for him each night when he came home, and if his guess was right, she was at this very moment out on their balcony showing his brother just how much she loved him.

Court pressed a palm against the door. "Why can't you give me that, G.G.?" he whispered. He dropped his hand down to his side and turned away from her door. An hour later, he gave up trying to work. His eyes were bleary and his mind was on the woman in his guest room.

After making sure all the alarms were set, he took a quick shower, and then climbed into his bed, alone. It seemed ridiculous that Lauren was in his home, yet she was in one room and he in another. He got that she worried about him when he was on the job, but neither one of them knew what tomorrow would bring. He could lose her to a horrible car crash, but he'd never walk away from her because something *might* happen. Life was a gamble. He'd count himself a lucky bastard for every day he had with her.

Tired from lack of sleep the night before, he drifted off to the sound of rain. Sometime later thunder boomed, waking him. Lightning lit up the room, followed by the sound of an explosion in the distance and another long rumble of thunder. The clock on his nightstand went dark and his ceiling fan slowly came to a stop. A transformer had obviously been hit, and he wondered how long the power would be out.

He liked storms, and if the lightning weren't hitting so close, he'd go out on his balcony and watch it. His computers all had surge protectors and were connected to backup batteries, so he wasn't worried about them, but he should probably get up and check on things. Before he could do so, his bedroom door eased open.

"Court?" Lauren whispered.

She was damn lucky he'd realized it was her before he'd gone for the gun on his nightstand. He was going to have to talk to her about sneaking into bedrooms, but it could wait. Pretending to be asleep, he watched under hooded eyes as she crept to the other side of the bed, holding back a smile when she eased onto the mattress with the stealth of a cat up to no good.

The explosion must have scared her. She inched the covers up to her chin and stilled. He waited until her breathing evened, and when he was sure she was asleep, he inched up behind her, spooning her. She let out a little sigh, as if even in sleep, she knew he held her.

"What am I going to do with you, G.G.?" he said quietly. It seemed like he asked himself that question a lot where she was concerned.

The alarm box on his nightstand buzzed twice, waking Court. That particular alert indicated something was happening on his balcony. He slid out of bed, and pulled on the sweatpants he always kept nearby. Grabbing his phone, he brought up the balcony camera, switching to night vision. Two men wearing all black knelt as they opened backpacks.

Court picked up his gun, then went around the bed, and scooped up Lauren. "Wake up," he commanded. "Lauren, wake up!" He stopped at the door to his safe room, setting her on her feet, holding her upright as she swayed into him.

"Mmm?"

"Listen," he said as he pushed the button to open the door. He put his hand on her chin, lifting her face. "Remember the ladders to Alex's and Nate's condos? I need you to go down to Alex right now."

She blinked her eyes, finally waking up. "Why? What's happening?"

"Just go. Now. Don't forget to push the buzzer like I told you so he knows it's you coming through. Go, G.G." He pushed her into the room, then closed the door behind her. At least she had on boxer shorts and a camisole, so he wasn't sending her naked to his brother.

Next, he closed the guest room door, using his phone to lock it. Back in his room, he tugged the mannequin head with a short, black wig on it from under his bed, and put it facedown on the pillow. He pulled his spare pillow over, turning it lengthwise, and then dragged the covers up to the mannequin's neck. In the dark, it looked real enough.

As he'd always been a planner, he'd readied for something like this happening. His brothers had laughed at his mannequin head when he'd shown them, but he'd ignored them. He believed it paid to be prepared, so screw them. Leaving his bedroom door open, he went to where an oversized chair sat in the corner, and squeezed in behind it.

Still using his phone, he switched all the alarms in his condo to silent, keeping the ones his brothers would hear on buzzers. He intended to catch these bastards, and didn't want any alarms to scare them off. If this were his lucky night, it would be the Kozlov brothers trying to break in. From under the chair, he hauled out a bulletproof vest and slipped it on. Again, from under the chair, he removed a steel box holding extra guns, ammunition, and night vision goggles.

"Come on in, boys, I'm ready for you," he murmured.

As he watched on his phone, one jimmied open his sliding glass door, setting off a silent alarm, then both crept inside. A message from Nate popped up at the bottom of his screen.

Status
Court typed an answer.

2 armed men inside tell Alex stay w girls
Nate's response was immediate.

Done on the way
Court messaged back.

Come in thru safe room

Returning his attention to the men, Court followed their movements on the screen as they crept down the hall. One tried the handle of the guest room. Finding it locked, they continued toward him. He hit record, activating the cameras mounted in the corners of his room.

Another message from Nate appeared at the bottom of his phone.

Inside

Nate would be watching the monitors now, seeing the action as it unfolded, so Court didn't bother answering. Once the men entered the bedroom, his brother would be able to sneak up behind them.

Just as the men slipped in, lightning lit up the room. "She's not here," one of them whispered. "Must be in the room that was locked."

"Boss said this one don't see the sun rise."

Idiots. Their whispers had grown louder, and if that had been him in the bed, they would have woken him. Both lifted the guns in their hands and proceeded to empty the chambers. They were beyond idiots. Now they had no bullets left to shoot him with.

"Move an inch," he said, rising, his weapon aimed at the one to his left, "and you'll be the ones not seeing the sun rise."

They froze. Then one, apparently the stupidest one, reached behind his back.

"I wouldn't if I were you," Nate said from behind them. He put his gun to the stupid one's head. "Although I'd love it if you gave me a reason to pull the trigger."

The smarter one put his hands in the air. Court moved from behind the chair, keeping his weapon trained on his guy. "Facedown on the floor, both of you, hands spread out to your sides."

The alarm clock lit up, letting them know the power was back on. Nate reached over to the light switch and flipped it up.

"Let's see what we have here." Disappointed they weren't the Kozlov brothers, Court relieved them of their guns. In searching them, he found backup weapons on each. All in all, a good takedown since no one was killed or wounded. But they'd put Lauren in danger, and that pissed him off.

"Names?" he said. When both stayed silent, he sighed. "Who sent you?" More silence. "Or I could just shoot you in the nuts. Make sure you don't add to the world's overpopulation."

"Jason Metcalf," the smarter one said. Dumber kept his mouth shut.

"Who sent you, Jason?"

"Don't know. Swear I don't. A friend called, said he had a job for us. Some dude wanted you dead and the lady brought back with us."

"The friend's name?"

No answer. Court poked the barrel of his gun against the man's groin. "You have 'til the count of three, Jason. Your friend's name. One. Two . . ."

"Don't shoot me! His name's Hank Banks."

"Shut up," Dumber said.

Metcalf glared at his partner. "Hey, man, it's not your nuts he's about to shoot off."

Court exchanged a glance with Nate. They were familiar with the name Hank Banks. The dude acted as a middleman for what he advertised as "odd jobs," connecting people who didn't want to get their hands dirty with men like these two. Banks was as slippery as a snake, never staying in the same place long enough for law enforcement to track him down.

"Where are you supposed to take the woman?"

"We want a lawyer," Dumber said.

Nate snorted. "That might work if we were the cops."

"Who are you, then, if you ain't cops?" the dumb one said.

"Someone you don't want to mess with." Court pulled off his vest, then went to a drawer and grabbed a T-shirt. After putting it on, he took some plastic ties out of the steel box. Once they had the two men secured, their hands behind their backs, he and Nate walked them into the living room, ordering them to sit on the sofa. Court sat in a chair across from them while Nate walked out onto the balcony. His brother would call Rothmire, find out what he wanted to do with the idiots.

"Now," he said, "let's try this again. What are you supposed to do with the woman?"

"What woman. I don't see no woman," Dumber said.

"Jason, my man, should I shoot his nuts off? If not his, it's going to be yours if one of you doesn't answer my question." He pointed his gun at Metcalf's groin.

"His! Shoot his," Metcalf yelled, squeezing his legs closed.

Court shifted his weapon to Dumber. "His it is."

"No, don't shoot mine," Dumber cried, also squeezing his legs closed. "We were supposed to take her to the corner, and he was going to pick her up."

"He? Banks?"

Metcalf nodded. "Yeah, man."

Banks wouldn't have any reason to come after Lauren himself, so he had to be working for Stephan Kozlov. Sirens sounded in the distance. "Neighbors must have heard you two dumbasses shooting your guns and called the cops."

"There're ropes dangling from the roof onto your balcony," Nate said, walking back inside. He glanced at the two men, giving them an eye roll. "Idiots are lucky they didn't fall and crack open their heads."

"Too bad they didn't."

"Agreed. Come in the kitchen a minute." Court eyed the two men. "Either of you move an inch, you're dead."

They could see the men from the kitchen, and as he listened to Nate, Court kept watch on them.

"One of your neighbors heard the gunfire and called 9-1-1, so we're not going to be able to keep this quiet. Rothmire said to let the cops take them in, and he'll send Rand or another agent to talk to them, see what we can learn," Nate quietly said.

"I figured that when I heard the sirens. They said they were supposed to take Lauren to the corner, and Banks was going to pick her up from there." The sirens were louder, sounding like they were in the parking lot. "Unfortunately, he probably split by now after seeing all the police cars."

The thought of those two getting their hands on her made him want to shoot their nuts off anyway. And what was she thinking? That he was up here wounded, or worse, dead? She already had a problem with his job, and this sure as hell wasn't going to help.

"I need to call Alex, tell him to let Lauren know I'm okay."

Nate put his hand on Court's shoulder. "Did that when I was outside."

"Thanks, bro." He wanted to get the two idiots off his hands so he could go down and show her in person that he was fine. "Open the door so the cops don't break it down." He put his gun in a kitchen drawer, then returned to the living room.

"If you want to avoid an attempted kidnapping charge, you'll tell the cops you planned to burglarize my place."

"Why should we do that?" Dumber said.

Man, the dude really was too dumb to live. "Well, for one thing, you'll do less time for a burglary than you would if you're found guilty of trying to kidnap someone."

Metcalf eyed him with suspicion. "Why are you willing to let us cop to that instead of kidnapping?"

Give the man a gold star for having some brains. "Because I don't want the woman involved in this. She doesn't deserve the problems it would bring." He shrugged. "Your choice, though. Whether you do more time or less makes no difference to me. The cops will be coming through the door in about sixty seconds. Which is it gonna be?"

"Burglary," Metcalf said.

"Smart man. You?" he asked Dumber.

"Burglary."

At least he was on board, but he'd said it begrudgingly, as if he were the one doing Court a big favor and not the other way around.

The detective who followed the cops in suspected that there was more to it than a simple burglary. If he decided to get too nosy, Rothmire would call the man's captain, have him call the detective off. After the cops hauled off the supposed burglars, and the detective was gone, Court followed Nate back into his bedroom.

"Fuckers murdered my bed," he said, staring sadly at his shot-up mattress.

CHAPTER
TWENTY-FOUR

"That was gunfire," Lauren cried. "What's happening up there? What if Court's hurt?" When Court had tossed her into his safe room, and closed the door behind her, she'd stood there for a moment, still half asleep, wondering what was happening. Then his order for her to go to Alex had sunk in. It had taken a few seconds to remember the sequence she was supposed to use when pressing the buzzer, but as soon as she had, the trapdoor below her had opened, Alex's face appearing beneath her.

Apparently, some kind of alarm had gone off, letting Alex know there was trouble. About the same time, the trapdoor above her had opened as well, and Nate had appeared.

"Stay with Madison and Lauren," he'd called down to Alex. Then he'd closed the trapdoor in Court's closet when she was halfway down the ladder.

After Lauren had descended into Alex's safe room, he had closed and bolted the trapdoor behind her. Now she sat on the sofa next to

Madison, wearing the robe her friend had loaned her, sick with worry. Whatever was going on had to be something to do with Stephan. Damn her ex to hell. Was he in Court's home right now? If he so much as put a scratch on Court, there was no place Stephan could hide from her. No place!

"He'll be okay," Madison said, grabbing her hand when she tried to stand. "Our guys know what they're doing."

Madison couldn't know that. What if it were Alex up there? She'd be dying inside, too, thinking the worst. At least the lights were back on. That was good, right?

"They're okay. Trust me," Alex said.

This was what she didn't think she could live with, the waiting to see Court walk in the door, safe and whole. Unable to sit still, she stood, and went to the glass door leading out to the balcony. The storm was moving away, but thunder was still rumbling in the distance. As she stared out, lightning flashed. She squinted.

"What's that?" she said.

Alex walked over. "What?"

"Is there a light on your balcony?"

He reached over and flipped a switch. "Damn. Stay here."

As he walked out, she eyed the gun stuck in the waistband of his jeans, another reminder of just who and what the brothers were. She watched as he tugged on one of the two ropes dangling from somewhere above them.

"What's he looking at?" Madison said, walking over.

"It looks like ropes." There were two of them, so she assumed there were two men. Had they come for her or had they come after Court? There was no way Stephan would have scaled down the side of a building, so was it someone with a grudge against Court?

She couldn't stand not knowing what was going on up above. There hadn't been any more gunfire, thank God, but the silence was just as bad. Sirens sounded in the distance, seemingly headed their way. Someone must have called the police.

"Well?" she said when Alex walked back inside.

"They came down from the roof. Wasn't expecting that." His phone buzzed. "All cool up there?" he said.

"Is that Court?" she asked.

He shook his head, mouthing, "Nate."

"Yeah, I'll tell her." He stuck the phone back in his pocket. "Court's fine. He and Nate will be down as soon as they can."

She wanted to sink to her knees in relief. "I need to do something while we wait. Can we bake a cake? Cook a pie? Anything?"

Madison laughed. "You don't *cook* a pie. I vote for wine and Alex's secret stash of salted caramels."

"Hey, you know about those?" Alex said, narrowing his eyes.

"I know all your secrets, babe." Madison lifted onto her toes and kissed him, then headed for the kitchen.

"You're an evil woman, Mad, stealing my stash."

Lauren smiled as Alex trailed after his wife. She wanted what they had, wanted it with Court. All she had to do was accept Court for who and what he was. Right now, though, she just needed to see for herself that he was unharmed.

Two glasses of wine and a handful of Alex's quickly dwindling caramel stash later, she leaned her head back on the sofa and closed her eyes. "What's wrong with me?"

"You're drunk?" Madison said.

She peeked out of one eye. "No. I mean why can't I accept—"

The front door opened and Court walked in, followed by Nate. She jumped up and ran to Court. He held out his hands, and she leaped into his arms, wrapping herself around him. "You're okay. Oh, God, I was so worried."

"I'm fine. Promise." With her legs still hugging his hips, he carried her to the sofa, keeping her on his lap when he sat.

"Who were they? Why did they break in?" As he told her the details, her heart sank. "And they were supposed to kill you and kidnap me?" Stephan was truly losing his mind.

"But they didn't accomplish either," Court said. "That's the important part. And we kept your name out of it, so you won't have to make any kind of statement."

That was a relief, anyway. "Thank you." Embarrassed she was straddling him in front of his brothers, she scooted off him.

"I, for one, am off to bed," Nate said, standing. He touched her shoulder as he walked past. "Try not to worry, Lauren. Stephan Kozlov's digging his own grave. He's making dumbass mistakes, leaving a trail a three-year-old could follow. Two, three days tops, we'll have him in custody."

She gave Court's brother a grateful smile. "I hope you're right."

"He's always right," Alex said. "Annoying if you ask me."

"No one asked you, baby brother." Nate winked at her.

It had only been a few days ago when she'd thought Nate was cold and intimidating, but he was growing on her. "Can we go home now . . . I mean up to your place?" she asked after Nate left. She wanted time alone with Court to talk about all the things going on in her head.

"Well, that's a problem. They murdered my bed."

"They what?" She blinked, wondering if she'd heard him right.

"I assume that was the gunfire we heard?" Alex said.

"Yep. I'll have to go bed shopping tomorrow." Court looked at her, grinning. "Can I bunk with you tonight?"

"I don't understand? Why would they do that?" Then it hit her, confirming her worst fears about the situations his career required he put himself into. "They thought you were in it."

"But I wasn't." He took her hand, pulling her up with him. "The sun will be up soon. Let's try to get a few hours of sleep."

"I'll return your robe tomorrow . . . Today, I guess I should say," she mumbled to Madison, giving her friend a hard hug.

"No problem." Madison laughed. "Or keep it. I don't care. All that matters is everyone's safe."

Court held her hand as they rode the elevator one floor up, but he didn't speak or even glance at her once. She peeked at him, seeing that he looked tired. Although she'd wanted to talk about tonight and all the things she was feeling, he needed his rest. The things she needed to say could wait a few hours.

When they walked down the hall to the guest room, she noticed the door to his bedroom was closed. She was glad. She didn't want to see his *murdered* bed and imagine him in it while someone was shooting.

"Go on to bed. I'll be there in a few minutes," he said, letting go of her hand.

"Okay." She blinked away tears as she watched him walk away, his bare feet silent on the wood floor. He was a beautiful, amazing man, and he deserved to be loved, and she wanted to be the woman who made him happy. There had to be a way to conquer this fear of losing him that was haunting her.

She crawled into bed, leaving a lamp on for him. A good fifteen minutes passed. What was he doing?

After shoving the mannequin's head back under his bed, Court stripped off the bullet-ridden comforter and sheets. Not wanting Lauren to see his shot-up mattress, he got a flat sheet from the linen closet. Lauren was freaked out enough as it was about his dangerous job without seeing the shredded mattress. As he worked, his resentment grew. Exactly what did she want from him?

One minute she was telling him she couldn't handle the danger he faced, the next, she was wrapped around him, holding on for dear life. He loved her, wanted her, needed her, would give his life for her. But that apparently wasn't good enough.

"To hell with that," he said, heading for the guest room. He stood over her and then pinned her to the bed, and stared into her eyes. "I can't do this, Lauren. This back and forth with you. You want me to leave the FBI? Is that what it's going to take to make you happy?"

"And do what?"

"I don't have a fucking clue. You got any job openings at your bookstore? Need a damn stock boy?"

Tears pooled in her eyes. "Court, please . . ."

"Please what?" He was a bastard, making her cry. He pushed off the bed. "Go to sleep. We'll talk tomorrow." They were both on edge and stressed by the night's events, and he needed to get away from her before he said more hurtful words. He closed the door behind him as he left the room.

The difference between him and his brothers was that he was a long-term planner. Alex lived in the moment, and Nate might plan for tomorrow but fully expected Murphy's Law to turn his plan on its head, which he took in stride.

Court went out onto the balcony, his place to think. Unlike Nate, he didn't find it easy to shrug off derailed plans, and Lauren had unquestionably run his train off the tracks.

As much as he'd tried for six years to forget her, he'd never forgotten how her mouth tasted against his, how soft her skin felt each time he'd trailed his hand over her hips, her stomach, her breasts. The new Lauren tasted just as delicious, but was curvier than her younger self and her face was more mature. She'd lost that inner sparkle that had first attracted him to her, though, and he blamed Stephan Kozlov for that.

The question still plagued his mind. What was he going to do about her? As he watched the sun come up over the ocean, the answer remained as elusive as ever. Thinking of her not being in his life sent an ache straight through his heart. Yet waiting around for her to walk away when all was said and done didn't sit well. If he had to choose between her and the FBI, which would it be? Why couldn't he have both?

Didn't she realize that by not giving them a chance she was letting Stephan win? Maybe Madison could talk some sense into her. He'd stop by the bookstore later, ask his sister-in-law for advice, and maybe some help. In the meantime, he needed to find Lauren's ex-husband before the bastard pulled another stupid stunt.

"Where's Lauren?" Madison asked when he arrived at High Tea and Black Cat Books.

"At my place. She's tired from not getting much sleep last night." He'd told her he had an errand to run, and she'd promised not to leave or answer the door. She'd seemed relieved when he'd said he'd be out for a while, as if she couldn't wait to be rid of him. The tension in the air between them when she'd walked into the kitchen this morning was almost visible.

Still angry with her for not thumbing her nose at her ex-husband and grabbing what she wanted—namely, him—he'd kept his mouth shut. The best thing he could do was give them a few hours apart to think things through, so he'd left.

"Hello, Court," Madison's mother said, walking over and giving him a hug.

"You're beautiful as ever, Angelina." He liked Angelina. She'd had a difficult time after her husband's murder and her twin brother's arrest, but she'd lifted her chin, stiffened her shoulders, and soldiered on. He couldn't help but respect that.

"You Gentry boys could charm the stars right out of the sky." She patted his arm.

"Aw, shucks, Angelina," he drawled. "Run away with me. We'll leave all our troubles behind and travel the world, you and I."

She giggled. "Bring your brothers along, and it's a deal."

"Hey," Madison said, "I don't care if you are my mother. Alex isn't going anywhere without me."

They chatted a few more minutes, and then Angelina left to help a customer. Now that he was here, Court wasn't sure how to ask his questions. "I'm sorry Lauren's not been able to work this week."

"We're managing. The important thing is that she's safe. I just hope you catch Stephan soon so she can get her life back. She's not herself right now."

"No, she isn't." He silently thanked Madison for giving him an opening to ask about Lauren. "Can we talk for a few minutes somewhere private?"

"Sure. Let's go to the office."

He closed the door behind them. "I won't take much of your time, but I don't know who else to talk to. You're her best friend, so I'm hoping you can help me figure out what's going on in her head."

"She's scared. Who wouldn't be?"

"I know, and I get that." He hesitated. Talking about his feelings wasn't something he knew how to do, even with his brothers. Although he didn't doubt he could go to either one with a personal problem, they were guys. They'd just tell him to suck it up or something stupid like that.

"Has something happened between you?" Madison asked.

"Yeah. She said she can't deal with my job. That it's dangerous, and she's worried I'm going to die."

"I know she loves you."

240

"She said that, too, but obviously not enough if she's willing to walk away from what we have." He went to the window and looked out as he collected his thoughts. It was hard to bare his soul, even though Madison was now family. "I don't want to lose her, but if she walks away again, it will be for the last time." He turned, facing her. "I don't care if she changes her mind a week later, I can't . . . I just can't."

It was impossible to explain to Madison how much she'd hurt him that first time, so he didn't even try, but he meant it about no more second chances. If she did leave, she would devastate him all over again, but it would be for the last time.

"Just give her some time, Court. Do something about Stephan so that's off her mind, and then—"

"And then what? She wants me to quit the FBI so she doesn't have to worry about me."

"She said that?"

"Not outright, but that's what she wants."

Madison shook her head. "That's not the answer. You'd end up resenting her for it."

"Probably." He let out a weary sigh. It wasn't fair to expect Madison to have a magic answer that would fix everything. "Did you ever consider that you'd be happier without Alex because of his job?"

She smiled. "Never. Even if I knew I'd only have him for one day, I'd still want him, and I'd thank God for each minute we were blessed with." She put her hand on his arm. "But Court, that doesn't mean Lauren loves you any less. It's because she loves you so much that she's afraid. We just need to figure out how to get her past that."

And how to do that, he hadn't a clue. "I've taken up enough of your time. I guess the only thing I can do is let it play out, see what happens."

"Why don't you tell her you have to go to Aces and Eights for a few hours tonight. I'll get her to come down. We'll order pizza, open a bottle of wine, and have a long talk. Maybe I can help her see how miserable she'd be without you, and that the reward of being with you outweighs the risk."

"I'd appreciate that. I'll get her to call you."

She hugged him. "I really do believe you two are meant for each other. Things will work out. You'll see."

He wasn't so sure about that. "I'm glad Alex was smart enough to marry you. It's nice to have a sister to talk to."

As he walked to his car, his phone buzzed, Lauren's name coming up on the screen. His heart skipped several beats. She only called when there was trouble.

CHAPTER
TWENTY-FIVE

Tired from being up half the night, Lauren decided to take a nap after Court left. It was either that or sit and worry. He hadn't said where he was going, which left her imagination to run wild, wondering if he was out looking for Stephan.

She put her phone on the nightstand, turned on the fan over her bed, crawled under the covers, and closed her eyes. How long was she going to be a prisoner, unable to walk down the street or go to work without worrying that Stephan would show up? She was going stir-crazy and missed being at the bookstore. Missed Hemingway. Was he lonely at night, all by himself in the store? She should talk to Madison about bringing him home in the evenings.

With her mind spinning in a thousand different directions, she gave up on taking a nap. At home when she was worried or restless, she cleaned. No reason she couldn't clean Court's condo. He was a neat guy, didn't leave shoes scattered around or clothes draped over chairs, but she'd noticed a thin layer of dust on the furniture. She found cleaning supplies under the kitchen sink, including furniture polish. Impressive a single guy living alone even had some, much less a bottle of the expensive brand.

She'd finished dusting and polishing the furniture in the living room and was heading to the guest room when her phone rang. Pulling it out of her back pocket, she glanced at the screen to see Julie's name. She smiled as she answered.

"Hey, Jules, this is a nice surprise."

"It's Daddy. Lauren, you have to come to the hospital."

Lauren dropped the furniture polish and cloth on the dresser. "What happened? Which hospital?"

"I don't know what happened. He was working in the yard. I heard yelling, so I went to see who he was talking to. I think he fell and hit his head on a rock. He wouldn't wake up. The ambulance took him to Jackson Memorial. I'm in the emergency room. Th-they won't tell me anything, Lauren." She started to cry.

"I'm on the way, baby. Just hang tight, okay? Call me back if they give you an update." As soon as she disconnected, she grabbed her purse, then ran out the door. When she reached the lobby, she ran up to the doorman. What was his name? George?

"George!" That wasn't right. "Jorge," she corrected. "I need a cab. I mean really fast. My father's in the hospital."

Bless him. Without questioning her, he picked up the phone. After a brief conversation, he said, "There's one two minutes away, Miss Lauren."

"Thank you."

"I will pray for your father."

She nodded her thanks, then ran out to meet the taxi, jumping in as soon as it pulled to a stop. "Jackson Memorial, the emergency entrance. Please hurry." Her phone was still clutched in her hand, and she scrolled to Court's name.

"Something happened to my dad," she said when he answered. "They took him to the emergency room."

"I'll come get you. Be there in ten minutes."

"No, I got a cab. I'm already on the way." At his hesitation, she knew he wasn't happy she hadn't waited for him, but this was her father.

"Which hospital? I'll meet you there."

"Jackson Memorial. You don't have to come if you're busy. I can call you when I know something."

"Dammit, Lauren, is that how little you think of me? I'll see you soon." He disconnected.

Lauren dropped the phone onto her lap. She hadn't meant to insult him, but she had. It was almost as if she were testing him, fully expecting him to get tired of her crap and decide she wasn't worth the effort. Unconsciously, maybe she had been doing that. If he was the one to walk away this time, she wouldn't have to feel guilty for ending the relationship. But if he did leave her, it would crush her.

Everything was so confusing, but right now, her attention needed to be on her father. As the taxi approached the hospital, she frowned, recalling Julie's comment that her father had been yelling at someone. Her dad never yelled. He was soft-spoken, slow to anger, and got along famously with his neighbors. She couldn't think of a soul he would have been arguing with.

She eyed the meter, then pulled out enough money to include a tip, handing it over when the driver came to a stop at the curb. "Thanks," she said as she scooted out of the cab. As she ran for the emergency room entrance, a couple standing next to a car in the parking lot caught her attention.

Her steps slowed, then came to an abrupt halt. "No," she whispered. "Please, God, no."

Run, her brain screamed. *Run*, her heart begged. But she couldn't. Not when Stephan had his hand wrapped around Julie's wrist. With feet that seemed to be encased in concrete, Lauren forced herself to walk to them. When she reached them, she met her sister's terrified eyes, then forced her gaze away, looking for anyone who could help.

"If you call for help, I will hurt her."

She looked at the man she hated with every fiber of her being. "Let her go, Stephan."

He smirked. "I do not think so."

Her ex-husband was a handsome man with his blond hair, sculpted face, and vivid blue eyes. He was also big and strong and cruel. On the ice, he had delighted in giving an opposing player a bloody nose, a black eye, and more than once a broken bone. Unfortunately, he enjoyed hurting people off the ice just as much.

As she studied him, a shudder snaked down her spine. His body had always been muscular, but now his arms and chest rippled with muscles like those of a weight lifter's. He'd had six years with nothing better to do than bulk up, and he'd obviously taken full advantage of whatever equipment had been available to him. Her mouth dried as fear curled its tendrils around her, turning her into a statue and stealing her ability to think.

"He came inside and told me you were in his car." Julie's lips trembled. "He said he would kill you if I didn't come with him."

Lauren tore her gaze away from Stephan's hold. Tears streamed down her sister's cheeks, her eyes pleading with Lauren to do something. Realizing she'd been holding her breath, she sucked air back into her lungs. Only one thing mattered and that was getting Julie to safety. That meant putting herself back into Stephan's punishing hands, and the mere thought of that made her feet want to run. She pushed her toes down, anchoring her shoes to the ground.

Get yourself together, Lauren. She swallowed hard, suppressed another shudder, then forced herself to look straight at Stephan. "Julie said Dad was arguing with someone. It was you, wasn't it?"

"He refused to call you to come home."

"You bastard. What did you do to him?"

He shrugged. "I might have pushed him. Was not my fault his he. hit a rock. After the ambulance took him away, I realized Julie would call you and you would come here." He grinned. "And so, here you are."

"What do you want?"

"Finally, you ask the right question. I want what is mine. You, wife. You owe me, Lauren, and I intend to collect."

Julie whimpered, and Lauren had the urge to whimper right along with her. "Let her go."

He eyed Julie. "Maybe I will keep you both. She reminds me of you when I first met you, when you were still fresh and young."

"I'll kill you before I'll let you touch her." His laugh grated across her skin, and she dug her nails into her palms, the pain welcome, reminding her that she had to be clever if she was to get Julie away from him.

"You do not have the power here, *Ангел*."

Angel. An endearment she hadn't heard in over six years, and one she'd once loved. Before he'd shown her his true self. He lifted the hand he'd been holding behind his leg. Lauren gasped at the gun he held.

"Please, Stephan. I'll do whatever you want, if you'll let her go."

"She cries too much." He put the gun to Julie's head. "She gets on my nerves."

Julie's eyes widened, and then she fell to her knees as her sobs filled the air. Stephan kept one hand wrapped around her wrist, forcing her arm to stay up behind her, while pressing the gun harder against the side of her head.

Lauren bit her teeth down hard on her bottom lip. Why hadn't she brought her own gun? Court had taught her how to kill a man, even if only on a paper target. If she had her gun now, she would shoot Stephan without a second thought. Without even a first thought.

"I'm yours, Stephan." She took a few steps toward him. "But only if you let her go."

"Come closer," he said.

"I will when you let her go."

He glanced from her to Julie, and then back to her. His smile was that of the spider inviting the fly into his web. She knew that smile and what it meant, oh, God, she did. She walked to him anyway. It was the only way he'd let go of Julie. She prayed that was true.

As soon as she was within reach, he pushed Julie away. "Run, Julie," Lauren yelled. Julie crawled across the pavement, still crying, and when she was out of reach of Stephan, Lauren turned to follow her. In her mind's eye, she visualized grabbing Julie by the hand and pulling her to safety. She darted a glance around. Where was a cop when you needed one?

She'd only taken a few steps when she was jerked back by the collar of her T-shirt. Julie struggled to her feet, then stopped. "Go, Julie," Lauren cried as Stephan dragged her away. He tossed her into the backseat of a car, following her in. She scooted to the other side of the seat, reaching for the door handle.

"Do not make me shoot you, Lauren. Do not doubt that I will."

At hearing a chuckle, she looked up to see Peter behind the wheel, peering back at her. "I vote that he shoots you. You are too much trouble."

Lauren dropped her hand from the handle, but stayed pressed against the door. "Why, Stephan? You had your pick of beautiful women. Why me?" That was something she'd always wondered. He'd dated models, an actress even, all gorgeous. Why her? She'd been a nobody, a simple girl living a simple life.

"They were all whores. Wanting only my fame and money. You did not care about any of that. You were sweet and pure." His face distorted. "You made me believe you were pure."

They'd already had the conversation as to her purity on their wedding night, and she had nothing more to say about that. "Where are we going?" she asked as Peter backed the car out of the space.

"To the airport. We are going home."

Oh, God. He really did plan to take her to Russia. The minute they stopped at a light, she would jump out. She would rather risk getting shot than get on a plane with him.

As they drove out of the hospital's parking lot, she peered out the back window. Julie was on her knees, crying, watching them disappear out of sight.

"I love you," she mouthed even though she knew her sister couldn't see her. "Take care of Daddy," she whispered as tears filled her own eyes.

CHAPTER
TWENTY-SIX

Court estimated he was only minutes behind Lauren in getting to the hospital. On the drive over, he'd calmed down considerably since talking to her. She was understandably upset and concerned about her father. He shouldn't have taken her suggestion that he not come to the hospital so personally. Part of it was because he couldn't figure out where he stood with her, and it made him crazy.

A few blocks from the hospital his phone buzzed, his Bluetooth announcing that it was Nate.

"What's up?" he said, answering.

"We got lucky on the car the Kozlovs are driving. It's a rental, a dark blue Buick Regal."

Nate gave him the license plate number, which Court repeated, memorizing it. As he pulled into the hospital's parking lot, looking for a space, he noticed a girl kneeling on the grass, crying. There was something familiar about her, and he drove toward her. When she looked up at his approaching car, he recognized her. Why was Lauren's sister out here alone, crying? Had her father taken a turn for the worse?

Still on the phone with Nate, he quickly briefed him on where he was and why. "Something's wrong. Lauren's sister is kneeling on the grass, bawling her eyes out. Hold on a sec." There weren't any open spaces, so he pulled up behind another car, then got out.

"Julie, remember me? I'm Lauren's friend, Court." Before he could ask what was wrong, she ran to him.

"You have to go get her."

Alarms screamed warnings in his head. "Lauren? Where is she?"

"He took her."

"Stephan? Tell me everything, Julie." He put the phone to his ear. "You hearing this?"

"Yeah," Nate said. "I'm putting a BOLO out on the car right now. Keep the line open so I can hear what she says."

Court put his hand on Julie's shoulder. "We'll find her, okay? I need you to tell me everything that happened."

Between sobs and hiccups, she got the story out. "He had a gun," she said. "Oh, and there was another man driving the car."

Peter. "So Lauren and Stephan are in the backseat?"

She nodded. "Please, you have to find her."

"Listen to me, Julie. I want you to go inside the emergency room." He put the phone to his ear. "Is Taylor available to come stay with her?"

"I talked to her a few minutes ago," Nate said. "She's in the office, catching up on paperwork. I'll send her over there."

"Julie, in about twenty minutes a woman named Taylor Collins is going to come stay with you. She has blonde hair and blue eyes and is very pretty. Until she gets here, don't leave the waiting room, don't talk to anyone but the doctors and nurses. I'll bring Lauren to you. I promise."

Surprising him, she grabbed him, giving him a hug. "Thank you."

Anxious to go, he unwrapped her arms from around his neck. "Go inside." He watched her until she disappeared inside the hospital, then jogged to his car. "Nate, get Rand to try to find the car on camera."

"He's already on it."

"Good. Until he gets a track on them and I hear different, I'm heading toward the airport. Based on the emails, Stephan's plan was to return to Russia with Lauren. He won't want to hang around now that he has her."

"If that's what he's doing, he'll have a private jet lined up."

"Yeah. That's the only way he could get her on a plane without any attention." Court put the blue light on the dash, and then turned his headlights to flashing. "And when I find Stephan Kozlov, it's not going to be pretty."

"I get it, bro. Just remember you're a federal agent who took an oath to uphold the law. I'm in my car heading for the airport, and I've got a helo standing by, ready to take to the air as soon as we have a firm fix on the car. SWAT's gearing up, ready to respond if there's a standoff."

"I'm not sure that's a good idea, overwhelming him like that. I'm guessing he's already decided he won't go back to prison. If he's backed into a corner, he'll take her with him." And that turned his blood to ice. "Just find the damn car."

"I'll go with your decision on this, Court, but they will be standing by should the situation go south. Hold on a sec. I've got another call coming in."

"Get out of the way," Court yelled at the driver ahead of him. As if the man had heard him, the driver glanced in his rearview mirror. Seeing the flashing blue light on the dash, the driver swerved into the right lane. "Thank you." He sped past.

"Rand found them. They're about four miles from the airport," Nate said, coming back on the line.

"I knew it. I'm maybe a mile or less behind them. Gotta go."

"Don't get stupid, Court. I know you want to go in with guns blazing—"

"Actually, no I don't. I'm going in like a fucking cat that the mouse never saw until it was too late." The lane ahead of him was clear, and he accelerated. "End call," he told Bluetooth.

As he sped toward Lauren, he formulated a plan. The trick would be figuring out which plane was waiting to take her to Russia. Minutes later, he spotted the Buick. He turned off his blue light. Still keeping his speed, he passed the car. For a few seconds, he considered ramming them, but Stephan had a gun and if he panicked . . . No, he couldn't go there. Lauren would not feel the pain of a bullet. Court would make damn sure of that.

The hardest thing he'd ever done in his life was race ahead, letting the car Lauren was in go out of his sight. Was she scared right now? Stupid question. Of course she was. He wished he could have blown his horn or something, letting her know he was near.

I'm coming for you, G.G. He swerved around a corner onto the service road that would take him to the private planes. As he drove up to the General Aviation Center, he spied a Gulfstream sitting on the runway, its powerful engines running.

Bingo! Court parked his car, and then ran to the plane. The stairs were down, waiting for its passengers. No one stopped him as he took the steps three at a time. The cabin door was open, and he pulled his badge out of his pocket when the pilot and copilot startled at his appearance.

"Did you file a flight plan for Russia?" he said. When they looked at each other, as if thinking what the hell was happening, he said again, "Did you file a fucking flight plan for Russia?"

"Yes," the copilot said.

"Then you get out of the plane and disappear." He shifted his gaze to the pilot. "I'm your new copilot."

"The hell you are. I don't know you."

Court turned his attention back to the copilot. "You aren't out of this plane in the next ten seconds, I'll see that you spend the next year behind bars."

The man scrambled out of his seat. He gave the pilot an apologetic look. "He has a badge. You don't."

Court pressed against the door, giving him room to get by. "Make yourself invisible. You don't say a word to the people coming to this plane, you don't give them a hint things aren't kosher."

"Got it," the man said.

Satisfied the copilot got his message, Court slid into the seat he'd vacated. "Here's the deal," he said. "The two men who are about to board kidnapped the woman with them. One of them has a gun. You will do everything I say when I say it."

The pilot stared at him with wide eyes. "Are you shitting me, man?"

"I am not. There are federal agents headed this way, but they won't be here in time to stop us from taking off. After we're in the air, you'll announce that you have engine trouble. Can you make it sound like your engines are failing?"

"You swear you're a federal agent? You could be flashing a fake badge, for all I know."

Court took out his phone, dialed the public number for the Miami bureau, putting it on speaker, and holding his cell out to the pilot. "Ask for Special Agent Court Gentry."

When the phone was answered by a woman's voice saying, "Thank you for calling the Miami office of the Federal Bureau of Investigation," the pilot waved a hand.

"Okay, you're real," he said. "Yes, I can make the engines sound like they're failing. Where do you want to land?"

Court pocketed his phone, considering for a moment before saying, "A small airport where there won't be a lot of people. Not too far away. Someplace other agents can catch up with us."

"Opa-locka would work." The pilot glanced at him. "My name's Gabe. Gabe Kerrigan. Just want to go on the record. I'm not going to be happy if there's even one scratch on my plane after this is over."

"Duly noted." Court pulled out a pair of sunglasses from his shirt pocket, sliding them on. "Also, one of the men about to board knows my face, so don't let anyone into the cockpit."

"You're just full of good news, Special Agent Court Gentry."

Court peered around the pilot, watching the approaching car. "Here they come. Greet them at the door. Make sure they don't come in here. Be cool. As far as you're concerned, nothing's suspicious."

"I should have called in sick today," Gabe said as he walked out of the cockpit.

Court called Nate. "You need to go to Opa-locka Airport," he said when his brother answered. "The pilot's going to fake engine trouble after we're in the air, then land there."

"Where the hell are you?"

"In the cockpit. I'm the substitute copilot."

Nate snorted. "Of course you are."

The car stopped, and Peter exited, opening the back door. Stephan stepped out, his hand gripping Lauren's wrist. Court growled. Although he was tempted to end this right now, according to Julie, Stephan had a gun. There were people all over the place who would be in the line of fire. Line crews fueling other planes, other pilots doing preflight checks, and a group of suit-clad men he assumed were waiting for their plane to be ready.

"How much time you need to get everyone in place?" he asked.

"At least thirty minutes. Longer if you can."

"Just keep them out of sight unless the shit hits the fan. If at all possible, I want this to go down quietly."

"Got it. Be careful, bro. I already sat by our baby brother's hospital bed, praying he'd live. I don't want a repeat, you hear?"

"Trust me. I don't plan to end up in a hospital bed. They're about to board. Gotta go." He pocketed his phone, and then waited for the passengers to get settled and the pilot to return to the cockpit.

The trio approached the stairs, Stephan on one side of Lauren, still holding on to her, and Peter on her other side. Stephan wore a lightweight jacket and had his hand in his pocket. Because Lauren wasn't fighting to get away, he assumed Stephan had threatened her. He wished he could let her know he was here.

Lauren tried to pull away from Stephan's grip on her arm. "I can walk up the damn stairs without your help," she said. She'd decided she'd take her chances and had attempted to jump out of the car, even with Stephan pointing a gun at her. Peter had laughed when the door wouldn't open.

"Childproof locks," he said. "Good invention."

As they walked toward the plane, Stephan said, "If you try to get away or warn anyone, I will shoot you and the person you talk to. When we get on the plane, you will not speak to the pilots or I will shoot them."

She didn't know if she believed him. Would he really shoot someone when that would send him right back to prison? If it were just her he'd threatened, she would chance it, but to cause an innocent bystander to be killed? She couldn't risk it. It looked like she was going to Russia.

"Peter, please don't let him do this," she pleaded, hoping he would talk sense into his brother.

Stephan pushed her up the stairs. "Get on the plane, Lauren."

With each step, her heart pounded harder, making it difficult to breathe. Court must realize by now what had happened. He would have talked to Julie when he arrived at the hospital, and would be looking for her. How would he even know where to search? It was too late to regret that she hadn't waited for him to come get her, but all she'd thought about was getting to her father.

Was her dad okay? She was sick with worry about him, sick at the thought of leaving American soil, and sick that she'd ever had any doubts she could live with the danger Court faced. One wrong step, and she could die today. What was the difference, then, between her and Court? He could lose her as easily as she could lose him. All that counted was being with him and being thankful for each day they had together.

The pilot stood just inside the door of the plane. "Welcome aboard," he said as they approached.

For one brief moment, she was sure she smelled Court's scent, but that was only wishful thinking. She paused, wanting to grab the pilot and tell him she was being kidnapped. Stephan must have sensed her thoughts because he pushed her past the pilot with a jab to her back. She was directed to a seat, and Stephan sat next to her on the aisle with Peter across from them. What she really wanted to do was curl up in a ball and cry, but she willed her tears away. She'd be damned if she'd break down in front of her bastard of an ex-husband.

"We'll be taking off in a few minutes," the pilot said, standing a few seats in front of them. "Once we're in the air, I'll let you know when you're free to move around. There are refreshments in the galley. Feel free to help yourself."

The entire time he spoke, giving them emergency procedure instructions, it seemed to her that he was watching her with unusual interest. Should she try to send him a message? If she blinked her eyes real fast, would he catch on? But what if he did? There was nothing he could do without putting himself in danger. To avoid the temptation of trying to signal him, she turned her face to the window.

Once his instructions were finished, the pilot told them to buckle up, and then returned to the cockpit, closing the door behind him. As she waited to hear the plane's engines start, her heart pounding so hard she could hear it in her ears, she wished she'd had a chance to tell Court she'd been wrong.

The engines roared to life, and the plane began to move, taking her away from her home, from her father and sister, from Court. "I'm sorry," she whispered as the landscape grew smaller below her.

"My only regret is that I did not have the opportunity to meet your boyfriend," Stephan said.

She kept her face to the window, ignoring him.

"I fully intended to teach him a lesson for touching what is mine."

She squeezed her eyes closed.

"Did you really think I'd be pleased to hear of your whoring ways?"

When she didn't answer, he put his hand on her sex, squeezing hard. Memories of the night he'd done the same thing when he'd beaten her exploded through her mind like her own personal horror movie . . . featuring a monster named Stephan.

"Are you listening to me, Lauren?" He squeezed harder.

No, she wasn't listening to him. She bit down hard on her bottom lip to keep from giving him the reaction he wanted. He had always liked seeing her afraid of him. It had taken her a while, but she'd finally figured out that it was the power over her he craved.

And then there was Peter. He sat across from her, watching her as if she were a science project he couldn't figure out. Well, she'd never been able to figure him out either. He was more contained than Stephan, held his thoughts and feelings closer. Although Stephan's temper was explosive, she believed Peter was more dangerous, but in a stab-you-in-the-back way. She hated them both, and that hate was growing with each minute they traveled farther away from all that she loved.

She pushed Stephan's hand away. He chuckled, letting her know that he'd allowed her to do that. "You won't get away with this," she said. "Either one of you."

"We already have, wife."

"I. Am. Not. Your. Wife." When he smirked, she wanted to slap him, but she turned back to the window. He hated it when she ignored him, so she'd do just that. How hard was it going to be to escape and get out of Russia? How was he even getting her into the country? She'd never gotten a passport. She had to assume they had a plan. The only way she could figure was that they'd bribed some official to look the other way. It was also possible Peter had obtained a fake passport for her.

Suddenly, the engine noise changed. It sounded like one of the engines was shutting down, then restarting. She frowned as she stuck her face to the window, trying to see what was happening. She'd noticed when walking up to the plane that the two engines were back by the tail. It was impossible to see them, but the plane gave a little bounce, and then whichever engine was having a problem quit and didn't come back on.

Her earlier thought returned. She'd been worried about Court dying, but it was going to be her. Stephan had taken her phone away earlier, so she couldn't even call Court and tell him how wrong she'd been. That she'd consider each day she had with him a blessing. *I love you, Court. I hope you know that.*

"This is your pilot. We have a problem with our left engine and will have to return to Miami. Rest assured we can land with one engine, so there is nothing to worry about. Please stay in your seats and keep your seat belts on."

Stephan and Peter began to speak to each other in Russian, their conversation sounding agitated. She trusted the pilot when he'd said landing with one engine wasn't a problem. That they were returning to Miami was the best news she could have received. It would be her last chance to escape.

CHAPTER
TWENTY-SEVEN

"If I didn't know better, I'd think we really were having engine trouble," Court said as the pilot banked the plane to return to Miami. "Is there any reason I can't use my phone?"

"Not really. Make your call, but finish it before we land."

Court called Nate. "It's me. I've got you on speaker so the pilot can hear. His name's Gabe Kerrigan. We're headed back now," he said. "We should be landing in Opa-locka in . . ." He glanced at Gabe.

"Twenty minutes."

"Since we're coming in for a supposed emergency landing, I think you could put some of the SWAT team guys on a fire truck and also have some pose as airport personnel."

"Gabe, give me five minutes to talk to the tower so they know what's going down before you radio in," Nate said.

"Will do," Gabe said. "I think you're right about one of the men having a gun. He kept his hand in his pocket when they were boarding."

Court nodded. "Nate, the trick will be separating Lauren from the Kozlovs. Peter will recognize me, so I'm going to have Gabe handle the evacuation. He'll send her down the stairs first. You grab her and get her to safety."

"I'll be one of the firemen," Nate said. "Hopefully, Lauren will keep cool when she sees me and not give the game away."

"I think she's smart enough to know to keep quiet, but be prepared for anything. See you on the ground." He disconnected. "You good with your role?" he asked Gabe.

"Beats flying to Russia. Wasn't looking forward to that."

"You flown there before?"

"I speak Russian, so yeah, quite a few times when we get a charter for this route. Twice for one of the men back there. Last time, he brought another guy back with him."

Court would bet his paycheck that had been Vadim. "You've done well. Just keep on keeping your cool. The objective is separating them from the woman."

"They really kidnapped her, huh?"

"Let's say they're trying to."

"She someone important? She worth a big ransom or something?"

She was worth all the money in the world. "No. The man's obsessed with her."

Gabe shook his head. "Don't get that. One woman's pretty much as good as another."

Court disagreed, but he kept his opinion to himself.

"Time to put this baby on the ground and rescue a lady in distress," Gabe said.

As the pilot communicated with the tower, Court leaned back in his seat, closed his eyes, and mentally visualized how the operation would go down. He considered the different things that could go wrong and how he should react. By the time the wheels touched down on the runway, he was ready to rescue his lady in distress.

When Gabe stopped the plane at the end of the runway, several fire trucks and emergency vehicles headed toward them, along with a few cars with the airport's logo on them.

"Go do your thing, Gabe. Remember, you want to get the woman out of the plane first. As soon as that happens, I'm going to step past you. When I do, you park your ass back in the cockpit, where you'll stay until I say you can come out."

"Got it." The pilot unbuckled his harness. "I'll *so* get free beers off this story when all's said and done."

"First one's on me if you pull this off. Leave the cockpit door open so I can hear what's going on."

Court was impressed with the man and how well he'd adapted when his plane was being taken over. Standing back and letting an untrained civilian take the lead wasn't at all to Court's liking, but it couldn't be helped. The plan was a good one and should go off without a hitch. Which was exactly why he was on edge. What should be easy often wasn't.

Keeping his face averted, Court slipped over into the pilot's seat so he could see out the window where the emergency vehicles had come to a stop. Nate stood on the bottom step, outfitted in a fireman's uniform. Rand Stevens, also impersonating a fireman, was jogging up the stairs. Alex leaned against the hood of a fuel truck. Their SWAT team members were scattered among a few people he didn't recognize.

Reassured his team was here, he returned his attention to what was going on inside the plane. He'd give anything for a camera mounted in the cabin. At least he could hear the conversation between the pilot and passengers. He had to give Gabe credit. There was no waver in his voice, no hint that all was not as it should be.

"Did I not promise we could land safely on one engine?" Gabe said, a hint of humor in his voice. "I won't know whether we can continue on in this plane or if we'll have to wait for a replacement until maintenance takes a look at the engines. There's a very nice passenger lounge at this airport where you can wait. As soon as I know more, I'll give you an update."

"Why did we not return to Miami International?"

Court wasn't sure which brother was talking, but it was a question he would have asked, too.

"Because of the emergency landing, Mr. Kozlov, we were diverted here. It's a smaller airport and not as much of a problem if one of their runways is shut down until the plane can be moved."

Good answer, Gabe.

"We will stay in the airplane until you report back your intentions," one of the brothers said.

Come on, Gabe, give them a reason why they can't.

"Sorry. No can do. They won't tow the plane to maintenance until everyone is off." There was a slight screech as the cabin door opened. "Ladies first."

This was it. Court tensed. As soon as Lauren was off the plane, he would be able to breathe again.

"No, my brother goes off first, next my wife, and then me."

Shit. He was ready to kill Stephan Kozlov where he stood. *She's not your wife, asshole.* There had been no sound from Lauren all this time. She had to be frightened out of her mind. How could he let her know he was here?

Lauren tried to pull her arm away from Stephan's hold, but he dug his fingers into her skin. She winced, which no doubt pleased her ex. How was she going to get away if he wouldn't let her out of his sight? But somehow she would because she was *not* getting back on this plane or any other bound for Russia.

She glanced at the pilot, who was looking back at her with concern. Was he suspicious that something wasn't right? If so, that was good and bad. He could be an ally, but that could get him killed. As much as she longed to signal him somehow, she couldn't bring herself to do it. Stephan was edgy, and there was no telling what he'd do if he caught on. She smiled, hoping that would allay any worries the pilot might have about her.

"Well, my mama taught me ladies always go first, but whatever," the pilot said. "The sooner everyone's off the plane, the sooner we can get it to maintenance."

Someone in the cockpit—the copilot?—started humming "Just the Way You Are." Her heart stuttered. It sounded just like Court, but that was impossible. Who else would hum that song at this precise moment, though? She had thought for a brief moment on boarding that she'd caught a whiff of his scent. Could he really be on the plane?

"Who is that?" Stephan asked.

The pilot glanced behind him, a frown on his face. "My copilot. He tends to hum when he's bored."

A fireman appeared in the open doorway. "Everyone okay here?"

Lauren eyed the man. She couldn't remember his name, but she'd danced with him at Alex and Madison's wedding several months earlier. Since he didn't give any indication of knowing her, she didn't show any sign of recognition. Was he really a fireman, or was he an FBI agent like Court and his brothers?

Almost certain that was Court in the cockpit and the fireman wasn't a fireman, she felt her knees almost buckle in relief. Somehow Court had done the impossible and put himself on the plane before they'd even boarded. The humming stopped, and although she realized he'd only done it to let her know he was here and it was better not to raise Stephan's suspicions, she wished he'd keep doing it because it soothed her nerves.

Next to her, Stephan tensed, as if suspecting something wasn't right. He glanced at his brother, and a message passed between the two of them. She needed to act before they had a chance to think things through and decide there really was something going on.

"Well, I for one am getting off this plane. Where's the ladies' room?" She jerked her arm away, but before she could step away from Stephan, he wrapped his arm around her waist, pulling her against him.

"You stay with me, wife." He nuzzled her ear while pushing the barrel of the gun he had in his pocket into her spine.

Lauren shuddered. Sweat pooled under her arms and down her back. She'd been raised to believe God heard prayers, so she prayed that no one would die because of her.

"Out, all of you," the pilot yelled, as if he'd lost patience with them. Then he stepped into the cockpit, disappearing from view.

The fireman-hopefully-FBI-agent didn't flinch at the pilot's outburst. He kept his gaze steadily on her. She widened her eyes, asking him what she should do now.

He stepped inside the plane. "Glad to see everyone's okay. I imagine an emergency landing is frightening, but you're nice and safe now. The ground crew's waiting to tow the plane, but can't do that until you leave." He held out his hand. "Ma'am, I'll help you down the stairs."

"Thank you." She reached for him, had her fingers on his.

"No," Stephan said. He poked her back again, reminding her that he had a gun. "Peter, we will follow you down."

The fireman smiled as he stepped back. "See you at the bottom, then."

Peter muttered something in Russian, then stepped out. Stephan pushed her forward. At the doorway, the sun hit her eyes, and she paused, halfway out, blinking against the bright light.

"Oomph."

At hearing someone grunt behind her, she glanced over her shoulder, trying to see inside the airplane. Another grunt sounded as two men wrestled in the confines of the cabin. They rolled over the seats, and she caught a glimpse of Court's face before they fell to the floor. She almost cried out, but snapped her mouth closed, realizing she would distract Court.

They were fighting over the gun, Court holding it away as Stephan tried to point it at him. Not only was Stephan bigger and bulkier than Court, he knew how to play dirty. Lauren looked around for something she could hit Stephan over the head with.

Suddenly, she was shoved from behind, causing her to stumble into the plane. Peter tried to push past her, but then he seemed to jerk back. On her knees, she glanced behind her to see Nate and the pretend fireman hauling Peter down the stairs. The pilot stood at the door to the cabin, watching the men fight.

"Do something," she said.

"He's got a gun. I'll just make things worse." He grabbed her hand, pulling her up. "You're going to distract the FBI man. Get in the cockpit."

The plane's galley was right in front of her, and she headed for it. The heaviest thing she could find was a bottle of wine. She grabbed it, hefting it in her hand. It should put a nasty bump on Stephan's head when she smashed it on his skull.

Back in the cabin, she watched for a chance to knock Stephan out. With his hands still wrapped around Stephan's wrist, forcing the gun away, Court somehow managed to hook a leg around Stephan's, flipping him over, and then straddling him. Their heads were facing her, and if Court would only lean away, she could slam the bottle down on Stephan's forehead.

Stephan twisted his head, looked straight at her, and then his lips lifted in a smile so disturbing that she shivered. Suddenly, a loud crack filled the air. It took a second to process that Stephan had pulled the trigger. It took another second to feel the sting in her leg. The wine bottle fell from her grasp and rolled down the floor toward the two men. She rubbed her palm over the burning pain. When she lifted her hand, she stared stupidly at the blood running down her fingers.

The bastard had meant to shoot her, had tried to carry out his promise that if he couldn't have her, no one would. She fell to her knees, reaching for the dropped bottle. By the time she finished with him, Stephan was going to wish he'd never laid eyes on her.

"Get her out of here," Court yelled.

She lifted her gaze to see him staring at her. Before she could tell him not to worry about her, that he needed to concentrate on Stephan, she was pulled against a hard body. As she was dragged out of the plane, her last glimpse was of Stephan wrestling his gun free of Court's hold.

"Let me go." She glanced up at Nate. "I'm okay. You have to help Court."

He tossed her into Alex's arms, then raced back up the stairs. Before he reached the top, another gunshot sounded. Lauren stared at the doorway as Nate disappeared into the plane, tears falling down her face.

"Please let him be okay," she whispered. "Please, God."

"He's too mean to die," Alex muttered. "He better be too damn mean."

Court wasn't mean. He was everything a man should be. Honorable, caring, hardworking. And he loved her. But as she stood on the tarmac, not knowing what was happening inside that plane, whether Court was hurt or worse, it confirmed the truth she'd been coming to accept. She would take even one day with Court if that were all they were blessed with over not having him at all.

"These guys need to take a look at your leg," Alex said, picking her up and carrying her to a stretcher where EMTs waited.

She grabbed his hand. "I'm fine. Go see to Court."

"He would want me to stay with you."

"Please. What if he's shot? Go to him, Alex."

He glanced over at the plane. "He better not be."

He called to the fireman. "This is Rand. He's one of us. He'll stay with you."

One of the EMTs poked at her thigh. "The bullet's still in her leg. We need to get her to the hospital."

Lauren gritted her teeth when the EMT prodded at the wound. Her leg was throbbing, but she didn't want him to know how badly it hurt. They'd want to take her to the hospital. She needed to be here for Court.

"Don't leave her side," Alex said to Rand, then raced to the plane. Against her protests, the EMTs shoved the stretcher into the back of an ambulance.

"You can ride up front with me," one of the EMTs said to Rand.

"Please, don't leave," she said to the one who got into the back with her. "He might need you more than me."

"Who's he, love?" the man said with a Spanish accent as he pressed a square of gauze to her leg.

"Court Gentry. He's an FBI agent. I think he might have been shot." She tried to push his hand away. "He's special," she whispered as the ambulance sped away.

CHAPTER
TWENTY-EIGHT

Court reached for the wine bottle rolling toward him. Stephan Kozlov was a mean sonofabitch and outweighed him by a good thirty pounds or more, but Court had rage on his side. The fucker had shot Lauren.

When he'd been sure Lauren was on her way out of the plane, he'd jumped out of the cockpit, deciding that the risk of taking Stephan down using the element of surprise outweighed letting him walk down the steps, still in control. He'd expected a fight. The man was obsessed beyond all reason with having Lauren.

Because of his strength, Kozlov managed to angle the gun at Court's chest. It was too confined in the cabin to use his martial arts skills or this fight would have already ended. Court grabbed the bottle, bringing it up and smashing it down with all his might on the man's head. The gun went off, the bullet whizzing past Court's ear, and then the weapon fell out of Stephan's hand. That was too damn close. Before Court could grab it, Nate whisked it away.

"Should I shoot him? He tried to kill you. I think I should shoot him."

Court pushed up. "If anyone's going to shoot him, it's going to be me. You're the one who said to remember I'm sworn to obey the law where this asshole's concerned." He glanced down at the unconscious man. "Get him out of my face before I really am tempted to put him out of his misery."

Alex ran up behind Nate. "Bro, are you okay?"

"I'm fine. Where's Lauren?"

"With the EMTs."

He glanced out the doorway. "Where?"

"They took her to the hospital."

Court glared at Alex. "You should have stayed with her."

"Rand's with her. She insisted I come see if you'd been shot."

He held out his hand. "One of you gimme your keys. I have to get to the hospital. You two can deal with this piece of shit and his scumbag brother."

Alex tossed his car keys to him. "Go see about your lady. We got this covered."

"Call me later," Nate said.

He lifted a hand in acknowledgment as he ran down the stairs.

"Lauren Montgomery," Court said to the emergency room receptionist. "She was brought in with a gunshot wound."

The woman typed Lauren's name on her keyboard. "She's being prepped for surgery."

"Where is she? I need to see her."

"Are you family?"

"I'm her fiancé." He eyed her name tag. "She thinks I was shot, too. Please, Debra. She needs to know I'm okay." Her eyes widened.

Apparently, Debra thought she had a Bonnie and Clyde on her hands because she scooted her chair back, putting more distance between them. Court was losing his patience. Time to bring out the big gun. He whipped out his badge, setting it on the counter. "Where is she?"

The badge seemed to reassure her—she walked her chair back to the counter. "Is she really your fiancée? Not someone you're going to arrest while she's on the operating table?"

"Yes, Debra. She really is my fiancée." He leaned toward her. "Swear you won't tell her I said this, but I will arrest her and put her in protective custody if it means keeping her safe."

That got him a smile and directions to the surgery department. "Thank you." He took a few steps, then returned to the counter. "Her father was brought in earlier today. Can you tell me if he was admitted? William Montgomery."

She keyed in his name. "Yes, he was. The Montgomery family doesn't seem to be having a good day."

"I intend to see that their day gets better." After getting William's room number, he went in search of Lauren. Unfortunately, they'd already taken her into surgery. His pleading to get an update on her condition fell on deaf ears since he wasn't family, nor did his badge impress the nurse. All she'd tell him was that the patient wasn't in critical condition. Although he knew that, it was a relief to hear it.

While he waited for Lauren to come out of surgery, he decided to go see Lauren's father. The elevator door opened and he got in, not realizing it was going down instead of up. When it reached the lobby, he noticed a gift shop. He should get something to take to William.

A shelf with green plants caught his attention, and he headed for it. He picked up one in a pretty blue pot, and as he carried it to the cashier, he noticed a display of stuffed animals. Sitting on the floor was a huge teddy bear with a heart-shaped patch sewn on its chest with the words *I love you*. When he picked it up, the damn thing came to his waist.

Ten minutes later, he walked into William's room, the bear draped over one arm and the plant in his hand. Julie—her eyes red and puffy from crying—sat by her father's bed, holding his hand. Court glanced at William and saw that he was asleep. As soon as Julie noticed him, she jumped up. He set the plant next to another one already on a shelf.

"Where's Lauren?" Julie whispered.

He motioned for her to follow him into the hallway. When she gave the bear a puzzled look, he said, "It's for Lauren. She's going to be okay, but she was shot in the leg and is in surgery right now."

"Stephan shot her?" At his nod, she scowled. "I hope you killed him."

Court swallowed a grin. Bloodthirsty little thing. "No, but he and his brother will go to prison for a very long time."

"Well, that's something, anyway. Are you sure she's okay? Can I see her?"

"I'm hoping you can get more information from the nurse than I was able to since you're family. How's your father?"

She glanced into the room. "He has a concussion, so they're holding him overnight. He should be able to go home tomorrow."

"Can you leave him for a few minutes?"

"Yeah. If he wakes up, he'll think I'm either in the cafeteria or in the waiting room, watching TV."

"Good. Let's go see what you can find out." Still carrying the bear, he led her to the elevator.

"Where did Stephan take her?"

"His intention was to take her to Russia with him. I wasn't about to let that happen." He told her a scaled-down version of the events.

"Wow. So you're an FBI agent. That's totally cool."

He wished her sister thought so. A different, friendlier nurse was at the desk. Julie found out that Lauren should be out of surgery in about thirty minutes, and then she'd be in recovery until they moved her to a room.

"Why don't you go back and stay with your dad. As soon as your sister's coherent enough to talk, I'll come get you." He wanted to see Lauren alone first, find out what was going on in her head. There was a good chance she'd tell him she couldn't be with him, but he'd already decided he'd just have to change her mind.

An hour later, a nurse and a man in scrubs rolled a gurney past the waiting room. Court's eyes zeroed in on the patient's pink-tipped hair. He gathered up the teddy bear, dropped the cup of god-awful coffee into a wastebasket, and then followed them.

"How is she?" he asked the nurse, the same one who'd given Julie an update.

"She'll be groggy when she wakes up. The doctor will stop by later to check on her. He'll give you an update." The man wearing scrubs, who Court now realized was an orderly, left, and once he was gone, the nurse said, "Her leg will hurt for a while, but she'll be fine."

Court let out a relieved breath. He'd been afraid that she'd have permanent damage. Now all he could do was wait for her to wake up. He pulled up a chair, set the bear on his lap, and closed his eyes. Although he was determined to find a way to get her past her fears, he hadn't a clue how to go about that.

They'd certainly had an odd relationship, falling in love so fast when they were young, and then not seeing each other for six years. Now that she was back in his life, he didn't want to lose her. He needed a plan.

Alex had won Madison back by kidnapping her and taking her on a romantic getaway. A bit drastic, but it had worked. Court didn't see that working with Lauren after all she'd gone through. He needed something bigger, something that would prove to her that he'd do whatever it took to keep her. There was only one thing he could think of that would make her happy. Did he love her enough to make the sacrifice?

What was that antiseptic smell? Lauren tried to open her eyes, but someone had glued them shut. She tried again, finally forcing them open. She yelped. There was a bear sitting in a chair staring at her. Blinking to clear her vision, she pushed herself up.

Everything came flooding back, Stephan kidnapping her, getting shot, her worry about Court. She needed to find someone who could tell her if he was okay. When she moved her legs to get out of the bed, pain shot up her leg.

"Ah, that hurts," she moaned, pressing her hand against her thigh.

"You shouldn't be moving around," the bear said.

She was obviously hallucinating. What kind of drugs had they given her? "Bears don't talk," she muttered. The bear stood, but the fog that had clouded her eyes cleared, and it was a relief to realize it was a giant teddy bear being held by a man. She studied the forearm wrapped around the bear.

"Court?"

He peeked around the bear's head. "Who did you think it was?"

"A talking bear."

"Oo-kay. I think you're still a little loopy, G.G."

"You weren't shot?" She reached for his hand, ending up with a bear paw instead. "Why are you carrying around a teddy bear?"

"No, I wasn't shot." He held the bear away, studying it. "He's a handsome devil. I got him for you."

"Why?" Hurt flashed in his eyes before he blinked them, and she regretted her question. It was still a puzzle why he'd bought her a giant bear.

"Because he bears an important message."

Her eyes settled on the heart-shaped patch, and then she looked up at him. "Is the message from the bear or you?"

"It's from me." He set the bear back on the chair, then eased onto the edge of the bed, being careful not to bump her leg as he took her hand. "I love you, Gorgeous Girl. I have from the day I watched you plant your face in the sand and come up laughing."

"You just liked my sexy green bikini."

"That, too." He glanced down at their joined hands. "I don't want to leave the FBI, but I will if that's what it takes. What if I asked for a transfer instead? I'd make a good analyst. That will probably mean a relocation, so will you come with me? If that's not good enough, I'll resign."

Two days ago, she would have jumped at his offer, although she would hate leaving her family and the bookstore. Even now, she was tempted because if he were sitting behind a desk, he would be safe. He would hate sitting behind a desk, though, and he'd be miserable if he left the FBI. She couldn't do that to him.

"When Stephan pointed a gun at me and I knew he intended to kill me, it solidified something I'd been thinking about." She turned her palm up, linking their fingers. "I worried about losing you when you could have just as easily lost me."

He scrunched his eyebrows together. "What are you saying?"

"That I love you. No conditions. The FBI is in your blood, and I don't want to take that away from you. It would change who you are. I love you, Special Agent Court Gentry."

Hope flared in his eyes. "Are you sure? I swear, Lauren, don't pull my chain on this. I mean it when I say I'll quit or take an analyst position if that's what it takes to make you happy."

"*You* make me happy, just you." She glanced away from his penetrating eyes. "If you still love me, that is."

He put his finger under her chin, lifting her face. "Look at me, G.G. I told you six years ago that I loved you. I told you two minutes ago that I still love you. I don't say things I don't mean. Not then. Not now." He leaned forward and kissed her.

Lauren closed her eyes with a sigh. She inhaled his familiar scent, soaked up the heat radiating from his body, and shivered as his lips fluttered across hers like butterfly wings. It was the sweetest kiss a man had ever given her.

"Stop molesting the patient."

"Go away, bro," Court said, his mouth curving into a smile against her lips.

She pushed away from Court, her cheeks heating as Alex walked to her bed, Nate stepping up behind him. Both Court's brothers smiled at her, and it was the first time she really felt that Nate accepted her.

"We thought you'd like to know that Peter is spilling his guts, hoping for leniency," Nate said. "Stephan will go away for a very long time, considering the charges against him. Kidnapping, attempted murder, assaulting a federal agent for a start. Also, according to Peter, both he and Stephan were involved in extortion and racketeering before Stephan went to prison."

"Thank you. That's the best news you could have given me. Will Peter go to prison, too?" He deserved to.

Alex shrugged. "Don't know. His lawyer's angling for deportation back to Russia in exchange for information. Supposedly he has a lot of dirt on some bad guys on the FBI's radar. Guess we'll have to wait and see how it all goes down. He'll either go to prison or be deported with no chance of ever returning to the good old USA."

"Either way, they'll never be a threat to you again." Court squeezed her hand. "You'll probably have to testify at some point."

"Bring them on." She looked forward to facing Stephan in a courtroom. She'd done it once, and she'd enjoy it even more this time.

Court grinned. "That's my girl."

"Any other questions?" Nate asked.

"Yeah, when can I get out of here?"

CHAPTER TWENTY-NINE

Eight months later...

They'd met at the beach and would get married at the beach. Court glanced at his watch again. In four hours, he and Lauren would exchange vows. About damn time. It had taken seven years for them to get to this day, and he wanted to get the wedding over so they could start on their honeymoon.

"I think the battery in my watch is slowing down."

Alex snorted. "Your battery is fine. You're just anxious to put a ring on her finger."

"Truth." Court lifted his bottle of beer, taking a swallow. It was Sunday, the day they always closed Aces & Eights. Madison, her mother, and Julie had kicked him out of his condo this morning. Apparently, it took all day to get a bride ready for her wedding. Who knew? He'd talked his brothers into hanging out with him for a few hours, and after lunch, with nowhere else to go, they'd ended up at Aces & Eights.

"Nah," Nate said. "He's anxious to get the wedding over so he can get to the honeymoon."

Court clicked his bottle against Nate's. "An even bigger truth."

"Your turn's next, big brother," Alex said.

Nate choked on the beer he'd just swallowed. "No. It isn't."

"Come on." Alex waggled his eyebrows. "You and Taylor?"

"There is no *me and Taylor*. I don't know why you keep implying there is. She's a friend. Nothing more."

"Right."

Court could tell by Alex's sarcastic retort that he still believed there was something going on between Nate and Taylor. Court hadn't made up his mind. He didn't care. He just wanted to get married. If their mother were still alive and knew his wedding was today, would she have wanted to come?

"Where do you think our mother is right now?"

"I wish I knew," Alex said.

When Nate didn't comment, Court glanced at him. His big brother was an expert at blanking his face. Ever since he'd come to the conclusion that he'd been wrong about their mother, Court had wanted to tell his brothers the secret he'd kept all these years. It was time to do that.

How would they react? He took a deep breath. "There's something I want to tell you that happened the day she left us."

Alex set his beer down, his eyes searching Court's. "Why do I think you're about to turn my world on its head?"

"Because I am." He met Nate's gaze. "You've always refused to talk about her, and I think you're keeping your own secrets. Maybe it's time we get everything in the open."

Nate's lips thinned. "I'm not harboring any secrets, nor do I want to hear yours."

When he stood, Alex hooked his leg under Nate's, pulling his feet out from under him. "Sit down, bro. I don't know what the fuck your problem is, but you're going to listen to what he has to say even if I have to tie you to your chair. We had a mother who loved us. That much I know. Yeah, she walked out on us, but if he knows a reason good enough that I can forgive her for leaving us in that bastard's hands, I want to hear it."

"And if I don't?"

"Tough shit. Listen anyway." Alex nodded at Court. "Go ahead."

What the hell was Nate's problem? Court took another deep breath. This wasn't going to be easy to get through. "That morning, before she left, I ripped my pants and was hiding behind the couch from the old man." He relayed the story he'd kept to himself all these years.

"When I realized that I had everything wrong about why Lauren cut me out of her life six years ago, I started thinking about that day and the possibility that I'd also been wrong about our mother. She was no more a whore than I'm the Easter Bunny. Unless she lost the baby, we have a sister or brother out there somewhere."

When he finished, he searched his brothers' faces. Alex seemed stunned. And Nate? Court couldn't tell what was going through his mind. "Say something, one of you."

"We have to find out," Alex finally said.

"I plan to." He met Nate's gaze. "Don't you want to know?"

"Raising you two clowns was more than enough for me. Do what you have to do, but leave me out of it." He stood, then scowled at Alex. "Knock my legs out from under me one more time, and I'll take you down."

"Damn," Alex muttered after Nate walked out. "What's his problem?"

Court didn't know, but something was eating at his big brother. "Wonder if he'll show up for my wedding?"

"Are you nervous? I'm nervous. I've never officiated a daughter's wedding before."

Lauren smiled at her dad. "I've waited too many years for this day. No, I'm not nervous because Court and I were meant to be."

He took her hand, then reached for Julie's, bringing the three of them together in a circle. "I wish your mother were here to see her beautiful daughter on her wedding day."

"Me, too," she whispered.

"No, don't cry," he said at seeing the tears pooling in her eyes. He smiled at Julie, her eyes also teary. "Either of you. I know she's watching right now with that beautiful smile of hers on her face."

"She would have loved Court." Lauren knew that in her heart.

"Yes, she would have." He hugged her, then said, "I need to get out there. I love you, daughter. You couldn't have chosen a better man to love, and this time I'm saying that knowing in my heart it's true."

Lauren held her father close for a moment. "It is. I love you, too. See you in a few minutes."

Court and her father—although as different as night and day—had spent time together the past few months and had formed a bond that had surprised her. Her guess was that for Court, her dad—who continued to call him son—filled a role he'd longed for since he was a boy. Sometimes she had to brush tears away when watching them together, talking and laughing, Court doing his best not to let a curse word slip and occasionally failing.

After her father left, she walked to the mirror that had been set up in the cabana. "Where's my lipstick?"

Julie handed her the tube. "I hope I look as beautiful as you on my wedding day. If Daddy marries me and my future husband . . ." She sighed. "I wish I knew who he was. Anyway, if he does, will you give me away?"

"I would be honored to." When she'd married Stephan, she'd wanted her father to give her away, so a minister friend of his had performed the ceremony. Considering how that marriage had turned out, she'd wanted her dad to marry her and Court. In her mind, his pronouncing them husband and wife seemed the right thing to do. Like a blessing—she was getting it right this time.

Since her father was officiating, she'd decided the best person to give her away was her sister. Unusual, but so was getting married barefoot. The beach was special to her and Court, since that was where they'd first fallen in love.

A section behind the hotel where the reception would be held had been roped off for the wedding party. All the guests were barefoot, their shoes left on the deck already set up for dinner and dancing.

Lauren took one last glance in the mirror. She'd fallen in love with the ankle-length white slip gown the minute she saw it. It was slit up to her knee, showing a little leg when she walked. Her only jewelry was her mother's diamond stud earrings and the diamond tennis bracelet Court had given her for her birthday. She'd intended to do away with the pink tips in her hair, but Court had begged her not to.

"I'll think I'm marrying the wrong woman without them," he'd said.

Madison came into the cabana, and handed her an oblong velvet box. "A wedding gift from the groom."

Inside was a sterling silver bracelet with a tiny heart dangling from the chain, a purple stone in the middle of the heart. It was pretty, but she'd prefer to wear only the tennis bracelet. It was a gift from the man she loved, though. She took it out of the box, then held out her arm. "Would you put it on me?"

Madison rolled her eyes. "It's an anklet, silly."

"Oh. That's so cool. Did you help him pick it out?"

"Nope. I suggested an anklet because you'd be barefoot, but he picked it out all by himself." Madison knelt and hooked it around her ankle on the side with the split in the gown. "And, it's platinum, not silver, so don't lose the damn thing."

Lauren held out her foot, admiring the anklet. It was the perfect wedding gift. She smiled, thinking how she'd thank Court appropriately later tonight. "I'm ready to go get married."

She followed Madison and Julie out of the cabana. Along with giving her away, Julie would serve as her maid of honor, and Madison was her bridesmaid. Both wore pale purple gowns and carried bouquets of lavender. Lauren had chosen a bouquet of white orchids with purplish-pink-tipped petals for herself. Nate and Alex would stand with Court, all three barefoot in their tuxes. There was something crazy sexy about that.

November was the perfect time for a South Florida beach wedding. She slipped her arm through her sister's as they walked past the guests seated in white folding chairs. The weather was beautiful, and a flutist sat off to the side, her music hauntingly beautiful. A crowd had gathered outside the roped-off area, many taking pictures on their phones.

When Lauren caught her first glimpse of Court, she wondered if it were possible for her heart to burst from happiness. His lips curved into a beautiful smile, and then his gaze traveled over her. When she reached him, she flashed her leg, showing him she wore the anklet. His smile turned wicked, the heat in his eyes sending a delicious shiver down her spine.

"Who gives this woman to be married to this man?" her father asked.

"I and my father do," Julie said, smiling at their dad, who beamed with pleasure at being unexpectedly included.

Lauren squeezed Julie's arm in approval. Julie put Lauren's hand on Court's, and then stepped to the side. Court brought her hand to his lips, and placed a kiss on her fingers while holding her gaze. That hadn't been in the rehearsal either, but the gesture made her knees weak. He never let go of her hand after that.

Later that night, she danced under the moon with her husband, at times wanting to pinch herself to make sure she wasn't dreaming.

On the day she'd given him up to protect him, she'd thought he would never be hers again. Had believed she'd never again know his touches, his kisses, never see the heat in his eyes when he looked at her.

"What are you thinking, my wife?" he whispered into her ear, pulling her closer. "I like saying that by the way. *Wife.* I'm going to keep you up all night just so I can say, *Come for me, wife.* So what are you thinking?"

"I don't remember." How was she supposed to think when he said things like that? "You did that on purpose." But there was something she was thinking. Stephan had called her *wife* as a way to remind her that he owned her. It was funny—although nothing related to Stephan was funny—how Court calling her wife made her feel special and loved, knowing her new husband would never think he owned her.

He chuckled, his breath tickling her neck. "Yeah, I like messing with your mind."

"Maybe I'll just go to sleep, *husband.* It's been a long day," she teased, smiling up at him. She liked calling him husband, a word she'd never used with affection where Stephan was concerned.

"Like hell you will."

"Then you'll just have to find ways to keep me awake." She licked his neck, smiling against his skin when he growled.

"Trust me, Mrs. Gentry, I'm very talented at *ways*," he said, his mouth so close to her ear that his warm breath sent her mind to all kinds of naughty thoughts of the wedding night awaiting them.

Over Court's shoulder, she noticed Alex walk onto the dance floor with Madison. The two of them stared into each other's eyes as they swayed to the music. The brothers had grown up being abused mentally and physically. Their mother had left them in the hands of an abuser, but somehow, they'd risen above their environment and could be proud of the men they'd become.

Court and Alex had found love and happiness. She hoped Nate's turn would come soon. Her money was on Taylor. She'd seen the longing in both their eyes when they looked at each other whenever they thought no one was watching. She scanned the guests, most of them FBI agents, searching for Nate and Taylor. There was Taylor sitting at a table with her fellow agent Rand Stevens.

"Where's Nate?" she asked. As Court's best man, Nate had stood next to his brother during the marriage ceremony, but she hadn't seen him since the photographer had finished taking the post-wedding photos.

"He left."

Lauren leaned away, peering up at him. "Really?"

Her husband's eyes turned troubled. "Yeah. Said he needed to get away for a few days. I don't know what's going on with him to answer the question you're about to ask."

She glanced back at Taylor, noticing that she seemed sad. Before she worried more about her new brother-in-law or the beautiful FBI agent, Court danced her to the railing of the deck.

"We'll worry about him tomorrow," Court said, as if reading her mind. "Tonight is ours." He gave her a wicked grin. "I have an irresistible urge to start making good on my promise to keep you up all night." He pressed his hips against her, letting her feel his arousal. "Yeah, really irresistible. Let's blow this joint."

Although they should say good-bye to their families and guests, she grabbed his hand, pulling him with her as she skipped down the steps of the deck so they could sneak away.

The band started playing "Just the Way You Are."

"Our song," Court said, drawing her to him. "One last dance before we go."

They were away from the lighted area, and she danced with her husband, their feet bare on the sand, to the sounds of the Bruno Mars song and the waves crashing onshore. When the song finished, Court kissed her, long and deep.

He broke away, cradled her face in his palms, and stared into her eyes. "I only want one thing, Gorgeous Girl. I want us."

She put her hands over his. "It's all I've wanted since the first time you said you loved me."

"I promise you'll never be sorry you married me, Lauren Gentry."

"And I'll make the same promise to you. I love you, Mr. Gentry."

"Love you more."

She laughed, swatted his chest, then took off running. "Do not."

"Oh, you're in trouble now, Mrs. Gentry."

"I'm counting on it."

He caught her, scooped her up in his arms, and carried her to their room, where he kept his promise to keep her up all night.

EPILOGUE

Kinsey Landon unfolded the letter she'd found in her mother's Bible. She'd read it a hundred times since her mother had died, and each read still knocked the ground out from under her feet. Wanda Landon had once been Wanda Gentry, something Kinsey had never known. Why had her mom kept her past a secret? Kinsey picked up the pages she'd dropped and read the letter again from the beginning.

> *My Darling Kinsey,*
>
> *If you are reading this, then I am no longer with you. Please don't cry too much, sweetheart. I've been blessed to have you in my life, and having you has kept me sane.*
>
> *You see, I had three sons who were taken from me, and my heart has cried each day from missing them. Without you in my life, I don't know how I would have gone on.*
>
> *I know I should have told you about your brothers, and I planned to, but I kept putting it off, unsure of how*

to explain walking away from my sons. You see, I left them for you.

The first time you asked about your father, I told you his name was John Landon and that he was dead. That was a lie, sweetheart. Maybe he's dead by now, I don't know, but your father's name was Gordon Gentry. He was not a nice man, Kinsey, but I would have stayed with him for my sons.

When he learned I was pregnant with you, he refused to believe he was your father. He demanded I get rid of you, and when I refused, he tried to beat you out of my stomach. I knew then that to protect you, I had to leave.

It was the hardest decision of my life, leaving my boys with that man, but if I'd tried to take them, he would have hunted us down. My heart is still broken because I didn't have the courage or means to defy him.

But there was a life inside me. You. I had no choice but to protect you, my sweet girl. Fortunately, a man your father sometimes hired to do odd jobs took pity on me and helped me escape by driving me to the bus station. I will always owe him for that act of kindness because he helped me save you.

I have to believe that I instilled in my sons a sense of honor and a love of learning so they could grow to be fine young men. I know in my heart they grew into men I would be proud of. If you are asking where they are today, I don't know. All I can tell you is that their names are Alex, Court, and Nate Gentry, and that the last time I saw them, they were living in Ocala, Florida.

From the moment I knew you were in my belly, I have loved you, Kinsey. Please forgive me for not being honest with you before now.

You are a beautiful, intelligent woman, and I'm so very proud of you, daughter. If you should decide to find your brothers, please tell them why I left. Tell them that I never stopped loving them.

I only ask one thing of you, Kinsey. Be happy. I love you through eternity.

Mom.

Kinsey dropped the letter onto her desk. Had her mom ever tried to find her sons, learn what had become of them? Kinsey swiveled the chair, staring out the window. She would never know the answer . . . but she had brothers? It was almost impossible to wrap her mind around that.

When she'd discovered the letter, her first reaction had been to start looking for them, but then she'd hesitated. What if they didn't want a sister? What if they'd grown up to be like their father . . . her father? From the little her mother had shared in the letter, he hadn't been a good man.

She'd been in her last year of school when she'd found the letter and had elected to concentrate on her studies and get her degree before deciding what to do. She'd needed the time to let the news of her "family" sink in. After all, she'd gone twenty-two years without them in her life. What did one more matter?

Even now, a year later, she still wasn't sure what to do. Some days, she missed her mother so much she *did* want to find them, believing that they would understand and share in her grief. It would give her comfort to know she wasn't alone in mourning the best woman she'd ever known.

From her earliest memory, it had been just her and her mother. She'd never doubted she'd been wanted and loved, and it was hard being alone now, never again able to pick up the phone and hear her mother's voice. She still couldn't look at her mother's picture without crying.

"I didn't even get to say good-bye to you, Mom," she whispered. The heart attack that had instantly killed her mother had taken that chance away.

She'd graduated two days ago, and now it was decision time. Did she want to find them, and if she did, how would it change her life? Did they hate their mother for leaving them, and would they resent Kinsey for being the reason? If so, she wasn't sure she could bear it on top of the ache already living in her heart. She almost wished her mother had taken her secrets to the grave.

ACKNOWLEDGMENTS

The book world is a fascinating place. My first book was published in 2013, and the biggest thing I've learned since then is how much I don't know. What I do know, however, is that I've made so many amazing friends—some I've met and some I probably never will meet, but they are all just as dear to me. I now have friends in close to every state in the United States and in countries all over the world that I talk to almost daily on social media. I am truly blessed.

Thank you to the readers who write me, telling me how much you love my books, especially my heroes. Thank you for leaving reviews! You have no idea how much an author appreciates that. Thank you for the online chats we have about everything under the sun. I love those so much. Thank you all for just being awesome!

There is one special reader and now a long-distance friend I want to tell you about. Her name is Brandy Morrison. Brandy has Turner's syndrome (look it up). It's not easy for her to read my books, but she tells me she devours every one of them. Books make her happy, so I'm honored to be one of her favorite authors . . . well, after Kristan Higgins, Susan Mallery, and Jill Shalvis. But hey, those are some big names to follow, so thank you for such an honor, Brandy.

If an author is really, really lucky, she finds the perfect critique partner. I got super lucky in finding two. Jenny Holiday, from a tentative exchange of manuscripts before either of us were published, we've evolved into a partnership that I know we both believe is special. I am blessed to have you not only as a critique partner but also as a dear friend. (Y'all need to go read Jenny's books. They're so good.)

Miranda Liasson, my Golden Heart Lucky 13 sister, friend, and critique partner, you're a treasure. I love our long phone calls. You're just so easy to talk to about everything. Which reminds me, it's my turn to call you. (Y'all go read Miranda's books, too. You'll be glad you did.)

Montlake Romance, how do I ever thank you for taking a chance on a relatively unknown author? With this one, we're on our sixth book together, and it's been more thrilling than riding the highest roller coaster in the world (and I do love those). Maria, Jessica, Melody, Elise, and everyone else at Montlake, I adore you!

To Jim, I couldn't do this without you. Even though you never complain, I'll try to stop burning dinner when I'm on deadline . . . But no promises, okay? I love you Mr. O. Always have, always will.

Then last (and definitely not least) there's my agent, Courtney Miller-Callihan. Wow, Courtney. What an amazing journey we're on. I couldn't have done it without you . . . Seriously! So, to the best agent in the world, thank you for believing in me. Raising a glass of wine (and you know how much I love my wine) to you, and saying, "Cheers! Here's to dozens and dozens of more fabulous years together."

ABOUT THE AUTHOR

Bestselling, award-winning author Sandra Owens lives in the beautiful Blue Ridge Mountains of North Carolina. Her family and friends often question her sanity but have ceased being surprised by what she might get up to next. She's jumped out of a plane, flown in an aerobatic plane while the pilot performed death-defying stunts, gotten into laser-gun fights in Air Combat, and ridden a Harley motorcycle for years. She regrets nothing.

Sandra is a Romance Writers of America Honor Roll member and a 2013 Golden Heart Finalist for her contemporary romance *Crazy for Her*. In addition to her contemporary romantic suspense novels, she writes Regency stories.

You can connect with Sandra on Facebook at Sandra Owens Author, on Twitter @SandyOwens1, or through her website, www.sandra-owens.com.